Preacher

The Cosantóir (Protectors) MC | Book 2

Michael Geraghty

Hold Fast Publishing

Chapter 1

Cillian Meehan rushed up the old church's broken stone steps, straightening the thin navy blue tie he wore so that the knot looked its best. He paused at the worn wooden doors that led into the chapel, took a deep breath, and stealthily moved inside so as not to disturb the mass that was already underway. Cillian had been late to Sunday services more than he liked over the last month or so. With so much going on with work and with the Cosantóir lately, his priorities have been jumbled. He hated missing church services and knew that it grounded him in some way when he could be there, away from all the distractions he often had in his everyday life.

He slid surreptitiously into the pew at the back row. However, as soon as he sat down on the old wood, a loud creak moved through the room, causing much of the congregation to turn and look to see who it was making the ruckus. Cillian gave a crooked smile as he sat and caught Father Mike's eyes from the pulpit. Father Mike gave a quick nod and smile and continued with his homily. The priest's voice echoed loudly as he talked about the importance of making yourself available to help others when you can.

Most of the early 8 AM mass patrons were older and preferred the small setting instead of the later masses on Sunday held in the larger, more modern church at the front of the property. The old place of worship showed signs of wear. With dwindling numbers in the congregation, the parish had fewer dollars to put into upkeep and maintenance, putting continued use of the facility in danger.

Cillian passively sat in the back row, bowing his head and giving replies. Anyone watching him would see that he silently mouthed the words the priest was saying before providing the response. Cillian's years as a priest left the indelible mark of reciting mass all the way through, right down to many of the gospel passages read. When it was time for the offering, the white-haired gentleman in the back row across from Cillian nodded to him, indicating he should grab the basket on his side of the church. Cillian concurred and picked up the wicker basket to pass along each row.

It was easy to see that people were putting fewer dollars into the offering. With many seniors on fixed incomes, while living in an area growing and becoming more expensive, there was less to go around. By the time Cillian had reached the front of the church, it had appeared that it was just a tiny layer of single bills coating the bottom of the basket. Not long after he had performed this task, Cillian returned to the church's altar bearing one of the gifts before Communion. As he handed the wine to Father Mike, Cillian heard him give a low whisper.

"Nice of you to make it," the priest said with a grin.

Cillian smiled back and sheepishly returned to his seat.

Father Mike called the congregation for Communion, and nearly everyone shuffled into line to receive. Cillian remained at the back, bowing his head and praying silently instead of going to the altar to receive. He avoided parishioners' looks as the sacrament procedure ended, and he stayed in place.

Once mass ended and Father Mike made his way down the aisle to the front door to greet the congregation as they left, Cillian let out a sigh. He smiled and said cordial hellos to many of the people going by. Most of the members knew him from the area, but few knew that he once stood at the altar himself. Cillian turned around to face the altar and the cross on the far wall behind it with the church emptied. He genuflected and crossed himself before he headed back outside and into the humid August air.

Late August in New York was notorious for its humidity and heat. This Sunday did not disappoint in those areas. Cillian emerged from the vestibule and stood on the front stone steps just paces away from Father Mike. He squinted as the bright sun hit his eyes, and he couldn't wait to return to the Hog House so he could change out of his suit and into more casual clothing. The suit only emerged on Sundays these days, since it was the rare occasion that he needed one. Cillian had hoped he could skirt by Father Mike without engaging in conversation. He saw that the priest spoke with Mrs. Caufield, an elderly local who was a regular at mass. He attempted to slide by Mrs. Caufield without arousing any suspicion. Unfortunately, Cillian's shoe caught one of the damaged areas of the stone. He stumbled forward, bumping the old woman's elbow, so she dropped her purse.

"Oh, dear!" Mrs. Caufield exclaimed frantically. Some of the contents had spilled out onto the steps. Cillian immediately bent down to gather the contents for her.

"I'm so sorry, Mrs. Caufield," Cillian told her as he gathered up her items. It was hard to miss the small silver cigarette case that had popped open, revealing the two rolled marijuana joints in them. Cillian quickly snapped it closed and handed it to the embarrassed woman.

"For my glaucoma," she told Cillian softly.

"Of course," he added as he watched her stuff the case back into her beaded white bag.

"Have a grand Sunday, Father," Mrs. Caufield told the priest. She smiled politely at Cillian.

"Mr. Meehan," she said with a nod as Cillian held her arm so she could maneuver down the steps herself.

Cillian stood next to Father Mike as the two men gazed at Mrs. Caufield as she tottered off towards her car.

"Glaucoma," Father Mike scoffed. "The woman can spot dust on top of my bookshelves in my office."

"We all need to relax a little bit now and then, Father," Cillian replied. "Have you ever?"

"Me?" the priest answered with a sly smile. "Maybe back in my seminary days, but not since then. You?"

"We'll save that one for confession, Father," Cillian replied.

"Everything okay with you, Cillian? I haven't seen you around much lately. You missed a few Sundays."

"Nothing earth-shattering." Cillian ran his hand over the short stubble on his head. "Some stuff with Conor and the Cosantóir went down that required my attention. I think we're back on track now."

"Yes, I read about some of that in the newspaper," Father Mike added. "Who knew all this was happening in our little town. How is Conor doing?"

"He's recovering," Cillian said. Beads of sweat were steadily forming on Cillian's forehead as the sun beat down on him. "He's home and in a wheelchair right now as he does some physical therapy. It might be a while before he can work or ride again."

"I'll be sure to include him in my prayers this week," Father Mike nodded. "Any chance you can get him to mass one day?"

Cillian chucked.

"I'm pretty sure I'm the only one of the Cosantóir you are going to see here, Father."

"You know, Cillian, you can just call me Mike," the priest confided.

"No, you're Father. You earned that title and keep earning it with all you do here," Cillian insisted.

"Is that how you felt about it?"

Cillian stood quietly for a moment.

"That was a lifetime ago now. I rarely think about it anymore."

Cillian knew this was not wholly true, and he disliked even telling a little white lie to the priest.

"I need to get going," Cillian said as he shook Father Mike's hand. "It was a great sermon today."

"What you heard of it, at least," Father Mike added with a wink. "Drop by anytime."

Cillian casually waved and made his way out to the parking lot. He strode over to his black Mustang and stood next to the driver's side door as he watched the church crowd disperse. He rarely rode his Harley to church, so it gave less of a reminder to those attending that the club was a big part of his life. Just as he climbed into his car, he saw Tina Brighton scurrying towards his vehicle.

Cillian hoped to pull out of the parking lot before she got there, but Tina exhibited uncanny speed navigating the gravel parking lot in her white high heels. In seconds, she was rapping on his tinted window.

"Mr. Meehan? Mr. Meehan?" she repeatedly asked while knocking on the glass.

Cillian sighed, his politeness getting the better of him, and he pressed the button to roll down the window. A forced smile rose to his lips before he spoke.

"Ms. Brighton," Cillian stated. "How lovely to see you this morning."

Cillian noticed the extra-curly brown hair Tina displayed, thanks to the added humidity of the day.

"Oh, Mr. Meehan, I am so glad I got you before you left," Tina said as she caught her breath. "I have a HUGE favor to ask you."

Cillian dreaded what was to come, but held his feelings in.

"Sure, go ahead," Cillian replied.

"Miss Burgess, our Sunday school teacher for eight to twelve-year-olds, needs to step out for just a few minutes. You know her family runs the funeral parlor down the street, right? Well, she got a call and needs to go down to the office. I think Mr. Murtaugh passed away. Poor old man... fighting illness for so long. My family and his have known each other for years..."

"Ms. Brighton," Cillian interrupted, "what do you need help with?"

"Would you mind, if you could, just sitting with her class for about five minutes while she runs down to the funeral home and unlocks the building? Her father said he would meet her there so she could come right back. I just need someone to mind the class while she was gone, maybe start the lesson for today..."

"Ms. Brighton, while I appreciate your dilemma, I'm not really the person you want to do that," Cillian told her. He moved to raise his window before she interjected again.

"Oh, please, Mr. Meehan. You're the only one left here who can help me. Father Mike has another Mass to prep for, and I did ask Mrs. Caufield while she was in her car, but to be honest, she didn't look like she could handle it. Her eyes seemed a bit glassy to me. I promise it will only be for a few minutes."

Cillian peered into the desperate brown eyes of the woman and let out a breath.

"Sure, but just for a few minutes. I don't mind sitting with them, but I really can't get into any lessons or curriculum."

"Oh great!" she exclaimed. "That's fine; just hang out with them for a few minutes. I'll meet you over at the community center building. Thank you so much!"

Cillian drove down the narrow gravel pathway past the cemetery attached to the church and in front of the community building. He climbed out of his Mustang and saw a few teenagers outside, waiting for their class to begin. A few of the boys gave him sideways glances, unsure of what he was doing there.

Cillian waited out front, keeping his distance from the teens, and shuffled his feet on the asphalt. He looked down at his black dress shoes and saw they had scuffs all over them. He knew they needed to be replaced, but he had worn the comfortable pair for many years and was reluctant to give them up.

Tina arrived at the building and flung open the door to the community center, leading Cillian to the small classroom at the end of the hall. The entire building felt stuffy and oppressive.

"Why is it so hot in here?" Cillian asked as they stood outside the classroom.

"Oh, the AC seems to be fussing today," Tina apologized. "We're hoping to get it fixed this week. Hopefully, it won't be too bad. We have all the windows open in there."

Cillian peered through the pane of glass on the door to see about ten or twelve kids sitting in the room waiting for class to start.

"Just five minutes, right?" Cillian asked again.

"Ten minutes, tops," she assured.

Before Cillian could change his mind, Tina had flung the door open to the classroom. All eyes turned toward him as they entered, and Cillian knew the kids were watching his every movement.

"Class," Tina said softly as the kids murmured to each other, not paying attention to her. "Excuse me?" she said again.

Cillian knew the gentle voice would not get the attention of preteens.

"Hey there!" he boomed. The students all snapped to attention and looked toward Cillian. He smiled and nodded to Tina.

"Guys, this is Mr. Meehan," Tina indicated. "He's going to sit with you until Miss Burgess comes back. You can start on your reading assignment for now. Tyler and Charlie, don't give Mr. Meehan any trouble," she said as she glared at the two boys together on the left side of the room.

"Thank you," Tina said softly to Cillian before she left the room.

Cillian scanned the room and saw ten sets of eyes looking back at him, wondering what he would do.

"Go ahead and do your reading," Cillian said with a wave of his hand as he sat in a folding chair at the front of the room. Even with the windows open, the room was stifling, and Cillian knew sweat stains were forming on his shirt.

Tyler and Charlie sat giggling and whispering to each other as they stared into a notebook. The older boy would do something different to try to make the younger one laugh louder, which worked like a charm with each passing moment.

"Something funny, guys?" Cillian said as he rose from his chair and strode over to stand in front of them. He was an imposing figure as he loomed over them. One thing Cillian had always done, even as a priest teaching, was use his size to his advantage. He looked more formidable than he actually was, but the students rarely saw that until they knew him.

"Tyler was just drawing something in his book," Charlie said, pointing to his friend as he ratted him out. Tyler shot a look back toward Charlie as the betrayal occurred.

"Mind if I take a look?" Cillian said as he took the notebook from Tyler's shaking hand.

Cillian casually looked down at the pages in front of him. Besides the word 'penis' covering one whole page, the other had a drawing of what he assumed was Ms. Burgess. Her hair was straggled and sticking up, she had a scowl on her face, and Tyler had drawn in stink lines coming from her body to indicate an unpleasant odor. The word 'Medusa' stood out underneath the drawing.

"You might want to put that away until later," Cillian said softly as he handed the book back to Tyler. "What are you supposed to be reading?"

"Boring stuff," Tyler replied.

"It's all stuff about confession," a girl from the other side of the room said as she held up her pages. "How important it is and what it is all about. I have some questions, though."

Cillian hesitated before he said anything. He knew that he was not supposed to be involved in any theological teachings at a school, according to the rescript of his dispensation. Sunday school might be outside those bounds, but Cillian still took his promises to the Church seriously.

"What's your question?" Cillian asked leerily.

"Well, if I already said I'm sorry to my Mom for what I did, why do I have to go to confession and repeat it? Isn't my apology enough?"

Cillian considered how best to answer the girl.

"Confession is our way of telling God how sorry we are for something. It lets you put things right with Him so that you know that you have been forgiven for what you did. Even though you have said you're sorry to your mother, it gives you the chance to let God know you have flaws and are strong enough to face up to them. He can forgive you of your sin so that you can be closer to God and Jesus and so that you can be healed."

The girl seemed satisfied with that answer, but then another girl piped up.

"My sister says God might be a girl, so why do you say Him?"

"I guess because, in the Bible, it always refers to God as Him, but who knows? God has no body. Your sister might be right. I don't think any of us knows the real answer to that. I think it's better to think of God as you want God to be, even though the Church teaches us to call God Him and calls Him Father."

"Yeah, they call Him Father," Tyler said. "So he has to be a dude."

"Not necessarily," Cillian answered. He sat back down in the folding chair and began to take off his jacket to cool off. "We call God Father because we are children of God, and He looks at us as His family and takes care of us."

Cillian noticed that none of the kids really paid attention to him and instead were staring at his arms. He looked down and realized that his several tattoos were now visible, including the Cosantóir logo.

"Whoa, look at all that ink!" Tyler said as he got up from his chair to look at the various tattoos. The other kids all followed suit, and Cillian had a crowd around him examining his arms. One child was looking at the words on his right forearm.

"What does this one say?" he asked.

"For I can do all things through Christ who gives me strength," Cillian told him.

"Cool," the boy said softly.

"My Mom says that only bad people get tattoos, especially that one," the girl who questioned Cillian before noted as she pointed at the Cosantóir logo on his left bicep.

"Your family sure has a lot to say," Cillian told her with a laugh. "That tattoo doesn't mean I'm a terrible person. It just means I am part of a club."

"She says it's a club that does naughty things," the girl shot back.

"I would say she is misinformed about what we do," Cillian replied. "Do you like to go to the Irish Festival coming up in town?"

The girl nodded and smiled, and many of the others chimed in with emphatic yeses.

"Well, because of my club, we can have that festival every year. So when you come this year, make sure you come looking for me so you can say hi."

The door to the classroom swung open, and a woman stood with her mouth agape.

"Who are you, and what are you doing?" she yelled. "Why are you showing the children tattoos? Back in your seats, children," she ordered.

The kids moved back to their seats while Cillian stood up and draped his suit jacket over his arm, covering some of the tattoos.

"I'm Cillian Meehan," Cillian said politely. "Tina asked me to watch the class until you got back. I assume you are Ms. Burgess?" Cillian knew full well it was her and realized Tyler's crude drawing of her was not far off, as her hair stuck out wildly.

"Yes, I am," she insisted as she stood straight and looked up at Cillian. "You were just supposed to sit here and watch the class, nothing more. Not show them blasphemous drawings on your arms. It's a sin."

"Actually, Pope Francis has indicated that tattoos can be helpful..." Cillian started before Ms. Burgess interrupted him.

"Don't bring the Holy Father into this," she stated. "I can take it from here, thank you."

"No problem." Cillian rolled his eyes as he made his way to the door.

"See ya, Mr. Meehan," Tyler said with a wink and smile.

"Bye, Tyler," he answered as he winked back and pointed his finger.

As Cillian closed the door, he could hear Ms. Burgess getting inundated with questions about God being female, about confession, tattoos, and other queries all at once. Cillian smirked as he made his way to his car. He tossed his suit jacket onto the passenger seat next to him and rolled down the driver's side window so he could stick his left arm out, proudly showing off his ink to anyone that walked past.

Cillian started the engine and revved it loudly, letting the vehicle idle for a moment. He reflected on his short time with the young students and what they had discussed. It was the first time he had been in a position to talk about religion in any way to children in many years, and he enjoyed it.

A few side glances from parents as they walked past his car and his arm to the community center caused him to pull his arm back into the car, close the window, and crank the AC up for his drive back to the Hog House.

Chapter 2

Everywhere Annabella turned, there seemed to be another stack of boxes. She thought she had been making progress with unpacking. Still, the reality was barely a dent had been put into the belongings moved from her previous home. All the furniture she managed to get was in place, but clothes, keepsakes, and the kitchen items were still looming all around. The kitchen was more like a darkened forest, with a small clearing where the table resided. Even the wooden table was studded with more packages than she could count.

Annabella let loose a deep sigh as she pulled one of the wooden kitchen chairs over to the empty spot she had made so she could reach a bit of counter space to set up her coffeemaker. She sat down and poured what was left in the carafe into her favorite coffee mug, emblazoned with the Wonder Woman logo on it. Leo had never let her leave that mug out anywhere because he saw it as embarrassing. Now that she was free from him, it was more empowering than ever to use it as often as she could.

Annabella strolled toward the living room and reached the curtains at the front window. She pulled them back to let the warm sunlight shine through onto her. With her eyes closed, she allowed the warmth to envelop her. She took a moment to let her mind escape the reality of her current situation. She was alone for the first time in her life, divorced from the husband she had known for the last twenty years, and her college-aged daughter mostly living on her own. Leo had fought her every step along the way in the divorce, doing his best to make sure she got as little as possible from his fortune. Her lawyer did the best she could for Annabella, making sure she at least got some alimony and proceeds from selling one of their homes. At the same time, Leo kept the primary residence in Bronxville. The truth was that Annabella would have walked away with the clothes on her back as long as she could walk away.

Here she was, in a new area she barely knew, feeling like she was growing up all over again. Annabella opened her eyes and walked down the short hall to the left of the living room, and looked into each of the two bedrooms there. The movers had been kind enough to set up her bed for her, so she had a place to sleep last night, but little else around her had been unpacked. The second room held boxes of her daughter's things. Annabella was still unsure if Makenna would even visit the house, let alone spend any time living there. Makenna had been glad to go away to Vassar. The young woman was getting ready to start her third year there and already had an apartment with two girlfriends off-campus.

In the distance, Annabella heard the familiar opening chords of Beethoven's Fifth Symphony. Annabella patted the front pocket of the shorts she was wearing and realized her phone was in the kitchen. She dreaded going to get it because she knew who was on the other end. Makenna had thought it hysterical to change the ringtone for Annabella's mother's number to the gloom doom of the opening bars of Beethoven's Fifth.

She strode slowly towards the kitchen, hoping against hope that her mother would hang up or the call would go to voicemail before Annabella could pick it up. The phone continued blaring when she picked it up, and Annabella drew in a deep breath and pressed the green button on her cell to answer it.

"Hi, Mom," she said as cheerfully as she could.

"Oh, you are awake," her mother replied. "It's past ten, so I figured you would be up already, but I never know what you are doing anymore."

"I've been up since 7:30," Annabella replied through her gritted teeth, still trying to sound as sunny as possible. "I was thinking about going to Mass at 11 if you want to join me." Going to church was always a good peace offering to her mother and the one thing they could agree on.

"Well, I've already been and back, Annabella," her mother answered. "I go to the early service on Sundays. I thought you would know that by now."

"Sorry. I don't know what I was thinking," Annabella said sarcastically.

"Don't take that tone, Annabella Rose," her mother scolded. "You and your father, always with the sarcasm. I didn't like it when he did it, or the two of you did it together, and I'm sure not going to take it now."

"I apologize, Mom," Annabella offered. Whenever her mother whipped out the 'Annabella Rose' in conversation, she knew her mother was distraught. "Why don't you come over for some coffee then? You haven't seen the house yet. It's got a nice little yard in the back where we can sit outside and..."

"Sit outside?" her mother said, shocked. "It's ninety degrees out there! It is August, you know."

"Okay, well, we can sit inside, and I'll turn the air conditioning on."

"Sit where?" her mother asked. "I'll bet your house is still riddled with boxes over there. I'm surprised you even have air conditioning there. Is it central air?"

"No, Mom, it's not," Annabella answered. She knew she was doing her deep breathing to calm down now. "I have a unit in my bedroom and one in the living room. It will all work fine. And yes, I have a lot of boxes around still. I just got here on Friday. I still have the stuff to sort through and put in the basement to clear things out."

"Why didn't you just have the movers take care of it for you? Really, Annabella, you should have thought these things through."

Her mother let out an audible annoyed sigh.

"You know, you wouldn't have to deal will all of this if you had just..."

"Mom," Annabella snapped, "don't even say it. I was not going to stay with Leo any longer. I wasn't happy."

"All I'm saying is that you had a good man who was an excellent provider. He made sure you had what you needed, took you on nice vacations, bought you nice things, and introduced you to a lot of influential people..."

"None of whom bothered to clue me in that my husband was cheating on me for years," Annabella shot back. "Having nice things is not a loving relationship, Mom. Do we really have to have this argument again? If that's what you called for, I do have a lot of unpacking to get to, so..."

"Fine, I'll leave it alone," her mother told her. "No, the reason I called is that I wanted to know if there is anything I should get in for Makenna."

"Get in for Makenna? Why?"

"Because she is coming to my home today to stay with me," her mother huffed. "I want to make sure we have food she likes and is comfortable."

"Why is Makenna coming to stay with you?" Annabella asked.

"She called me on Friday and asked if she could stay the week with me. I assume it's before she goes back to school for the fall semester. She is still going to school, right? You do have money to pay for her education?"

"Leo is taking care of her tuition, Mom," Annabella said with an eye roll. "It was part of the divorce decree. I just didn't know she was looking to come to Monroe to stay with you. I wonder why she didn't call me?"

"Probably because she knew you would have piles of boxes around. She couldn't very well sleep on the floor for a week," her mother chided.

"I don't know what you should get for her, Mom," Annabella retorted. "She's twenty years old and lives on her own. I know she likes Coke Zero, macaroni and cheese, and cheeseburgers."

"Oh my," her mother told her scornfully. "I do hope she's eating better than that. You really should tell her..."

Annabella cut her mother off.

"She's staying with you, Mom. Just ask her when she gets there, or call her up. She clearly talks to you about what she's doing. I have to go. I have a lot of unpacking to do. I'll talk to you later."

Annabella hung up the phone and tossed it onto the kitchen counter. Talking with her mother was draining. It was never a conversation, but more like a lecture on what Annabella was doing wrong with her life. Dealing with Marcella Foley had been like that for as long as Annabella could remember. Her mother was always a stickler for organization, respect, and traditional ways, even when they became outdated.

The real puzzle for Annabella was why Makenna had not reached out to her. Her daughter knew she was moving into the house this week, but she had not spoken to Makenna since the previous weekend. Makenna never mentioned plans to come to the area for a visit. As far as Annabella knew, her daughter had spent the summer working at an internship for the Poughkeepsie Journal and living at her apartment there.

Annabella reached for her phone again and called Makenna. She could only imagine what ringtone her daughter used to identify her calls.

Probably something like 'the Bitch is Back,' Annabella thought.

She was surprised when Makenna answered instead of letting it go to voicemail.

"Hey, Mom," Makenna chirped. "What's up?"

"Hi, honey," Annabella said smoothly. "I was just calling to check in. What are you up to? Getting ready for school to start?"

"Yeah, everything is pretty much set for that. I still have until Labor Day to relax some."

"Great," Annabella told her. "Since you have some free time, maybe you can swing over here. You can help me unpack, and we can spend some time together. I feel like I have hardly seen you this summer with you working your internship."

"Well, I figured you had a full plate, so I was just giving you space," Makenna said hesitantly. "I do have some stuff planned this week already, but I am sure I can find some time to come by and see the place."

"Why not just do it when you come to spend the week at your grand-mother's?" Annabella added.

"Oh... yeah," Makenna said quietly.

"Why wouldn't you tell me you were coming to Monroe? You knew I was moving this week. I have to find out from her you're coming to the area and not even going to see me or stay with me?"

"I thought you had enough to do this week and wouldn't want me around. Dee and Reese are coming with me, and it was just easier to ask Grandma if we could stay with her. You don't have the room at your place. Besides, she's always complaining that I never stop by her and spend time with her."

"I complain about the same thing, Mac!" Annabella yelled.

"I'm sorry, Mom," Makenna told her. "How about before I go over to Grandma's tonight, we swing by your place? We can help you do all the unpacking, have some pizza, and hang out. It will be fun. We can be there in about an hour."

"Sure," Annabella said calmly. "That would be great. Thank you."

"You okay, Mom?" Makenna asked. "You sound a little frazzled."

"No... I'm fine. It's just been a hectic week. Actually, it's been a wild year or so. I'm just looking to get settled, I guess. Having you here will be a big help, especially if you'll be around for the week."

"Sure," Makenna said with hesitation. "Okay, we'll see you in a bit. Love you."

"Love you too," Annabella answered. She hung up the phone and smiled.

Something going right for a change, Annabella thought as she sipped her coffee.

Chapter 3

Cillian removed his tie as he drove his car up the hill toward Hog House. As one of the senior members and an officer in the Cosantóir, he was afforded one of the garage's parking spaces built behind the home. He pulled into the garage and got out of the vehicle, walking across the dry, dusty ground. The lack of recent rain had dried everything out, and the gravel dust covered the bottom part of his black dress pants as he approached the back entrance.

A couple of club members sat on the covered back porch. One quietly sipped on a bottle of Corona while the other, clad in just a black leather vest and a pair of jeans, lounged on the swing while he puffed on a vape pen. The strong piney scent of the weed permeated the air on the porch.

"You all dressed up for a funeral, Preacher?" the man on the swing said with a laugh.

"It's Sunday," Cillian replied as he loosened his tie. "I'm coming from church. Maybe it wouldn't hurt you to go with me next week?"

"No church in the world is gonna let Bug in," chortled the biker sipping his beer.

"Fuck you," Bug shot back. "I went to church when I was a kid. I was even an altar boy," he said proudly as he took another hit.

"If they could only see you now," the other man laughed.

"Hey, where do you think I learned to smoke this stuff?" Bug answered. "We found the priest's stash one day after mass. He knew his stuff. No offense, Preacher."

Cillian smiled and nodded before excusing himself indoors. He headed straight for his room in the Hog House and closed the door behind him. He gazed around at his sparsely decorated room before walking over to the large closet. He hung up his suit jacket and dusted off his pants before hanging them back up and placed his tie on his tie rack before changing into his black t-shirt and jeans. He ran his hand through the stubbled hair growing on his head before sitting down at his desk and flipping on his laptop.

Music echoed from down the hall as the Hog House was already in full swing for Sunday. Sunday was the one day where nearly everyone involved with the Cosantóir was off work, except for the few Sandhogs who volunteered for weekend work to get extra cash. Much of the crew would go for a Sunday ride when the weather was good, and it was almost time for them to head out for the day.

A loud knock at the door got Cillian's attention.

"Come on in," he replied as he scanned over his email.

Liam O'Farrell, the vice-president of the Cosantóir and de facto leader since his father, Conor, had been injured and hospitalized, filled Cillian's doorframe.

"Preacher, we're heading out for ridin' in a few. You comin' with us?" Liam asked in his husky voice.

"Not today," Cillian answered. "I promised your Da I would swing by the house and see him this morning. He said he had club business to discuss."

"He never mentioned a damn thing to me," Liam said as he scratched the dark beard on his chin. "I can go with you and have Demon lead the ride today."

"Nah, it's probably nothing," Cillian added. "You know your Da since he got out of the hospital. He's getting itchy being in that chair all day and wants to micromanage everything at work and with the Cosantóir. I'm sure it's nothing. Where are you riding today?"

"Up 17 to Bethel Woods and back down. Some of the boys want to swing into the casino while we're up that way. Friday was payday, and they've got cash burnin' a hole in their pockets. Eejits. They'll blow the fuckin' wad in two hours and then be begging me to help them out for the next two weeks. They'll be surprised when they're all eatin' peanut butter sandwiches for lunch 'til next payday."

"Want me to talk to them?" Cillian asked. One of his roles with the club has always been to try to counsel members about nearly anything.

"No way!" Liam bellowed. "Let them learn the hard way, like my Da did with me. They all make good money. They need to learn to take care of it. Besides, I can convince them to get drinks for me while I'm up there."

"Liam, let's go," a voice yelled from the bar.

"Say hi to Da and me brother while you're there," Liam said as he backed out of the doorway and closed the door, making sure to duck his head so he didn't hit it on the top of the frame.

Cillian went back to reading his email and saw one from Seanán Clarke. It had been over a year since he had any contact with Seanán, never before via email. It was a simple message from his old friend:

I'm just checking in to see how you are doing. Nothing to worry about. Just an old friend wondering how you are. God Bless.

S

It was more unlike Seanán to reach out to Cillian this way, and it caused him to worry. Cillian knew that Seanán had health issues and was into his eighties now, and his lack of contact with his mentor allowed guilt to spread through him. Cillian picked up his cell phone and quickly dialed the number he had.

"Good morning, St. Brendan's rectory. This is Evelyn speaking," the cheerful voice sang into the phone.

"Good morning," Cillian replied. "Could I speak with Father Clarke, please?"

"I'm sorry, Father Clarke is attending masses this morning. If it's an emergency, I can have one of our other priests get in touch with you."

"No, no, it's not an emergency. That won't be necessary," Cillian answered. "Can I leave him a message?"

"Certainly," Evelyn told him.

"Just let him know that Cillian Meehan called and if he could phone me back..."

"Father Meehan?" Evelyn squealed into the phone. "Father, it's me... Evelyn Byrne. I don't know if you remember me. I was a teenager in the parish when you were here. You taught English here at the high school, and I was in your class in tenth grade."

"Yes, I do recall you, Evelyn. It's nice to hear your voice, but I'm not..."

"We were all so sad when we came back after the summer break and you were gone. As much as I love Father Clarke, I have to say you were my favorite here at the parish. Are you planning to come and visit? Where are you serving now?"

Cillian cleared his throat.

"I don't know if I'll be visiting anytime soon or not, and, actually, I left the clergy a long time ago."

There was a brief silence on the other end of the phone, one that Cillian always expected whenever he ran into anyone that knew him as a priest or as part of his parish years ago.

"Oh... I didn't realize," Evelyn stammered. "Is... is there anything else you would like to tell Father Clarke?"

"No, that was it," Cillian offered. "Thank you so much. It was nice to talk to you, Evelyn."

"It was nice to speak with you as well, Father... I mean Mr. Meehan. Have a blessed day," Evelyn replied.

"You as well," Cillian said as he hung up.

Incidences such as the one he just experienced were commonplace for Cillian, as they likely are for many priests that have left their vocation. However, Cillian never got used to it. Leaving the priesthood left a particular hole in his heart. People often did not know how to relate to him, especially if they knew he was once a priest. The loneliness that situation created for him was something he had never been able to shake. Going from the clergy where everyone in the parish knew you, respected you, and wanted to talk to you to someone that people no longer knew how to relate to or even call you was devastating. Cillian had left his parish area shortly after receiving his dispensation and never looked back. He started his life over in Harriman, where he knew practically no one all those years ago.

Cillian grabbed his helmet from his room and walked out toward the bar area. A few members were strewn about the room on the couches while a couple of others sat at the bar, getting their drink on early. Cillian nodded to Rory, a member and former Sandhog injured on the job a few years back. Rory smiled and moved to the end of the bar where Cillian passed.

"Mornin', Preacher," Rory beamed. Rory noticed the helmet tucked under Cillian's arm. "I think you missed the club heading out, but I'm sure you can catch up."

Cillian glanced down to where Rory was wiping down the bar to see his gnarled left hand. Cillian recalled the day on the tunnels' job where there was a small slide that seemed inconsequential until he looked down and saw Rory's hand pinned under rocks and mud. By the time he was freed, his hand was mangled, and he lost his index and middle fingers. Cillian convinced the Cosantóir to hire Rory as a bartender for the Hog House to still feel part of the family, even though he wasn't a Sandhog anymore.

"No, Rory, I'm on my way over to Conor's. If anyone is looking for me, they can get me on my cell. It should be a quiet afternoon around here for you."

"No troubles," Rory said confidently. "Gives me time to catch up on my reading."

Rory reached under the bar and pulled out a textbook on refrigeration and appliance repair.

"I'm taking some classes at the tech school," he said proudly. "I'm using some of the worker's comp settlement you helped me get. I figure it's a good skill, right? Those repair guys make as much or more than Hogs, and it will let me do some the repairs around here if we need them."

"That's great, Rory," Cillian offered. "I'm glad to hear it. Keep it up. I'll see you later."

Cillian trod across the wood floor to the front porch and made his way down to his Harley. He hadn't needed to put the tarp over his bike in a while, since it had been so dry lately, and he just hopped on for the ride to Conor's place.

Before going to Conor's, Cillian made a pit stop at Dunkin' Donuts. He knew Maeve, Conor's lady, probably made coffee already, but Conor almost expected a donut and coffee delivery when he invited Cillian over. Many years ago, it had become a tradition that Cillian still kept up, no matter what day of the week or time.

Cillian scanned the parking lot for an open space to park, which was a challenge on a Sunday morning in the summer. He walked into the store and waited patiently in line. He noticed a tall young man with glasses leaving the counter with a tray of iced coffee and iced tea in his hand and held the door open for him as he exited.

"Thank you so much," the man's voice cracked as he adjusted his glasses.

"No problem, son," Cillian said politely. The woman entering simultaneously with her little girl huffed a bit as the door swung close to her.

"Watch it!" she barked at the young man, who apologized and kept walking. The woman sighed deeply when she looked at the line.

"Tara, let's just go," she told the girl. "It's too crowded here. Mommy just wants to get home."

"Mom," the girl whined, "you told me if I was good at church, I could get a pink frosted donut! You promised!"

Cillian looked back at the mother and the little girl. Tara stared up at Cillian's large frame. She seemed slightly intimidated by his size and the visible tattoos on his arms. She moved closer to her mother and hugged around her leg as her mother looked down and then glared at Cillian.

"Cillian!" A voice yelled. "Hey, Preacher!"

Cillian looked up and saw Annie, one of Dunkin's managers and Demon's daughter, waving at him from behind the counter. Cillian smiled and waved to her before she bade him to come to the far counter.

He slowly walked over to the pickup counter, getting more stares and glares from people waiting, including the Mom.

"Hey, what gives Annie?" a young man with a neckbeard and glasses yelled. "I'm waiting ahead of him!"

"Quiet down, Elvin!" Annie shot back. "You get the same small coffee in your very particular way every day and never leave us a tip. You can wait."

Annie reached over and grabbed the steel thermos from Cillian's hand.

"The usual today?" Annie asked with a smile.

"Yes, please," Cillian said quietly. "Annie, I can wait; it's no big deal. The whole patience is a virtue thing, you know."

"It's no big deal. The line is moving fast."

Annie walked off to fill the thermos as Cillian turned to look at the store. Even the seats were filled, including a familiar face sitting at a table by the front window.

Annie returned, handing the thermos and a box of donuts to Cillian.

"Six glazed, six jellies," Annie offered.

"Thanks," Cillian said as he held up his cell phone so Annie could scan for payment. He then reached into his pocket and grabbed a ten, and handed it to her.

"See, Elvin?" she yelled as the young hipster got close to the counter. "This is why he gets treated well! It's a tip!" She held up the ten for all to see as Elvin tried to hide his head.

"Annie, can I get a pink frosted donut and a plain donut as well, please?" Cillian asked.

Annie strode over to the donut rack, grabbed the last pink frosted off the shelf, and bagged it along with the plain.

"Here, on me," Annie smiled. "Tell my Dad I'll see him at home."

"Will do," Cillian nodded. He saw the line still creeping along and walked over to the table by the window. There sat an older, white-bearded gentleman in his dark clothes and yarmulke.

"Good morning, Meyer," Cillian said. He reached into the bag and handed Meyer the plain donut. Meyer looked up from his laptop screen and smiled at his friend.

"Cillian... A sheinem dank... you're too kind," Meyer said as he picked up the donut.

"My pleasure," Cillian stated. "Don't work too hard. Enjoy the sunshine," he said as he patted his friend's shoulder.

Cillian saw that the mother and little girl were still waiting their turn, so Cillian approached them. He bent down in front of Tara, so he was at eye level with her.

"This is for you, for being so good at church today," Cillian said with a smile.

Tara hesitated and looked up at her mother for approval. The mother sighed and nodded, and Tara took the bag. She looked inside, saw the pink frosting, and beamed.

"What do you say, Tara?" the mother encouraged.

"Thank you," she said softly as she took a bite of the yeasty dough, getting sprinkles all over her dress.

"Have a good day," Cillian said as he offered his hand to Tara, and she shook it.

Cillian stowed his thermos and donuts in his saddlebag and took off towards Conor's home. The ride over created a warm breeze against his body as the humid air sped toward him. He reached Conor's driveway and turned to head to the house, parking his bike under one of the giant oaks that spread in front of the house, so it stayed in the shade.

Cillian knocked on the front door and heard Maeve yell, "Come in." As soon as he entered the house, Jameson, Conor's pit bull, bounded to the front door to greet Cillian. His tail wagged rapidly as he jumped up and put his paws on Cillian's waist.

"Nice to see you too, Jameson," Cillian laughed. The dog had already put his snout towards Cillian's left pocket, knowing what was to come next.

"You lookin' for something?" Cillian questioned the dog as Jameson then sat obediently in front of him. Cillian pulled a bone-shaped biscuit from his pocket and placed it on Jameson's nose. The dog just sat, waiting for the following command. Cillian barely had the "okay" out of his mouth when Jameson snatched the biscuit into his mouth.

With a hearty laugh, Cillian paced to the kitchen. Maeve was pouring coffee into the mugs laid out on the table when he came in.

"Morning, Preacher," she said with a smile. Cillian walked over and gave Maeve a kiss on the cheek.

"How are you this morning, darlin'?" Cillian asked.

"Glad to be alive," she chuckled. Cillian held up the box of donuts and the thermos.

"He's in his office," Maeve offered.

The sounds of papers hitting the floor followed by the familiar Irish tongue yelling "Fuck!" got Cillian's attention.

"I'll go," Cillian told Maeve.

"Good, 'cause if I go in there, I'm smothering him with the first thing I find. He's been nothing but ornery since we got him home from the hospital."

Cillian walked over to Conor's office and lightly rapped on the door.

"What?" Conor yelled from inside.

Cillian swung the door open and saw papers strewn across the floor. Conor sat in his wheelchair, the chair caught between the corner of his desk and one of the armchairs in the room.

"I hate this fecking chair," Conor swore as he slapped his hands on the arms of the wheelchair. "The thing is harder to maneuver than a Harley."

Cillian gripped the chair and freed Conor from his trap before bending down to scoop up the papers.

"You won't need to use it much longer if you would actually do your therapy and walk around," Cillian scolded. "Maeve said you keep making the therapists cry and leave."

"What do they know?" Conor spat. "Snot-nosed twenty-somethings tryin' to tell me how to use my legs and arms. Eejits and arses."

"If you don't let them help you, you'll never get out of that chair so you can get back to work or get on your bike. Ease up on the therapists. Remember: Therefore whatever you desire for men to do to you, you shall also do to them; for this is the law and the prophets. Matthew 7:12."

"Cripes, Preacher, don't start in with the sermon, okay?" Conor said in frustration. He ran his left hand shakily through his gray hair, wincing when his hand hit the spot on his head where he had been struck by falling equipment.

"Just words of wisdom," Cillian said as he opened the box of donuts and handed a jelly donut to Conor. Conor grinned widely.

"Thank you, friend," Conor smiled. "I have to eat it fast."

"Why? Maeve saw me come in with them."

"Yes, but she'll want me to eat just one. If I eat fast, I can have two before she can stop me. She's trying to get me to be healthier. Isn't enough that I don't drink or do drugs anymore?"

Conor wolfed down the first donut and grabbed a second before moving his wheelchair behind his desk. He held a white porcelain mug out to Cillian to fill it with coffee from the thermos.

"You know, you pay a fortune for that coffee Maeve makes for you. You don't need me to keep picking this up for you."

"Preacher," Conor began, "some traditions are meant to carry on. This is one of them. Pour yourself a cup," Conor told him as he pointed to the tray of mugs and glasses by the far wall. Cillian poured out a mug and sat back down.

"Sláinte," Conor toasted before both men sipped.

"So, what did you need me for today?" Cillian asked. "I'm missing the ride today to be here."

"Eh, they were only going to Bethel. Fools looking to waste their money. You're not missing anything but the scenery. I need to talk to you about the festival coming up." Conor sorted through the papers that had fallen, stacked them neatly, placed them in a folder, and handed them to Cillian.

"What's all this?" Cillian asked as he flipped through the pages.

"That's everything to arrange and run the festival," Conor told him. "Permits, phone numbers, vendors, connections... all of it. I want you to take care of it this year."

"Why aren't you doing it?"

Conor nodded toward the office door, so Cillian would close it.

"Honestly, I don't think I'm up to it," he said solemnly. "Ever since all this," Conor pointed at the scar on his head and hand and then moved down to the wheelchair, "I'm having a rough go of it. Not just physically. That's a bitch of itself. Mentally, too. I can't concentrate like I need to. I look at the papers, and my mind wanders off. I'm... I'm not myself, friend, and I don't know when I will be. Don't say anything to Maeve or the club. Just tell them I delegated to you. That's all they need to know right now."

"Have you talked to your doctors about this?" Cillian asked with concern.

"The doctors are worse than the therapists. They just give me pills, which I won't take. I'll work through it in my own time. For now, though, I need you to do this for me, okay?"

"That's a lot on my plate," Cillian replied. "The Festival starts on Friday. How am I supposed to do all that and work?"

"Jesus, Preacher, in all the years I have known you and seen you working with the Hogs, how much vacation have you taken?"

Cillian sat back in his chair before answering.

"None," he admitted.

"Exactly. Eighteen years without time off. Stop working like a feckin' machine, man. Take some time for yourself. If all this shite has taught me anything, it's that life goes by too fast. Most of the legwork is already done. You just need to double-check stuff and be there on Thursday when they start to set stuff up to make sure it's right. It's all there in the papers. Enjoy the week alone away from the tunnels."

"I don't know, Conor," Cillian said. "I've... I've spent more than enough time alone. You know that."

"I know," Conor nodded. "Use the time to get out of your head. See what's out there. Forget about the past."

"Easier said than done," Cillian whispered. "And what if I don't want a vacation? What about Liam or Finn doing this?"

"Too late," Conor said, holding up his logbook. "I already cleared it with the union. They were happy to hear you were taking two weeks off. Hell, you could take six months out if you wanted to and still have time left to use. Liam can't do this. He's too short-tempered and will just piss people off. Finn is a probationary club member still. He's not in a position to do it. You're an officer. You'll be helping both of us, and the community, and the club. Besides, you're the better face to put forward for the Cosantóir than I am. Most of the area still thinks I'm a bad guy, and we're all crooks and hoodlums. Maybe you can change that."

"I'll do it," Cillian sighed as he put the folder down on his lap.

"Fantastic," Conor roared as he took a bite of his second donut just as Maeve knocked and pushed the door open.

"Maeve!" Conor yelled. "You know you aren't supposed to come in here." Conor felt helpless as jelly dripped down his chin.

"I'm just asking if Preacher wants anything, but I see that's already taken care of," she chided. "How many does that make, Conor Aiden O'Farrell? Time for your playmate to go anyway. You have therapy in ten minutes."

"Christ, woman, I threw the last one out of here Friday," Conor replied. "He was tearing up like a schoolgirl that skinned her knees," he chuckled.

"And I told the agency to send someone else, so get yourself ready, or I'll yank you out of that chair myself," Maeve ordered.

Cillian rose to leave, grabbing his thermos and the folder.

"I'll be in touch tomorrow," Cillian said to Conor.

"Wait," Maeve said, stopping Cillian at the door. "Take these with you." She handed Cillian the donut box, first taking a glazed donut out and biting half of it right at Conor.

"I swear, Maeve, if I could get out of this chair..." Conor growled.

"Do it!" Maeve taunted with a laugh as she left the room triumphantly, guiding Cillian out in the process.

"Go easy on him, Maeve," Cillian said as she walked him to the door. "He's dealing with a pretty rough patch right now."

"No worries, Preacher," Maeve said confidently. "I know when to push and when to back off. He's got a lot going on in that thick head of his right now, but with the right help, he'll get through it. Thanks for stopping by."

Maeve gave Cillian a hug before he made his way down the wooden steps to his bike.

The garage door opened as Cillian sat on his bike. Finn pulled out on his motorcycle and moved alongside Cillian.

"Cillian, I didn't know you were here for a social call," Finn smiled.

"More work than social," he said, holding up the folder before he put it in his saddlebag.

"What's all that?"

"Festival paperwork. Your Da wants me to run it this year."

Finn sat back on his bike.

"Really? I can't believe he gave that up. It seems like one of his favorite things. You're the perfect guy for it, though. I'm sure it will be fantastic. If you need any help, just ask."

"Thanks, Finn. I might take you up on that. Going for a ride?"

"Nah, just over to Siobhan's. We're going to brunch at Artistic Taste if you want to join us," Finn offered.

"No, you two go and enjoy time together," Cillian answered. "I've got plenty to do now."

"See you later then," Finn told him as he flipped his helmet visor down and drove off.

Cillian stowed his belongings and started up his bike. He reached the end of the driveway and sat there with his bike idling as he tried to decide where to go and what to do on his own.

Chapter 4

The Kitchen-Aid clattered onto the Formica countertop in the kitchen, even though Annabella took great pains to move it gently. She wiped the layer of dust off the top of the machine. Years of disuse of one of her favorite baking appliances left her worried that perhaps the mixer wouldn't work at all and would need to be replaced. Once Leo had hired kitchen help to work in their home, it marked the end of her cooking and baking days. As much as she loved and enjoyed it, Leo insisted it wasn't "her role in the relationship" anymore now that they were married. Still, there were times when he was away on business where she would give the staff time off to cook and bake herself and feel whole again.

After plugging the black mixer in, she tentatively flipped the switch, and, much to her delight, she saw the machine come to life. Annabella smiled and sighed, grateful that she would not have to spend extra money on a mixer right now. The purchase of the tiny house drained all of the money she received as part of the sale of the home she had with Leo. She had squirreled away some money over the last ten years of their marriage and hidden it in a bank account under her maiden name, so she had a cushion of an emergency fund, but she knew she would not be able to rely on that for long. Getting a job soon was a priority for her, not just for security but also for her confidence.

Annabella sat down on a wooden chair in the kitchen. She had been fortunate enough that the previous owner had left some old furniture in the large basement so that Annabella could fill out the house with things she did not have. Leo made sure it was difficult for her to get anything from the place to the point where she willingly signed away quite a bit in the divorce decree to walk away with her freedom and the small alimony check she was supposed to receive every month. Unfortunately, Leo was not always so prompt in living up to his end of the agreement.

Her eyes moved across the room as she gazed at the areas of worn paint in the kitchen. In a perfect world, she would have painted before settling in. In the past, Leo would have had contractors in within the day to repaint for her. It would have to be one of the many chores of homeownership that would have to wait. A faint breeze wafted through the window over the sink that peeked out onto the yard, providing Annabella with some comfortable air. The heatwave had begun right before she moved in, making a move more exhausting for all involved and slowing her progress on getting settled.

Annabella picked up her cell phone, connected to Spotify, and dialed up a 90s dance mix list to blast on the lone speaker in the kitchen. The first song to play was the Backstreet Boys, bringing her back to her younger years when she and her girlfriends would sing songs all day long and argue about Backstreet or *NSYNC (She always staunchly defended Backstreet). Annabella got out of her chair and began to work on putting away the load of glassware she had just finished washing. Her hips swayed along with the music as she lip-synced along with the lyrics, hitting all the right notes. She used a highball glass as her microphone as she sang out loud and danced her way over to the cabinet.

Just as she reached for another glass and belted out the chorus, a loud knock on the kitchen's screen door startled Annabella enough where she dropped one of the highball glasses and gasped. She looked up and saw a familiar face peeking through the screen but reacted to the sound of the glass hitting the tile floor and shattering.

"Shit!" she exclaimed with glass scattering across the white tiles.

The screen door opened immediately as Annabella bent down to pick up the large shard of glass lying at her feet.

"Anna, I'm so sorry," the woman said as she entered.

"It's not a problem," Anna answered. She tossed the chunk of glass into the nearby trashcan and turned to face her guest. She beamed widely and carefully stepped forward so the two could embrace.

"It's so good to see you, Erin," Anna said as she squeezed her friend tightly.

"No kidding," Erin replied. "It's been way too long. What's it been? Ten years?"

Anna stepped back and considered the question. "Yeah, I guess. It was probably at Jessie's wedding. Not a day I really want to remember."

"I didn't mean to bring it up," Erin said remorsefully.

"Not a problem," Anna said, standing up straight. "It was Leo who was an ass the whole day. He drank too much, humiliated the bartender, and then hit on Jessie's sister before fighting her boyfriend. On the ride home, he made me swear I wouldn't come back to the area again. That's all in the past now, though."

"Damn, Anna, you look amazing," Erin said as she looked at her friend from head to toe.

Anna blushed at the compliment.

"Stop, I look a mess right now. I'm covered in dirt and dust from this place." She brushed some of the dirt off her denim shorts and saw dust bunnies clinging to her black tank top.

"Yeah, okay," Erin scoffed. "You're better toned than me for sure. Do you work out eight hours a day?"

"Not quite, but I did my fair share. That's all done with now, though. I can't afford that personal trainer anymore. I have to find my own form of exercise." Anna laughed as she picked up the Kitchen-Aid again and lifted it over her head before putting it down on the counter.

"Hey, if anybody can keep it up, you can," Erin told her confidently.

Anna grabbed some cold bottles of water from the fridge and handed one to Erin.

"How's the place coming along? I was so happy when I found out you bought it. When we used to walk past this house, Mrs. Cromartie used to watch to make sure we didn't get too close to her lawn or garden."

"Mrs. Cromartie didn't put much into the place to keep it at its best," Anna lamented. "There's work to do inside and out. Even with all the work to be done, it wasn't cheap. Her son made sure to get every last nickel out of me that he could. But, it's mine. The house is small, but the basement is enormous, and there's an attic too that I haven't even looked at yet. I loved how she had trees around her for some privacy and a nice-looking lawn and garden. I'll have to do my best to keep it going."

"Just don't yell at me to get off your lawn when I walk past," Erin laughed.

"Well, I don't know how much time I'll have to do that" Anna said. "I've got to get myself a job so I can keep the lights on and maybe use the AC now and then."

"That's one of the reasons I stopped by," Erin grinned.

"What? To use my electricity?"

"Very funny," Erin replied. "No, I have a proposition for you. I know you're trying to get your life jumpstarted again. How about you come and work with me?"

Anna was speechless and surprised by the offer.

"You don't have to give me a pity job, Erin."

"Hey, it's far from that," Erin said as she drew her chair closer to Anna. "Listen, my catering business has done well, but I'm expanding. I just started with a food truck at the beginning of the summer – Erin's Edibles Express. It's been popular whenever we have gone out, but I don't have the manpower to do everything. I hire temps to waitress for me for catering, but I could use some kitchen help."

"Erin, I haven't done any real cooking in years," Anna told her. "Besides, I don't have any professional experience in a kitchen or anything."

"No, you don't," Erin admitted. "But I remember how good you were and how much we always loved to cook together. I think we can make it successful. I can't promise you a huge salary to start, but it's a job I know you can excel at and enjoy. You talked about cooking all the time when we were kids. What do you say?"

"I say when do you need me to start?"

"Great!" Erin said, clapping her hands. "Come over to my place tomorrow, and we can start to go over things. I'm bringing the truck to the Irish Festival this week, so we need to plan the menu and get you comfortable working everything."

"Thanks, Erin. You have no idea how much I needed this right now," Anna said as she rose from her chair to hug her friend. Anna choked up as she held Erin tightly.

"Hey, you're the one doing me a favor," Erin said softly. "By the way, I can be a real bitch of a boss. You've been warned."

"Oh, so nothing much has changed then," Anna stated as she chuckled and wiped her eyes.

"See? It's already like you haven't been gone! I'll see you tomorrow."

Erin gave her friend a kiss on the cheek as she walked out the screen door. Anna waved to her from the window as she watched Erin crossing the yard to head to her home down the street. Once Anna saw that Erin was out of sight and earshot, she let out a shrill yell.

"Yes!!" she said, pumping her fist in the air. "Take that, Leo!"

She took a big gulp of water and then heard Destiny's Child's "Independent Women, Pt. 1", come on over the speaker. Anna laughed heartily at the omen of the song and went back to dancing around the kitchen.

Chapter 5

Dust kicked up off the dry ground as another trailer ambled through to set up one of the carnival rides. Cillian spent the better part of the Thursday ensuring all the rides and booths arrived as scheduled to be inspected before opening on Friday. Running the Irish Festival proved to be more cumbersome than Cillian thought it would be. He now understood just why Conor was so eager to pass the chore along to someone else. At the beginning of the week, he had thought he would have little to do with the free time he suddenly had for two weeks. He had spent countless hours speaking with ride operators, vendors, and the town to make sure permits, insurance, security, and more were in place just so they could open the event on time. There were also checks to be written to pay for everything. As treasurer of the Cosantóir, he was well aware of how much the club spent each year to host the event. It was a significant expense, but it helped the club raise money to donate to various charities in the area, something few people recognized.

Cillian watched as the workers quickly went to work to get the Ferris wheel set up. It was the last of the rides that needed inspection before that end of the festival was completed. He walked from site to site, marking his checklist of various booths for games, food, activities, and more before reaching the large beer tent area set up. Tables and chairs were already in place, along with a dance floor, stage, and bar with a tap system. Over the years, the club learned that not everyone had the same passion for Guinness and offered other beers in the tent. However, they opted to use only local breweries, just like they used only local businesses as vendors. Kegs from Rushing Duck, Apex Brewing, and Long Lot were already rolling in to be stored in the refrigerated truck they rented for the weekend.

Cillian ducked under the tent to escape the scorching sun still going strong at 5 PM. He removed the green bandana he used to cover his head and used it to wipe some of the sweat off his brow and face. He walked across to where one of the round tables had already been set up, grabbed a chair, and sat down to go over his checklist. He pulled another chair over with the toe of his boot so he could prop his feet up. Within moments, a red Solo cup filled to the top appeared in front of him. He glanced up and saw Darryl, affectionately called Demon by the Cosantóir, standing beside him.

"Don't worry," Darryl told him. "It's not beer - Just some fresh lemonade from the truck setting up. They're making stuff for the workers."

Darryl pulled over another chair and sat his large frame down before he sipped from his own cup.

"I didn't even know you were down here," Cillian told him. Cillian sipped the tart, cold refreshment and let out a sigh. "Thanks, Demon. It's just what I needed."

"I came down to help load kegs into the truck," Demon responded. "They're a little easier for me to move around than some of the smaller guys here. It looks like we're all stocked and ready to go. You've worked your ass off the last few days, Preacher."

"Not really," Cillian said modestly. "Most of the hard work was already done. I just had to supervise and sign checks."

"Yeah, okay," Darryl laughed. "I've seen you with that clipboard in your hand every day, man. You've worked just as hard as if you were on-site with us."

"Work going okay?" Cillian asked. He had tried to avoid talking about work to keep his mind away from what he might be missing.

"You're not missing anything," Darryl assured him. "Same shit, different day and location. We show up and do our job and leave the nonsense and politics to the suits. No problems at all. Tunnels get dug right – that's all that matters."

"Fair enough, but it's been weird not going to work with you guys all week. I sit at the Hog House in the morning, and it's dead quiet. I have to get out of there and do something all day to keep me busy. It's like being back in the..." Cillian cut himself off.

"It's okay, Preacher, you don't have to say it," Darryl told him. "I get it. When I first retired from wrestling, I didn't know what to do with myself either. It was too much of nothing around the house, at least until Janet left me. She hated me tagging along everywhere. If I hadn't stumbled upon the club, I don't know where I would be now."

Darryl plucked his own bandana from his pocket to wipe the sweat off his bald head.

"I'll bet this will be the best festival we have had yet, thanks to you," Daryl boasted. He held up his cup of lemonade to toast Cillian. "Nice job, Preacher."

Cillian held his cup up to Daryl and smiled.

"Sláinte," Cillian offered as he finished off his drink.

"You done for the day now?" Darryl asked.

"I think so." Cillian flipped the pages of his checklist and placed the clipboard down on the table. "Now it's just pulling everything off tomorrow. I'll get down here early in the day just to make sure we are ready to go."

"Then how about I treat you to dinner?" Darryl asked as he nodded his head toward the Empire Diner across the street.

"Sounds good. I'll meet you over there."

Cillian made his way over to the refrigerated truck with its system running loudly already. He double-checked the locks on the back and looked up at the cameras he had asked for to make sure nothing would get vandalized before he made his way across the grass to where his bike was parked. He darted his bike the short distance up the road and across the street to pull into the diner parking lot.

The lot was nearly full when Cillian pulled in and spotted Darryl's large, green motorcycle parked at the far side of the lot. Because Darryl was such a big man, he needed an oversized bike to carry his weight and frame. His Harley seemed more prominent than some of the small cars dotting the parking lot. Cillian parked his bike in the spot next to Daryl and stepped off his machine.

"Crowded for a Thursday night," Cillian noted as they walked toward the entrance.

"We're nearing the end of summer," Daryl replied. "The last roundup, I guess. It's too hot to cook anyway."

The men entered the diner and stood by the register, waiting for a host to greet them. Cillian noted the usual looks the Cosantóir got whenever they went out into town. People stared when they saw the leather and tattoos, but going anywhere with Darryl often elicited even more looks because of his imposing size. Customers gawked with unease while the two stood by the door. One young man wanted to squeeze by to exit with his takeout order and offered a meek 'excuse me' to Darryl.

"No problem, my man," Darryl said with a grin as he stepped to the side and held the door open before the man scurried out.

A young lady approached Cillian and Darryl with two menus in her hand.

"Just two tonight?" she asked.

"Yes, please," Cillian told her.

"Can we get a table?" Daryl added. "The booths are a little tough on me," he laughed.

"You got it," she said with a smile as she led the men to a table in the center of the larger dining room. The two received more glares as they sat down with their menus.

"Are they all staring?" Darryl said softly to Cillian.

"They always do," Cillian said as he flipped the menu pages even though he had pretty much memorized the offerings at this point in his life.

"Watch this," Darryl smiled. He stood up, rattling the wooden table and glassware on it. He took his leather jacket off and laid it on the chair next to him as the table around him watched on. Tattoos were visible on his dark skin, with everything from the Cosantóir logo on his left arm to the Sand Hog logo on his right. The demon tattoo that took up much of his back, a remnant from his wrestling days, had a claw that peeked through on the back of his neck. He turned his neck, cracking it loudly before he sat back down.

"Now everyone is watching," Darryl laughed.

"You two again?" the waitress said as she smiled at both men. "How you doin', honey?" she asked Cillian as she placed glasses of ice water in front of each of them.

"I'm doing well, Cathy; how are you?" Cillian shut the menu and grinned.

"Good, just like I was two days ago when you were here for breakfast and dinner," she laughed. "Let me guess – triple decker chicken salad on rye toast and an iced tea?"

"You know me too well," Cillian replied.

"What about you, Darryl?" she asked.

Darryl scanned around and looked at the booth to his left.

"What are you having there?" Darryl asked the older couple sitting at the booth.

"Me?" the woman replied shakily. "It's... it's the pressed prime rib sandwich. Why? Did you want it?"

"That looks perfect!" he grinned widely. "I'll have that."

The woman went to hand her plate to Darryl as he burst out laughing loudly, turning more heads.

"Oh no, Ma'am, I don't want yours, but thank you for the offering. I'll get my own and a plate of onion rings and an iced tea too, please."

Cathy took the menus and went off to get drinks as the customers moved their attention from the bikers to their own business.

"It's always fun going out with you," Cillian said as he rolled his eyes at his friend.

"Makes life interesting, doesn't it?" Darryl replied.

Cathy appeared with iced teas and a small plate that she put in front of Cillian.

"Extra pickles because I know you love them, honey," she smiled.

"Thanks, Cathy," Cillian said as he snatched one up and took a bite of the crisp sour.

Cathy put her hand on Cillian's shoulder and patted him before she walked off.

"You know," Darryl said as he reached over and took a pickle for himself, "she flirts with you every time we come in here."

"She does not," Cillian scoffed. "She's just friendly and good at her job."

"Yeah, okay," Darryl said. "She's always touching you, asking how you are, and making small talk with you. I never see her do that when I come in here with someone else. You're clueless, man. You should ask her out."

"Cathy's nice and all, but..."

"Here we go again," Darryl interrupted. "Preacher, you are always full of excuses when we talk about women. Cathy is friendly, she's pretty, and she clearly is into you. I don't know what's holding you back. When was the last date you had?"

Darryl's loud voice garnered attention from some of the booths around them as they watched. He looked around and smiled.

"See?" he said with a wave of his arms. "Inquiring minds want to know."

Cillian felt eyes upon him and shifted in his seat.

"Can we not talk about this right now?" he replied as he picked up his iced tea.

"You gonna answer me?" Darryl pressed.

"It's been a while, okay? It's not a big deal."

Cathy reappeared with plates of food balanced on her arms.

"Pressed prime rib sandwich with a plate of onion rings," she said as she placed the items in front of Darryl, "and chicken salad for you, honey," she said as she gave Cillian his food. "Can I get you guys anything else right now?"

"I think that's it, thanks, Cathy," Cillian told her. Cathy started to walk away before Daryl stopped her.

"Say, Cathy," Darryl started, "you have a boyfriend?" he asked bluntly.

"Why, you in the market?" she laughed.

"Maybe I am," Darryl said slyly. He could see Cathy staring at Cillian as Cillian picked up his sandwich and took a bite, hoping to avoid conversation.

"No, I'm not seeing anybody right now," she said, still looking at Cillian as she answered.

"Hard to believe, a nice woman like you alone. That seems like a shame." Darryl picked up an onion ring and chomped on it.

"Doesn't it?" she laughed. "Let me know if you guys need anything else," she said as she walked away.

"There you go," Darryl said as he grabbed his sandwich. "I put my foot in the door for you, Preacher. The rest is up to you."

"You're an ass," Cillian retorted.

"I've been called worse," Darryl said through a mouthful of meat and onions.

The two men made quick work of their sandwiches as Cillian steered talk away from his non-existent relationships to other topics. When Cathy returned to the table, there was nothing but crumbs left on each plate.

"Anything else?" she asked.

"Not for me," Cillian pushed the empty plate away from him.

"Can I get a piece of that blue velvet cake to go?" Darryl asked. "And get some for my friends over there," Daryl stated as he pointed to the booth where the frightened woman sat.

Cathy dropped off two plates of cake at the booth before bringing Darryl his boxed piece.

"On me, for your help," Darryl smiled as the couple looked at him.

Cathy stood holding the check, unsure of where to go with it.

"He's paying," Cillian insisted.

She handed the bill to Darryl, but before she could let go of it, Darryl gave it a tug.

"You coming to the festival this weekend?" Darryl asked.

"I have to work until 10 each night," Cathy said with a hint of remorse.

"It goes to 11 on Friday on Saturday," Darryl added. "You should come. It will be fun. Head over to the beer tent so we can serve you for a change."

Cathy looked at Cillian and smiled and then back at Darryl.

"I'm sure I can swing by for a beer," she said.

"Great, we'll see you then," Darryl said as he stood up and grabbed his leather jacket.

"See you then," she said to Cillian as she walked to another table.

"You're a menace," Cillian said through his teeth as they walked to the register to pay for their meal.

Once they were outside, Cillian berated his friend a bit more.

"What the hell, Demon?" Cillian said as he strode toward his bike. "Now she thinks I wanted her to come and will expect something."

"Chill, Preacher," Darryl said as he sat on his bike. "I don't think she has any expectations. You're going to be there anyway, so what's the difference? You said yourself she's a nice person. So you hang out and talk for a bit. It's not like you have to be like Liam and take her back to Hog House and..."

"Enough, okay?" Cillian said sternly.

"Geez, man, I was trying to help you out. Don't get your panties in a twist over it. Do whatever the fuck you want."

"I'm sorry," Cillian said. "I've... I've just got a lot of stuff on my mind right now with the festival, and... other stuff."

"No problem," Darryl said, offering his hand to Cillian to shake it. "Hey, we're brothers that are here for each other. You need something or someone to talk to, hit me up. You know that."

"Thanks, Darryl," Cillian said as he got on his bike. "You coming to the house?"

"Nah, I told Annie I'd come home and give her car an oil change. I swear that girl would drive that thing until it exploded. I'll see you tomorrow when the fun starts."

Cillian headed the short distance back to Hog House. A few bikes were parked outside, and the house seemed noisier than the usual Thursday evening.

Cillian walked into the house and to the entertainment room. Several club members were gathered at the bar watching the Mets on the big screen TV. A few others were scattered on the couches or tables throughout the room. One club member was making out with someone on the couch, and he had his right hand working up and under her shirt as Cillian walked past.

"Take it up to a room, Whitey," Cillian said over the din to get Whitey's attention. "You know the rules. Not in the main areas."

"Sorry, Preacher," Whitey apologized. He straightened himself up and rose, grabbing the woman's hand to help her off the couch. She pulled down the tank top she was wearing to cover herself.

"C'mon, let's go upstairs," Whitey ordered.

"Geez, he's uptight," the woman said. "Is he really a Preacher? He sure acts like it."

"Hey!" Whitey yelled. "Don't disrespect him. We do what he asks, or you can just take your ass home."

Whitey led the woman towards the staircase as Cillian made his way to the bar. He stopped at the corner and got Rory's attention.

"What's the score?" he asked the bartender.

"4-2 Phillies in the eighth," Rory answered. "We've got men on first and second though with one out, and Nimmo is up. You want a pint?"

"Please," Cillian sighed.

Rory poured him a Guinness, and Cillian took a sip as he watched the TV. The hopes and cheers quickly turned to groans of despair as the batter hit a sharp line drive that was snagged by the second baseman, who promptly flipped the ball to second for an inning-ending double play.

"Feckin' Mets!" a voice yelled as glasses were slammed on the bar.

Cillian took his beer, nodded to Rory, and headed toward his room. Once inside, Cillian sat at his desk, putting his clipboard and beer down before kicking off his boots and jeans. The cold air from the central AC Conor had installed a few years ago drifted down and gave him a comforting chill on his bare legs. He propped his feet up on his desk and picked up his Guinness, sipping as he went mindlessly through emails on his computer. He noticed he still hadn't heard back from Father Clarke. Cillian wasn't sure when he would have time, but he resolved to take a ride to St. Brendan's once the weekend festival was done to see his old friend.

He drained the rest of his pint glass and shut the laptop before moving over to his bed. He didn't even bother pulling the blanket down and just laid there, staring up at the ceiling. He thought about what Demon had tried to arrange with Cathy for him. She was friendly, and they had a good rapport with each other, but the idea of going on a date with her had not even crossed Cillian's mind.

Cillian closed his eyes, took a deep breath, held it for a few seconds, and then exhaled through his mouth. He had learned the relaxation tip long ago, and it always helped him clear his mind when he needed it. At that moment, however, it didn't seem to do the trick for him.

Chapter 6

The grassy areas around the lakes were filled with crowds of young and old enjoying the festival. Mother Nature deigned to give them a little break from the heat and humidity for the Friday, bringing even larger crowds out to enjoy the food and fun. Lines formed at nearly every ride and food booth, and the group at the beer tent was never-ending, with people waiting outside for the chance to buy beer or get a table. Cillian strolled around once more, checking in at various places to make sure everything was going well. Everyone had smiles on their faces, a good indicator that all were having a good time.

Following his most recent lap around the grounds, Cillian made his way through the crowd at the beer tent to get inside. Whitey had volunteered to act as the de facto bouncer to ensure they were not over capacity inside the tent. The town had police on-site to keep an eye on things, as was customary. Still, whenever the Cosantóir were involved, they were extra vigilant in case there were any problems. The last thing Cillian wanted was to have everything shut down because underage drinkers got served, drugs were on the premises, or a fight broke out. He had given a pep talk to the club members who volunteered to work the festival, harkening back to Patrick Swayze's speech in "Roadhouse" – be nice until it is time to not be nice. It would not be easy for some club members, but it was necessary for a public event like this.

Cillian went beyond the entrance and was greeted by raucous Irish music. Cillian had hired several local bands to play for the weekend, along with a DJ, and tonight it was the Irish rock band Tom Collins & the Mixers. People dotted the dance floor, and Cillian wove his way through the crowd to get to a far table where he knew Cosantóir members like Conor were seated. Cillian spied his friend, who was sitting in his wheelchair and holding court at the table.

"Preacher!" Conor exclaimed. "Take a load off." He pointed to the folding chair next to the wheelchair.

Cillian sat, grateful to be off his feet for the first time in what felt like days.

"Everything okay?" Conor asked.

"Looks like we're all running smoothly," Cillian said. He placed his cellphone on the table and sat back in the chair. His phone had been his lifeline all week and even tonight as people texted and called him with questions or minor problems that needed to be quashed.

"You look like you need a pint," Conor said, reaching over and tapping his friend's wrist. Conor gave a look to one of the Cosantóir standing nearby and nodded. The younger man came over immediately.

"Colin, can you get Preacher a pint and another ginger ale for me," Conor asked, holding up his empty glass.

"You bet," Colin replied and dashed off toward the bar.

"I could have gone up myself, Conor," Cillian chided.

"Nonsense," Conor insisted. "You've put in a lot of work here. You can get waited on a bit."

Conor glanced at the seated crowd, the dance floor, and the mob at the bar.

"Besides, you don't want to have to wait on that line if you don't have to. This is the largest opening night crowd I have seen. You did great work, Preacher."

"Nah, you had already done most of the hard work. I just put the pieces together," Cillian told him, leaning close to the wheelchair so Conor could hear him over the noise.

"Think what you want, mo chara," Conor smiled. Cillian always grinned when Conor used Gaelic to refer to their friendship. "This year, this is all you."

Conor looked over to his son Liam, seated across the table from him and enjoying a Guinness while flirting.

"Liam!" Conor barked, getting his son's attention. He waved his hand in an upward motion, and Liam knew just what his father was requesting. He rose from his seat and let out a resounding yell of "Hey!"

All eyes turned in Liam's direction as a hush formed in the tent.

"The Ceannaire has something to say," Liam told the crowd before pointing back to his father. He nodded back toward his father, and, in an instant, Maeve was up from her seat and wheeling the wheelchair out to the center of the dance floor. Maeve walked over to the band to grab one of the wireless microphones and hand it to Conor, who refused it.

"I don't need that damn thing to get people to hear me," he gruffed as he raised his voice.

"Ain't that the truth!" a voice yelled from the crowd, causing laughter.

"Listen up, all. It's been a rough few weeks for all of us, but it's great to see that we can rally around to help take care of our community when we need to. As you walk around tonight and enjoy everything at the festival this weekend, keep in mind all the hard work the volunteers and local businesses have put in to make sure you have a good time. Usually, I would love to take credit for all of this. This year, thanks to this thing," he said as he rattled the arms of the wheelchair, "I haven't been able to do all that I have done in the past. Thankfully, we had someone to step in and do the job for me... even better than I have done in the past. Preacher, come on out here and take your kudos."

Cillian slowly rose from his seat and made his way over to his friend to thunderous applause. Embarrassed by the attention, Cillian gave a slight wave to the crowd before reaching Conor.

"You're an arse," Cillian said, leaning down to his friend.

"Yes, I am," Conor smiled, shaking Cillian's hand. Colin arrived next to both men with their drinks, and Conor gripped his glass of ginger ale before holding it up. He nodded over to Maeve, who rushed to his side and helped the injured man up from the wheelchair so he could stand. Conor shakily got to his feet to even more applause.e no

"I guess those feckin' therapists have done some good so far," he laughed as he held his glass. "To Preacher," he toasted. "

Sláinte!"

The entire crowd held up glasses and joined in.

Cillian leaned over to his friend and replied, "Slàinte Mhaith," before sipping his pint.

Conor sat back down in his wheelchair, and Maeve helped get him back to the table as Cillian followed. Cillian got plenty of slaps on the back of his leather jacket as he moved toward the table.

No sooner had Cillian sat down next to Conor when Colin dashed over to the two men.

"We've got an issue at the entrance," Colin said urgently.

Conor turned his head to see what was going on and saw a bit of a ruckus.

"I got it," Cillian replied, signaling for Colin to come with him. The two men hustled through the maze of tables to the front, where Whitey loudly dealt with someone. Cillian had arrived just as a young man gave Whitey a shove. Whitey had pulled his fists back to engage, but Cillian stepped between the two.

"Is there a problem here?" Cillian asked, looking back and forth between the two. The young man and his two friends all looked to be of good size and in good shape.

"Yes, there is," the man said as he stepped closer to Cillian. "Your lackey here won't let us in to get a beer."

Cillian turned to Whitey for a response.

"I asked them for ID, and none would give it to me," Whitey pronounced. "Then he started mouthing off."

"You gotta show ID guys; those are the rules for everyone, no exceptions," Cillian explained. "We don't want the whole place shut down for a mistake. Just let us have a look at the ID, and you can come in."

"I tried to explain to your friend here that we didn't bring ID," the young man said belligerently. Cillian looked into the man's dark eyes and could see they were glassy. He figured the trio was either high or drunk already before they got here. "Just let us in." The young man tried to push his way past Cillian, but Cillian stopped him with a strong, flat palm against the man's chest.

"I can't do that," Cillian said sternly.

Cillian stepped closer to the man to speak more quietly.

"Look, you guys clearly have had something already, and you can't prove to be legal, so you're not getting in. Now, I can call the police over and have them remove you guys, or you can just go on your way, sober up, and enjoy the festival. Your choice."

"C'mon, James, let's just go," one of the men behind said.

"I want a fuckin' beer!" James said, pushing Cillian's hand down off his chest. He went to walk around Cillian before Cillian stepped in front of him again. The young man went to raise his fist to Cillian, but Cillian gripped his wrist tightly and held it in place. Colin and Whitey both stepped up to make sure the other two men backed down.

"Last chance," Cillian whispered to the youngster as he put pressure on the wrist.

James tugged his arm away and rubbed his now-sore wrist.

"Fuck this place," he spat as he turned around and left the tent area, his friends following behind.

Cillian watched as the trio walked away towards the rest of the festival. He noticed James looked back and sneered before giving Cillian the finger. Cillian tapped Colin on the shoulder.

"Get a message to the boys out and about to keep an eye out for those three," Cillian requested. Colin simply nodded and grabbed his phone from his pocket to spread the word. Cillian watched as the young men disappeared from view before his concentration was interrupted.

"Cillian? Hey you!" a voice repeated before giving him a light push to snap him out of his focus. Cillian abruptly turned and saw Cathy, the waitress from the diner, standing before him.

"Cathy... Hi, I'm sorry... I was just dealing with something."

"I noticed," she said. "I think you caught everyone's attention. Everything okay?"

"Yeah, just some kids causing trouble. It was no big deal."

The two stood in awkward silence for a moment before Cillian realized he should say something.

"Did... did you want a beer or a glass of wine from the bar?" Cillian asked.

"I would, but I've had a long day at work and still have to drive home. One drink is usually enough to make me... well..." she chuckled before she finished her sentence.

"Oh, sure," Cillian laughed.

"Maybe we can walk around a little bit, though?" she asked. "I just walked over and haven't seen the whole place yet."

"Sure, sure," Cillian answered. "Just let me go grab my phone."

Cillian raced back to the table and saw Conor engaged in fiery conversation, yelling something about how it was when he first started working in the tunnels. Cillian tried to slip in and grab his phone without notice, but he was spied by Maeve.

"Where are you off to?" she asked as Cillian gathered his phone.

"Oh... I'm just going to walk around a bit and check on things," he said as he looked back towards the entrance to the tent and saw Cathy waiting patiently for him. Maeve followed his gaze and then turned to Cillian and smiled.

"She's cute," Maeve said.

"Just a friend from the diner," Cillian rushed, hoping to stave off a litany of questions.

"I didn't say anything," Maeve told him, making a zipping motion on her lips.

Liam looked over and saw what the two were staring at.

"You gonna close that deal tonight, Preacher?" Liam guffawed.

"You're a pig, Liam," the woman sitting next to Liam added.

"Guilty as charged," he added, taking a slight bow. "We'll want details in the morning!" Liam yelled as Cillian turned to go.

"Pipe down, eejit," Conor interjected. "Go enjoy," Conor told him. "Never mind these arseholes."

Cillian simply nodded and walked off toward Cathy. The two meandered across the grass, taking in all the sights and smells of the festival. They walked past several food trucks making all kinds of treats. Everything from the local empanada truck to the fire department tent grilling burgers and hot dogs to typical carnival food like fried dough permeated the night air. They walked along quietly as Cillian wracked his brain, trying to come up with a conversation.

"They'll be fireworks tomorrow night if you come back," Cillian stated.

"Oh, that will be nice. I work the morning shift tomorrow, so maybe I can make it."

"Yeah, that would be great," he said, struggling for more to add.

The two walked by some of the carnival rides with their dynamic lights. They did stop to watch kids playing a ring toss game and then at the tent that had bowls of goldfish to throw a ping-pong ball into. Cillian did his best with small talk and began to relax a bit.

"So, do you ever get free time to do anything fun?" Cathy asked. "It seems like you're always busy with something."

"I keep myself occupied," Cillian added. "With work, the club, this festival, and other stuff, I barely have time to do much lately."

"I know," Cathy laughed. "I see you at the diner an awful lot. Don't you ever want a home-cooked meal?"

"I'm not much of a cook," Cillian admitted. "We have a kitchen at the house, but I don't go much beyond the microwave."

"Well, you need a real meal for a change," Cathy insisted. "Nothing against the diner. We have great stuff, but it's not the same. Maybe... I can cook for you sometime?" Cathy smiled.

Cillian gave a nervous laugh and looked up at the crowd. He caught a glimpse of the three young men from the tent now herding a couple of women into the shadows behind one of the ride trailers. The situation gave Cillian an uneasy vibe.

"Cathy... excuse me for a minute," Cillian said. "I have to go check on this."

Cillian jogged off before Cathy could reply. He worked his way through the crowd that waited to get on the Spider ride. The engine for the ride growled louder as he got near. Cillian turned the corner around the trailer and spotted the three young men with two girls who had their backs against the trailer.

"C'mon," he heard James telling the one girl. "I told you I'd get you some beer, but you're gonna have to do something for me," he said as he pressed his body forcefully against hers. His two friends held onto the other girl to keep her from interrupting.

"I guess you don't know what last chance means," Cillian said as he moved quickly and pulled James off the girl, sending the young man stumbling to the ground.

"You okay?" Cillian asked the girl. She was clearly shaken and nodded rapidly. Her eyes grew wide as she looked at Cillian, causing him to turn quickly as he saw James swinging a half-full beer bottle at him. Cillian sidestepped the swing so that James fell on the ground once more, his face hitting the grass.

"I've had just about enough of your interfering, Grandpa," James howled. He rushed toward Cillian, who moved two steps to his left to dodge James' sprawling tackle attempt. Cillian watched as the young man collided against the side of the trailer. Cillian pounced on him, pulling James' right arm behind his back while pressing his face roughly against the trailer.

"Let go of me!" James shouted. Cillian pushed on his arm every time he wriggled, bringing it higher up his back until he was yelling in pain.

"Now, I can dislocate your shoulder or break your arm... which will it be?" Cillian hissed into James' ear. James' two friends were now on Cillian, pulling him off their wounded comrade. One hit Cillian in the midsection with a soft punch. Still, it was enough to make Cillian wince so the boys could grab his arms. James turned, shaking his right arm as he tried to get the feeling back into it and approached Cillian.

"Time for some payback," James grinned. He picked up the now-empty beer bottle off the ground. "That's another beer you owe me, old man," James scowled. He moved toward Cillian, raising the bottle high over his head with the intent of hitting Cillian as hard as he could. As James brought the bottle down, his arm was intercepted and caught in the grip of a giant hand. James turned around to see a figure looming over him.

"Bad manners, asshole," Darryl rumbled as he plucked the bottle from James' hand and tossed it away. With just a fast turn of Daryl's hand, a loud crack went through the air as James' wrist broke. James crumpled to the ground with a wail.

Darryl turned his attention to the two men holding Cillian, though neither held onto his friend any longer. The two watched as Darryl loomed over them. He grabbed one by the collar of his t-shirt and tossed him towards James so that he barreled into his fallen friend.

"Fuck!" James squealed in pain again as his friend landed on him.

Darryl took two strides towards the last standing punk. Darryl's shadow engulfed the young man, and he begged for mercy.

"I think at least one of your friends needs to go to the hospital," Darryl said. "You sober enough to get them there, or do I need to call you a police escort?"

"I'll... I'll get them there, sir," the young man whimpered. He scurried over to gather up James and his pal before the three of them took off toward the parking lot.

"You good?" Darryl said to Cillian.

"Yeah, the kid caught me off guard," Cillian admitted as he stood straight. "Thanks."

"Anytime, brother," Daryl said. He turned his attention to the two girls. "You ladies okay?"

"Yes, thank you so much," the dark-haired friend said as she put her arm around the girl James was assaulting.

The four walked out into the light of the festival before Cillian stopped them.

"Do you know those creeps?" Cillian asked.

The dark-haired girl turned to her friend without saying anything before the girl lifted her head and looked at Cillian.

"Unfortunately, yes," she said as she stared at Cillian. "James lives here in town near my grandmother. He's been an asshole as long as I have known him."

Cillian stared at the girl, taking in her features. Her golden hair, her hazel eyes, even the way she stood all sparked memories for him. Before he could say anything, Cathy had reached the group with Liam. A couple of others of the Cosantóir arrived as well.

"What's going on?" Liam asked. "Your lady friend here said there was trouble."

"Same eejits who tried to get into the beer tent," Cillian remarked. "Darryl took care of them, and they fled."

"Want us to go after them?" Colin asked, turning to Liam for an order. Liam looked at Cillian and saw the Preacher shake his head no.

"Let 'em go," Liam commanded. "Preacher knows who they are. We'll settle it if we have to."

"Are you okay?" Cathy said, approaching Cillian and frightened by what was going on.

"I'm fine," Cillian said quickly. He looked back to the girls and took a step toward them. He gazed at the blond girl, who stepped back at the intensity of his stare.

"What... what's your name?" Cillian asked her.

"Makenna," the girl told him.

"No, your full name," he said with urgency.

"Makenna Mazza," she remarked. Makenna looked confusedly at her friend and then back at Cillian.

"Mazza..." Cillian said quietly. "Is your mother... Annabella?"

Chapter 7

Annabella spent the days ahead of the Irish Festival going over particulars with Erin and honing her knife and kitchen skills. She chopped an endless supply of vegetables for practice, checked the menu and recipes Erin planned to use on the truck so she knew them well, and went out and treated herself to a new pair of sneakers. If Annabella would be on her feet all day for days in a row, she needed to make sure she had something better than her beat-up pair of New Balance.

When Friday rolled around, Anna readied herself and strode to her car. Makenna pulled into the driveway behind her car just as she was getting prepared to leave, blocking her in. Annabella got out of her vehicle and watched as Makenna climbed out of her black BMW, a recent gift from her father, humming along to whatever music she listened to on her iPhone. She paid little attention to Annabella until she reached the point in the driveway where her mother stood.

"Hey," Annabella yelled.

Makenna idly walked past her mother, never looking up from her phone.

"HEY!" she screamed, finally getting Makenna's attention. Her daughter looked at her with shock.

"Oh, hi, Mom," Makenna casually offered.

"Hello," came a gruff answer. "You're blocking me in, and I need to go to work."

"Sorry. I just wanted to swing by to look through some of the clothes you might have. I'm looking for that cute pair of shorts..."

"Makenna, please move your car," her mother pleaded. "It's the first day of the festival, and I need to be there. Erin needs me to help her with setup and prep."

Makenna rolled her eyes and shuffled back toward her car. She got in and dutifully backed out of the driveway so Annabella could leave.

Annabella pulled up alongside her daughter and rolled down her window.

"I'll be at the festival until late. Do you have your key?" Annabella asked.

"I'm not staying here tonight, Mom," Makenna replied. "Dee, Reese, and I are all going to the festival later. We'll probably be out late and then just crash back at Grandma's house again. I've been there all week; why would I change now?"

"I just thought that since the house is a bit more settled, you might want to stay here."

"Mom, no offense, but you barely have room for yourself in there," Makenna pointed to the front door. "Honestly, I don't know how you do it. We had such a big house in..."

"That house wasn't all it was cracked up to be," Annabella huffed.

"It was beautiful... lots of rooms and property, a big pool, a staff... I don't know how you can say that."

"It was a prison for me, Mac," Annabella insisted. "Your father thought if he 'dazzled' me with all those things, I wouldn't notice or care about how I was being treated. I was just a polished trophy for him to bring out and show to his rich friends."

Annabella's face was getting flush with anger just remembering it all and how she put up with it.

She shook her head to clear the bad thoughts and looked back at Makenna.

"This place here... this is mine and yours too if you want it to be. This will be a home, not just a house. Anyway, I have to get going, or Erin will wonder where I am. Stop by the food truck and see me in action tonight."

"Sure," Makenna nodded. "We'll get over there if we can. See you later."

Annabella sighed as she watched Makenna walk to the front door and go inside. Annabella sped off towards the lakes, working the side roads to avoid getting stuck in too much traffic. It had been years she spent any significant time in Harriman and Monroe. The amount of traffic that existed now far exceeded what she recalled when she was younger. She sat idle in traffic on 17M longer than she had anticipated. Annabella kept glancing at the clock on the dashboard and saw the minutes tick away to the point where she was now late, causing her to panic. She rushed her car through the last of the yellow lights she came upon so she wouldn't get stuck again, making the tires squeal along the way.

A lone parking spot sat clear just outside of Airplane Park. Annabella snuck in just ahead of a large pickup truck, and she got some angry leers as she climbed out from the other driver. She hustled across the street and onto the grassy area around the lakes, now filled with the sounds and smells she remembered from festivals long ago. As she strode across the lawn, she spotted stands for all the carnival favorites – corn dogs, popcorn, fried dough, cotton candy – mixed in with carnival games and rides. The local fire department had their grills and smokers going so that the smells of burgers, barbecued chicken, and hot dogs emanated through the air.

She approached Erin's truck, going up the steel steps to the open door. Erin was inside making last-minute checks of inventory to be sure they had all they needed.

"Hey!" Erin beamed as she spotted Annabella.

"I'm sorry, I know I'm late," Anna replied nervously, checking her watch.

"Oh, please," Erin scoffed. "You're here; that's the important part. Ready to jump into the fire?"

"Let's do it," Annabella said enthusiastically.

Erin gave a brief tutorial on the truck's equipment, so Annabella knew where to find everything and how each item worked. Erin showed her the menu they were using for the evening, sticking to basics and food that was easy to carry around – wrap sandwiches, chili, sausage and pepper sandwiches, and beignets. She took a beige apron from Erin with the Erin's Edibles logo and put it on before she tied her hair up in a ponytail.

"Good idea," Erin noted as she did the same with her hair. "It's going to get hot in here. All I've got are these little fans, and once the flat top and fryers are going, it's a sauna in here. You got comfortable shoes on, right? We're on our feet moving all night. I'll try to go easy on you since it's your first day."

"Don't you dare," Anna said with determination. "Give me what you got. Where do I start?"

Anna spent the hours before the festival began chopping countless raw vegetables for wraps and preparing the beignet dough. She blended up fresh raspberries and blueberries for dipping sauces. She familiarized herself with the location of everything so she could reach for one thing while performing another task and not miss a beat. One of Erin's catering waitresses, a young girl named Olivia, was manning the window to take the orders. Olivia walked Annabella through the order process, using the register and the credit card reader they had for the tablet they used for orders.

When the first customer ambled up to the window, Annabella's butterflies in her stomach exploded into full panic mode, and her mind went blank. All she could see was Leo standing in front of her telling her she should just sit there and "be pretty for him."

"Hey," Erin said to her as she spotted the glazed look in Annabella's eyes. "You okay?"

Annabella snapped back again and took a deep breath. She held her hands up in front of her face and saw them shaking.

"Erin, I haven't worked in over twenty years," she whispered to her friend.

"You got this," Erin told her, placing her hands on her friend's shoulders. "Leo's not here to tell you any different. I know you can handle it, or I wouldn't have asked. Let's go and have some fun."

Annabella nodded and exhaled before she smiled. "What's up, Olivia?" she shouted.

Olivia grinned back.

"A Buffalo chicken wrap and a pressed veggie sandwich, please!" Olivia yelled.

Erin reached over and turned on music as she worked the flat top, and Annabella prepped the sandwiches.

"We're rolling, ladies!" Erin laughed.

Time sped by as the festival crowd picked up. A steady stream of customers made their way to the window, ordering everything on the menu. The beignets proved to be a hot item. Annabella found herself stationed at the fryer often, adding bits of dough that came to crisp perfection in moments. She would remove the beignets, place them on their checkered paper tray, sprinkle them liberally with powdered sugar, and then add a sauce on the side. Caramel, melted chocolate, and berry sauces flowed constantly. Annabella's apron was dotted with flecks of oil and snowy white sugar.

When they hit a lull and could take a breath, Annabella glanced at her watch and saw it was nearly 10 PM already. She stationed herself in front of one of the small fans. Even the tepid air the fan moved around helped to cool her sweaty forehead. Erin clanged up the metal steps and into the truck, handing a plastic cup to Annabella.

"Fresh lemonade from down the row," Erin said. Annabella nodded and drew the golden liquid through the straw. The chill sent goosebumps through her body.

"Here, Liv," Erin said as she handed one to the girl.

"I think things will quiet down now," Erin said. "There's only an hour left tonight. They'll be hitting the rides or the beer tent." Erin sat on one of the coolers and patted the space next to her so Annabella would sit.

"If I sit down now, I might not get back up," Annabella admitted.

"It hasn't been that bad," Olivia chuckled. "Wait until you do one of the weddings with us."

"You're just a kid," Annabella scolded the younger girl. "I'm 42 and haven't worked like this in a long time. I'm beat."

"Speaking of being a kid," Olivia said as she turned to Erin. "Since it's quieter, do you think this kid can leave the truck for a few minutes? My sister and her friends are over at the Spider ride. I promise I'll be back to help with clean and close."

"All right," Erin gave in. "You know I can't resist those big brown eyes. But you're handling the trash bags tonight, then."

"Deal!" Olivia said as she took off her apron and hung it up. She sped past Annabella and Erin and out the back door. Annabella watched out the order window as she spied Olivia racing towards the flashing lights of the Spider.

"She's great," Annabella said as she drew deeply on the straw of her lemonade.

"The best I've got," Erin admitted. "I hired her three years ago when I was starting up the business, and she was just sixteen and had no experience. Liv outlasted everyone else I have used, including men and women with more experience. She busts her tail. I wish I had a team of Olivias."

"I'm sure you do after working with me tonight," Annabella said as she opened another box of plastic utensils.

"Will you stop it?" Erin chided. "You've been fantastic. There's no way I could have done all this by myself back here. You've been a pro. You jumped in and got the job done. I'm impressed."

"Well, thanks," Annabella said modestly. "Let's see how I am tomorrow when I'm all sore and twisted like a pretzel."

"Pretzels!" Erin yelled as she sat up. "Shit! That's what I forgot. I premade all those pretzel sticks and forgot to bring them. Tomorrow. You need a bathroom break?"

"No, I'm good," Annabella said as she slurped the last of her lemonade. "I think I have just sweat it all away tonight."

"Well, I'm going to run over to the bathrooms. I'll be back in two minutes."

Annabella tried to busy herself, straightening and putting things away that she knew they didn't need any longer for the night. A rapid banging on the metal sill of the order window startled her.

"Hey in there," a voice yelled. "Let's get some service! Shake a leg, skirt!" The laughter of several young men hung in Annabella's ears as she inhaled to push down what she wanted to say in reply to the rude man.

"Can I help you?" she asked, painting a smile on her face. She recognized the smarmy look of James Weber. James and his family lived two houses down from Annabella's mother. He was the same age as Makenna but with twice the entitlement issues. More than once, Annabella had overheard Makenna talking about him and how he was constantly hitting on her whenever her daughter came up to visit her grandmother.

Annabella stared blankly at James, hoping he wouldn't recognize her. They hadn't seen each other in years, and she hoped that played in her favor.

James scanned the menu and sighed. Annabella got a strong whiff of alcohol when he did this and stepped back a bit.

"Just get the sausage and peppers, man," one of the other young men said. "We need to get to the beer tent."

"Sausage gives him the shits," the third man said with a laugh.

"Fuck off, Harry," James spat out. "Just give me some of the beignets."

Annabella nodded and went over to the fryer, quickly tossing the batter into the spattering oil. She walked back toward the window and saw James drinking something from a flask.

"What kind of sauce would you like?" she said politely.

"What?" James barked.

"The beignets come with a sauce on the side. Caramel, chocolate, or berry."

"The only thing he wants dripping on his fingers is Makenna," Harry roared as he grabbed the flask from James.

James said nothing but walked closer to the truck, staring at her. Annabella saw a hint of recognition in his eyes as he grinned.

"Shut up!" James yelled. "I'll take the caramel," James said sweetly. "I like sweet and sticky."

Annabella took a few steps back from the window, watching as James kept his eyes trained on her. Annabella leaped forward and gasped when she bumped into Erin behind her.

"I'm just pulling the beignets out for you," Erin said. "Sorry to startle you. You okay?"

"Yeah, I just need to get some of the caramel sauce," she said as she warmed some lightly before pouring it into a cup.

Annabella brought the paper tray over to the order window and passed it through to James.

"Five dollars," Annabella told him.

James took the tray and reached into his pocket, pulling out a twenty-dollar bill.

Annabella grasped the crisp bill, but James held onto it and wouldn't let go.

"I'm a little surprised to see you working here, Mrs. Mazza," he said.

"It's a job... and my name is Foley, James. You should know that. Your parents live right next to my mother and have all your life."

"Feisty," James said. "I see where your daughter gets it from."

James loosened his grip on the twenty so Annabella could take it.

"Keep the change," James said. "It looks like you need the tip. I'll make sure to let Makenna know I saw you."

James dipped his finger into the warm caramel and sucked it off his finger before walking away in laughter.

"Who's that asshat?" Erin said as she watched them walk away.

"James Weber. His family lives near my Mom's place. He's been a creep since he was a toddler."

"Well, it looks like whatever he's smoking, drinking, or doing only enhances that. You want to get some fresh air?"

"No, I'd rather stay busy," Annabella admitted. "I can start cleaning the flat top for you."

Irish music could be heard blasting from the beer tent as many of the food stations and trucks began to close up for the night. Erin and Annabella had made good work on the cleaning with few interruptions. It was only when Olivia came racing up to the truck that they went from the cooking area to the window.

"What's going on, Liv?" Erin asked the girl.

"A big fight," she said out of breath. "Sorry I'm back late, but I couldn't get through the crowd. All these people were standing around. The bikers were taking care of some dudes that practically raped these girls, I guess. At least that's what I heard."

"Are the police coming?" Annabella asked.

"Not if the Cosantóir is handling it," Erin answered. "They're the biker club that runs the festival. They have more of a take care of your own problems approach."

"Wow, you guys are almost done," Olivia marveled as she peered into the truck. "I feel bad."

"Don't feel bad," Erin told her. "Just get in here and do the rest! You can mop down the floor and get rid of all the trash, please. Why don't you knock off for the night, Anna?"

"Are you sure? I can stay until you're done."

"I want to make sure you come back tomorrow," Erin laughed. Erin pulled in the tip jar from the counter and quickly counted it out. "Here's your cut." Erin handed Anna a mix of a wad of singles and fives.

"Thanks, Erin," Anna replied as she hugged her friend. "I'll see you tomorrow."

Anna hung her apron on the hook and went outside of the truck. Even though it was still quite humid, the air outside felt significantly colder than the food truck's hot box. She passed Olivia coming back from the garbage area and glanced over to where there was still a crowd of people around. Since it was on her way back to her car, Anna strolled over to get a look at some of the commotion.

She instantly recognized the long dark hair Reese, Makenna's friend, sported. Anna quickened her pace over to the crowd now, worried about who might have been involved. It was then she spotted Makenna standing there in her shorts and tank top, with her friend Deirdre draping an arm over her shoulder.

Anna stepped quickly to her daughter.

"Makenna!" she said as she spun the girl around. She could see mascara streaks on Makenna's face, and she breathed rapidly. "Are you okay? What happened?"

"It... it was nothing, Mom," Makenna told her.

"Nothing? People are saying there was an attack. Were you girls attacked?"

Reese had joined her friends now and spoke up.

"We weren't... I mean, not really," Reese said. "I mean, James might have..."

"Did James Weber attack you? Let's get you to the police," Anna insisted as she put her arm around Makenna.

"Mom, he didn't attack me," Makenna insisted. "Jesus, Reese, way to go. He got a little carried away."

"Makenna, did he hurt you?" Anna looked into her daughter's eyes, but Makenna quickly turned her gaze to the ground so her mother couldn't read anything.

"He scared us more than anything," Reese went on. "They said they were going to get beer for us and didn't, and then he..."

"Reese! Shut the fuck up!" Makenna yelled.

"It doesn't matter," Anna told her. "Why aren't the police here yet? Should I call them?"

"No, Mom. We don't need the police. It wasn't a big deal," Makenna pleaded with her mother as Anna took out her cell phone.

"Don't worry about it, Mrs. Mazza," Deirdre chimed in. "Those guys over there took care of everything," she said, pointing to four or five men clad in matching leathers even though it was nearly 90 out.

"Yeah," Makenna agreed. "And one of those guys I think knows you. He asked if I was your daughter."

"Knows me?" Anna said aloud. "I don't know any bikers. He must be mistaken."

"No mistake," Makenna said. "He knew you were Annabella Mazza."

"Which one?" Anna asked. Makenna pointed to a tall figure with his back to the women. "That guy there. He's the one who came in and stopped James."

Anna put her arm around Makenna and herded her over toward where the bikers were standing. The women stood behind the men before Makenna tapped the biker on the shoulder.

"I just wanted to say thank you again," Makenna said to him. "My Mom is here too if you wanted to see her."

The biker spun around quickly and faced them. It took Anna a moment with the dim lighting around her to get a look at his face. The temples had gray around them, and the body and dress were much different. Still, that jawline and those blue eyes were something that Anna had never forgotten. She searched for words but found nothing as she stared at his familiar face.

"Hello, Annabella," the voice said softly. The moment he spoke, she heard the lilt in his brogue that brought it all together.

"Is it really you?" she said with awe. "Father Meehan?"

Chapter 8

C illian never imagined that he would ever see Annabella's face again. That initial moment where she was before him with her arm wrapped around her daughter, the woman he had just saved from a potential assault, shocked him. It had been almost twenty years since Cillian had seen her face-to-face, but the look was unmistakable to him. Her golden hair was longer than he recalled, but her face, right down to the way her brow wrinkled when she was caught in her thoughts, remained the same.

It was when Annabella called him 'Father Meehan' that the reality of the situation fell upon him. She had no idea that Cillian had left that life behind him long ago, but with her there now, all those feelings came roaring back like a freight train whizzing by.

"Preacher," Liam said as he nudged Cillian with his elbow, "I think she's talking to you."

Cillian snapped back to the present when he heard Makenna speak as well.

"You're a priest?" Makenna said, stunned.

"No..." Cillian stuttered. "I mean, I was... a long time ago when your mother and I knew each other."

"You look so different," Annabella said quietly. Cillian felt her gaze upon him, taking in everything about him from his graying hair to the leather jacket and jeans he wore to the team of the Cosantóir that was around him now.

"A lot has changed in twenty years... for me, anyway," Cillian admitted. "You... you still look like you're twenty." Cillian could see a rosy blush move to Annabella's cheeks even in the darkened area where they stood.

"Hardly," she said humbly. Cillian watched as Annabella instinctively brushed her hands over her clothing to try to straighten her shirt and brush her hair from her eyes.

The two stood in awkward silence, looking at each other before Makenna intervened again.

"Mom? Mom!" she insisted before Annabella turned to her daughter. "Can we stay with you tonight? I don't know if James will be back or not, and he's so close to Grandma's place it might be better if we were with you right now."

"Sure, honey, that's fine," Annabella offered. Cillian observed her putting her arm around Makenna.

"I don't think he'll be bothering you anytime soon," Cillian told Makenna. "I think Demon..." Cillian noticed a flash of worry cross Annabella's face. "I mean, Darryl... did enough to his wrist that he'll be away for at least the night."

"What did he do?" Annabella asked cautiously. Her eyes looked up into Cillian's. Cillian hesitated before answering, and one of the other girls jumped in.

"He snapped it like a twig," Deirdre replied. "I heard the bones crack."

"Oh my," Annabella answered. Cillian saw her eyes lock on him again. A mix of thankfulness and unease was visible on her face.

"He had it coming," Deirdre added. "Who knows what that perv would have done if you hadn't stepped in."

Annabella nodded without saying a word before holding her daughter tighter against her.

"Should… should we go to the police about it?" she asked Cillian quietly.

"You certainly can if you want to," Cillian answered. "I am sure they would be glad to get a statement and then go over and arrest him. They'll also come looking for me and the club as well, I'm guessing. That kid didn't seem like the type that would just roll over. I'm sure he'd want to press charges against me and the others as well."

"I don't want to cause any problems for you," Annabella admitted, "but I don't want him to think he can just get away with what he did either."

"Trust me, Mom," Makenna interjected into the conversation, "there's no way he thinks that now. He'll be too afraid to say anything to anyone. Let's just go back to your house."

Cillian picked up what Makenna told her mother and took a step toward both of them before they could walk off.

"Your house?" He asked. "So you're living in this area now? I thought your husband's business was down in Westchester."

"It was… I mean, it is," Annabella said, flustered. "What I mean is that Leo and I aren't together anymore. The divorce was finalized a few weeks ago. I have a little house over in Harriman on Church Street.

"I didn't realize," Cillian replied. "I'm sorry to hear that."

"Don't be," Annabella chuckled. "I'm sorry it took me so long to figure out what an SOB he is. I decided to move up this way to start over. I didn't know you weren't a…"

Cillian noticed Annabella catch herself. She clearly was going to say something about the priesthood and stopped.

"Do you live around here as well?" she asked, changing the topic abruptly.

"I do," Cillian answered. "Small world, I guess."

"Yes, I guess it is," Annabella answered with a slight smile.

Cillian's pulse raced when he saw her smile. Annabella's grin always made him weak, especially when she displayed the one small dimple she had on her left cheek.

"We should go, Mom," Makenna told her mother.

"Yes, okay, Mac," Annabella replied. "Thank you, Fa..." Annabella caught herself again.

"It's just Cillian now," he stated, trying to make her feel more at ease.

"Thank you, Cillian," she said softly.

"It was lovely to see you again," Cillian said with a nod.

Cillian turned to walk back toward where other members of the Cosantóir were still gathered, discussing the event and what they should do next. Before he could reach the other members, Cillian felt a tap on the back of his leather jacket. He spun around and saw Makenna standing before him.

"Thank you," she offered softly.

"You're welcome," Cillian smiled.

"My Mom would like to invite you over for dinner at her place. You know, to say thanks, and maybe you two can catch up."

Excitement coursed through Cillian's veins before he reined himself in.

"That would be lovely, but I'm kind of tied up with the festival for the next few nights."

"Oh, she's working here as well, over at Erin's Edibles food truck. It would probably have to be after the weekend, but we can arrange it."

Cillian looked past Makenna and saw Annabella standing just underneath the lights next to one of the carnival rides. The light encircled her as she glanced back to see Cillian.

"I'd love to," Cillian offered. "Let her know I'll meet up with her here tomorrow night, and we can talk about it some more, okay?"

"Absolutely," Makenna beamed before turning and racing back to her mother. Cillian watched as the women talked, and Annabella looked back in his direction. Cillian gave her a casual wave, and Annabella smiled and waved back.

"Who's the pretty lass waving at you, Preacher?" Liam said as he sidled up next to Cillian.

"Turns out one of the girls is the daughter of an old friend of mine," Cillian replied as he continued to watch Annabella walk away and into the darkness. "That was her. Annabella Mazza."

"She looks pretty far from Italian if you ask me," Liam scoffed.

"Italian on her mother's side, and the fella she married was Italian. Her maiden name is Foley. Her Da was a great man. One of the nicest people I ever met, and Irish through and through. Donal Foley. He was far too young when he passed."

"Where do you know them from?" Liam inquired.

Cillian sighed before answering.

"They were... they were part of my parish. I married Annabella and Leo and gave Donal his last rites. It was a long time ago. I haven't seen her in twenty years, maybe more," he said softly to keep the conversation from prying ears.

"Ahh, back in the B.C. days," Liam said with a laugh.

Cillian gave a confused look to his friend.

"B.C.," Liam insisted. "Before Cosantóir. Geez, Preacher, that was a good one. Anyways, how old was she when she got married? She looks like she could be that girl's sister, never mind her Ma."

"She was barely twenty-one when they got married. Bella has always had that look about her. She hasn't changed a bit," Cillian replied.

"Sounds like she was a bit more than the good church girl to you," Liam said before lowering his voice. "Speaking of which, don't forget you have your lady friend over there waitin' on ya." Liam nodded over toward where Cathy patiently waited for Cillian.

"Cripes, I forgot," Cillian said as he hustled over toward where Cathy stood.

"Is everything okay?" she asked concernedly.

"Fine," Cillian responded while forcing a smile. "Just some folks getting a little out of hand is all."

"People are saying those girls got attacked, and that you intervened."

"Not just me, thankfully, or things could have been worse. Darryl is the hero."

"It was brave of you to step in," Cathy said as she stepped closer to Cillian.

"Not really," he answered humbly. "It was the right thing to do."

"Well, that woman you were talking to seemed very grateful. Do you know her?"

Cillian hesitated before answering.

"Yes, I do. She's an old friend. We haven't seen each other in a very long time. It was a weird coincidence."

"I thought... I thought I heard her call you Father Meehan," Cathy asked inquisitively.

Cillian sighed.

"You did," he said resignedly. "That was also a lifetime ago."

"You were a priest?"

"Is that so hard to believe?" Cillian asked defensively while trying to smile through it. He had sensed the same shock and surprise in voices for many years.

"I'm sorry," Cathy apologized. "I didn't mean it to come out like that. It's just... it's just hard to picture, is all. You're in a motorcycle club, wear leathers, have tattoos... and you're kind of burly. I have a hard time envisioning you as a priest."

"Sometimes I do too," Cillian replied. "It's the truth, though. It's not something I advertise. Like I said, it was a long time ago."

The couple stood in a bit of awkward silence as the crowd began to disperse. Liam walked up to Cillian and Cathy.

"We're going back to the beer tent to finish out the night," Liam announced. "You comin', Preacher? I think you could use one after all that."

"Sure," Cillian assented. "We'll meet you over there."

"Oh, I should probably get going," Cathy interjected. "I worked a long day, and I have to work tomorrow too."

"Are you sure?" Cillian asked. "I'd be happy to get you a beer. I feel like I kind of left you in the cold."

"No, really, it's okay," Cathy told him. "I'm sure I'll see you at the diner soon. Have a good night."

Cathy put her hand gently on Cillian's arm, gave him a quick smile, and walked off toward the diner.

"I hope all that didn't mess things up for you," Liam said.

"No, I'm pretty sure I did that on my own," Cillian told him.

"Don't sweat it, Preacher."

Liam slapped the back of Cillian's leather jacket and pulled him along with him as they ambled to the beer tent.

"Plenty of fish in the sea, brother," Liam told Cillian as they paced along.

Cillian simply nodded in reply and gazed off into the direction that Annabella had walked.

Chapter 9

Annabella and Makenna walked together into the darkened parking area where Annabella's car sat. As Annabella searched her purse for her keys, she heard her daughter talking to her friends.

"I can't believe James would do that," Reese said in hushed tones to Makenna and Deirdre.

"I can," Deirdre added. "He's a prick. We need to avoid him," she warned.

"Easier said than done," Reese added. "He lives right next to Mac's grandmother. You know we'll see him again before the week is out. Maybe we should just go back to our apartment for the rest of the week. What do you think, Mac?"

"I don't think he'll be bothering us," Makenna said firmly. "Those guys taught him a lesson. One night at my Mom's should be fine."

Annabella was relieved to hear Makenna was so strong in her approach, something she lamented she hadn't shown when she was her daughter's age.

"The car is open," Annabella said loudly to break up the conversation.

"Oh, we're parked over there," Makenna pointed further down the lot where it was darker. Couples and families milled about, walking to their own vehicles as the festival night drew to a close.

"I can drive you over there," Annabella insisted. She watched as Makenna rolled her eyes and the girls began to file into the small car.

The girls were silent on the short trek to Makenna's car. Annabella pulled up next to her daughter's auto and watched as they switched over. She got Deirdre to roll down the window to Makenna's BMW.

"Follow me straight back," Annabella said.

"Mom, relax," Makenna insisted as she yelled over the music blaring in the car.

"I'll feel better about it, okay?"

Makenna rolled the driver's side window up as Annabella drove off toward her home. The drive took a bit longer than usual, with all the auto and pedestrian traffic milling around town at 11 PM. When Annabella arrived in her driveway, she waited patiently outside her car for Makenna and her friends to arrive. She noticed that the sensor light pointed at the driveway had not come on.

Something else that needs fixing around here, Annabella thought.

The time before the girls arrived gave Annabella a moment to reflect on her day. Pride coursed through her as she considered how well her first day of work in years had gone. She knew she would get better with each passing day and looked forward to tomorrow. Meeting up with Cillian was a complete surprise to her. Even with him looking vastly different from what she remembered, he still came across as the man she turned to, not just a spiritual advisor but a good friend that she was abruptly taken from.

Makenna and her friends finally arrived, toting McDonald's bags as they climbed out of the car.

"Why did you stop?" Annabella told her daughter. "I thought you were following me straight back."

"We were hungry, Mom," Makenna insisted. "I don't know what you have in the house for food, and it's too late for any of us to cook anything.

I got you a double cheeseburger and fries," she said as she crinkled the brown paper bag and handed it to her mother.

"Thanks," Annabella said before moving to the front door to unlock it.

"You should fix that light," Makenna said as they approached in the darkness,

"It must be the groundskeeper's night off," Annabella said sarcastically. "I'll have the butler make a note to speak with him in the morning. It's on the list, Mac."

"Someone's cranky," Makenna said as the group walked into the house.

"I'm sorry," Annabella answered. "It's been a long day. I'm tired and stressed about what happened with you girls."

The lights flipped on to reveal the small couch and recliner set up in the living room. A pile of broken-down empty boxes lay stacked on the floor next to the television, and boxes still to be unpacked sat on the sun porch just off the living room.

Annabella sat down in the recliner and kicked off her sneakers. The chair enveloped her body as she finally began to relax. Deirdre and Reese sat on the couch while Makenna sat on the floor around the glass coffee table in front of the sofa. They had already begun to dig into their meals before Annabella even opened her bag.

Annabella was munching on a few French fries when Deirdre spoke up.

"So, Mrs. Mazza," Deirdre began as she sipped her soda.

"Deirdre, you can call me Anna, or Annabella, or Ms. Foley if you like. I don't use Mazza anymore," Annabella interrupted.

"I'm sorry… Anna," Deirdre said with a sheepish smile. "So, where did you know the priest from?"

"He was one of our parish priests when I was younger, just before I got married to Makenna's father." There was a hint of disdain in Annabella's voice when she responded, and she meant it to be there.

"He's pretty handsome for a priest," Reese added. "Not the kind of guy I remember at church when I was growing up, for sure. I might have taken a stronger interest in religion if he was in charge!"

The girls all laughed, and Anna joined in with a chuckle.

"Well, I can tell you that he doesn't quite look the same as when I knew him, but he was always good-looking and was one of the nicest men I ever knew."

"Sounds like you had a bit of a crush on him, Mom," Makenna chimed in.

Anna felt the rush of a blush to her cheeks.

"I... I don't know about that," Anna said, flustered by the statement. "I was so young back then. He seemed much older than me – more insightful, mature – even though he was in his early thirties when I was about twenty. I had a lot to learn about life back then. Father Meehan... I mean, Cillian... was always willing to listen to me and had advice. I wish I had taken some of it back then. Now..."

"I wonder what he does now as part of that motorcycle gang," Reese added.

"You really think they're a gang and do like Sons of Anarchy stuff?" Deirdre said as she munched a chicken sandwich.

"Well, we'll get to find out next week," Makenna said with a smile.

"What are you talking about?" Anna replied.

"When I went to thank him before we left, I kind of invited him over to your place for dinner next week." Makenna smiled slyly.

Anna sat upright in the recliner, knocking stray French fries onto the carpet.

"Why did you do that?" Anna yelled.

"Relax, Mom," Makenna said calmly. "I thought it would be a nice thing to do for what he did for me. You said he's an old friend. Besides, the way he was looking at you, I think he might be interested in seeing you again anyway."

"Mac, this place is a wreck still! I have lots of unopened boxes, and I'll be working. I don't know if I'll have time to prepare a meal and get the place cleaned up and get ready for guests..."

"Mom, chill out."

Makenna rose from the couch and went over and knelt in front of her mother. She took Anna's hands in hers and looked at her face.

"Mom, don't get all worked up over it. Look... I know the last few months... hell, the last few years have been tough on you with everything with Dad. You're getting a chance at a new start here. He just seems like the kind of friend you might need in your life right now. You haven't seen him in twenty years. It will be fun. And Dee, Reese, and I will help you with everything. We can help you with the house, getting stuff to cook, whatever you need."

"Thank you," Anna sighed. "What day is he coming over?"

"Oh yeah, about that," Makenna said coyly. "I told him you were working at the festival tomorrow and that he can meet you there to talk about it."

"Makenna!" Anna yelled. "I'll be swamped working. This is a bad idea."

"Mom, you've spent years not socializing with anyone you wanted to see. It's time for you to do things that make you happy. If you don't want to see him, tell him that you don't have time when he comes by. I was just trying to help you. See how you feel tomorrow."

Anna nodded unconsciously as she thought about Cillian. She stood up from the recliner, blinked twice, and looked at the girls.

"I'm sorry. I guess I'm just worn out from today. I'm going to get ready for bed. You girls help yourself to whatever you can find. I think there are extra pillows and blankets in the closet in Makenna's room."

Makenna rose from the floor and gave her mother a hug. Anna was surprised by the movement and embraced Makenna, holding her.

"Thanks, Mom," Makenna whispered. "Love you."

"I love you too, baby," Anna replied softly.

Anna walked off into her bedroom and shut the door. She kicked off her sneakers and peeled off the socks and jeans she wore. Her shirt carried all the smells from the food truck, with oil, batter, condiments, and more, making her shirt look like a Jackson Pollock painting. Anna tossed the garment in the linen hamper in her room, and her bra quickly followed as she sighed in relief to feel free. She considered taking a shower, but exhaustion steadily overtook her body. Instead of getting revived by the hot water, she chose to pull on her oversized faded Mets t-shirt with Mike Piazza's name and number on the back. It was a shirt she had held onto for many years, one she kept tucked into the back of her dresser because Leo preferred her to wear something more glamorous and sexy to bed.

No one knew the origin of the Mets shirt but Anna. It was given to her as a gift on a trip to Shea Stadium for Game 4 of the 1999 playoff series against the Diamondbacks when Todd Pratt hit a dramatic home run in extra innings to clinch the series for the Mets. It was one of the standout moments for Anna and one that included Cillian Meehan. He had taken her to the game because he knew she was a big fan and bought that shirt for her. She still recalled the lingering embrace she gave him when they got back that day and how it made her feel.

Anna hugged herself and closed her eyes, thinking about what it might be like now to replicate that moment with him.

Chapter 10

Cillian maneuvered his way through the throngs to check in at as many places as possible to ensure all was well with the vendors, rides, and more. Saturday brought warm weather again, but it did not keep the crowds from filling the Goose Pond area, looking to enjoy all that the festival offered. He had shed his leather jacket for the daytime hours, leaving it at the beer tent while he walked around. He wore his black short-sleeved t-shirt that allowed some of his tattoos to peek below the sleeves and Cillian noticed that he garnered a few glances, much like the rest of the Cosantóir received all day and night.

After performing a check with the Fun House ride, the only place left to visit was the food truck for Erin's Edibles. Cillian had avoided going there, though he had walked past the location several times during his rounds. He needed to stop and make sure all was okay, and as interested as he was in going there, he felt nervous in the pit of his stomach.

He worked his way through the crowd and saw a long line already forming outside the truck. He waited patiently on the line, calming himself as he got closer and closer to the order window. When he arrived, he was greeted by a Latina girl with big brown eyes and a wide smile.

"Hi! What can I get you?" she asked.

"Oh hi," Cillian began. "I don't need anything, really. I'm with the festival. I was just checking in so I could find out if you guys have all you need or have any issues."

"Hold on, let me get the big boss for you," the girl said as she turned and said something out of Cillian's earshot.

Cillian straightened up, expecting to see Annabella come toward him. He spotted someone coming from the truck's back to the outside where he stood, but it wasn't Anna.

"Hi," the woman said to him. She was dressed in a light green v-neck t-shirt with 'Erin's Edibles' emblazoned on it. "I'm Erin. Olivia said you're with the festival."

"Oh, yes, I am," Cillian responded with some disappointment. "I'm Cillian Meehan. I organized things this year. I just wanted to make sure you guys are okay or if you needed anything."

Erin offered her hand to Cillian, and he received a firm, confident handshake.

"Thanks, Cillian. We're doing great. Business has been busier than ever. This is my first time doing an event like this, and it's been a wonderful experience so far. We're just trying to keep up with everything."

"Well, here," Cillian said, reaching into his back pocket to take out one of the cards he had made. "This has my name, cell phone, and email on it. If you need something or have any questions, just let me know."

"You bet!" Erin said. Erin turned to walk away before Cillian stopped her.

"Say, Erin, before you go... is Annabella here?"

"She's not at the truck at the moment," Erin replied. "She ran out to the bank to get us some more change. She should be back in a few minutes, though. You know Anna?"

"Yes, we're old friends," Cillian admitted. "I just wanted to stop over and say hi."

Erin grinned at Cillian.

"She didn't mention she knew one of the Cosantóir," Erin said as she pointed at the edge of the tattoo showing beneath one of Cillian's sleeves.

"Oh, I don't think she knew about that," Cillian replied. "We hadn't seen each other in a very long time... long before this."

"If you want to stick around, she'll be here," Erin answered. "I'd be happy to get you something to eat while you wait, on the house."

"No, no, thanks," Cillian rushed. "I'll... I'll stop by later on. Is she here the whole day?"

"Right up to closing and beyond. I'll tell Anna you stopped by, and we'll see you later?"

"Yep, perfect," Cillian said. "Thanks again."

Cillian quickly shuffled off towards the beer tent. He suddenly felt parched and needed a drink.

Anna arrived back at the food truck with a satchel filled with singles, fives, and ten-dollar bills. She stepped inside and saw Olivia and Erin both moving quickly to take and fill orders.

"Here's the cash," Anna said triumphantly.

"Just in time," Olivia said as she took the bag. "I think I have two singles left. Thanks."

Anna pulled a couple of order tickets down to get back to work when she noticed the t-shirt Erin was wearing.

"What's with the shirts?" Anna asked as she tossed potatoes into the fryer.

"Oh, right," Erin said as she continued to build a sandwich. "I got shirts for us to wear. They're in the box over there," Erin indicated with her head. "Grab a green one."

Anna scouted through the box of t-shirts and spotted the green-colored items. She looked feverishly for an XL or even a large but didn't see any. She pulled a medium shirt out and held it up to Erin.

"Erin, this is all you have? I can't wear this."

Anna held the t-shirt up against her body to show her friend.

"What are you talking about?" Erin answered. She glanced at Anna and walked over to her. "It will fit you fine. I've seen pictures of the form-fitting stuff you would wear at parties. This t-shirt is much more low-key than those things."

"It's too small," Anna insisted, tossing the t-shirt down.

Erin reached down and picked up the shirt.

"Stop it," Erin said. "You're in better shape than I am for sure." Erin reached over and tugged up on Anna's shirt, rapidly lifting it over her friend's head, so she stood in just her bra.

"Erin! What the hell?" Anna gasped.

"Stop. We used to get dressed in the same room all the time."

Erin pulled the green shirt over Anna's head. Anna reached back to pull her ponytail out of the shirt collar and faced Erin.

"See? It's too short." Anna indicated the slight gap between the hem of the shirt and her jeans. "And this v-neck is a bit much," she added as she glanced at her cleavage on display.

"When did you become such a prude?" Erin scoffed. "It looks great... Olivia, doesn't it look great?"

Olivia looked back and gave a thumbs-up and a wolf whistle.

"It's okay, Anna. You look great. In 2 minutes, we'll be so busy you won't have time to worry about it."

Anna rolled her eyes and went back to the grill and fryer. The lunchtime rush kept the three of them busy straight through until about 3 PM when they finally hit a lull. Erin went into the cooler and pulled out

3 bottles of water, handing one to Olivia and Anna. Anna immediately pressed the cold bottle to her forehead and sighed.

"I didn't think that rush would ever end," Olivia said as she sat on a stool. "The line stretched across the lawn at one point to the ride on the other side from us. Do we even have food left to sell?"

Erin walked over to the fridge and the coolers to look.

"We should have enough to get us through dinner before the fireworks," she answered. Erin shut the cooler and then touched the back of her jeans, feeling something in her pocket.

"Oh, I forgot," Erin said as she pulled out the business card. "Someone stopped by looking for you, Anna."

"For me?" Anna said with surprise. "I barely know anyone in this town."

"Well, he knew you... by name," Erin said, handing Anna the card. She glanced at it and saw Cillian's name. A flutter coursed through her body as she saw his phone number and email listed there.

"What... what did he say?"

"Just that he was looking for you, and he was an old friend," Erin added. "I'm an old friend, and I thought I knew all your old boyfriends. Since when did you hang out with bikers? Your mother must have had a stroke."

"He's not an old boyfriend," Anna insisted.

"Too bad," Erin said. "He's definitely worth looking at every day. Seems kind of shy, too. Not at all like the other Cosantóir I've met."

"It's the shy ones you have to watch out for!" Olivia added with a laugh.

"He's someone I knew a long time ago... before I got married. He was just a good friend," Anna told them.

"He's probably going to come back around later looking for you," Erin informed Anna. "Or you could just call him now."

"Only if we can listen in," Olivia said excitedly.

"I'm not calling him," Anna insisted and handed the card back to Erin. "We're going to be too busy. I'm sure we'll meet up eventually."

"Why not call him?" Erin said. "He obviously wants to see you, Anna."

Anna went over to the fridge and took out some vegetables that she began to chop as a distraction.

"Don't we have prep work to do?" she said, trying to change the subject.

"Whatever," Erin said disappointingly.

The lull didn't last long, and before they knew it, lines were forming outside the truck again. People ordered anything and everything – hot pretzel sticks, fries, salads, and sandwiches. Anna and Erin worked as an assembly line, cooking and putting orders together as rapidly as possible. Hours went by with little or no break at all in action. Things kept up even as the sun began to go down, and the crowd readied for the impending fireworks display to come once it was dark enough.

Anna secured five minutes to run over to one of the Port-A-potties to get a breather. Even then, she had to wait in a long line before she could gain access. She lingered a bit as she walked back to the truck, looking at the couples walking around holding hands or arm-in-arm. Young and old all enjoyed the atmosphere and fun. Anna heard loud music and laughter coming from the beer tent and walked over just to peek inside. The tables were filled with people, and she spied several of the men she saw last night at the ruckus that Makenna was involved in. She scurried away quickly before she could be potentially spotted by Cillian.

She returned to the food truck and saw just one person waiting at the window, speaking with Olivia. Anna walked to the back of the truck and stopped short as she saw Erin standing there with Cillian.

"Hi," Anna said shyly. She tossed a glare toward Erin.

"We had run out of bottles of water," Erin said to Anna. "I called Cillian, and he brought two cases over for us."

"Hi, Anna," Cillian smiled.

"Nice to see you... Cillian," Anna replied. She checked herself in time, so she didn't call him 'Father Meehan' this time.

"I'll go put these in the coolers," Anna said as she went to move inside the truck.

"It's okay, I've got these," Erin told her. "Talk to your friend." Erin grinned back at Anna. Anna wanted to give Erin the finger in the worst way, but she held back.

"I guess it's been a crazy day for you," Cillian said to Anna.

"We've been busy non-stop," Anna said as she brushed stray strands of her blonde hair from her eyes. "I guess you have as well."

"Not really," Cillian stated. "All the hard work was done ahead of time. Now it's just putting out fires if they come up. Is... is your daughter okay after last night?"

Anna warmed to the caring side of Cillian that reminded her of the past.

"Yes, thanks," Anna answered. "She was a little shook up, but okay. She and her friends were doing something else tonight. Thank you again for helping her last night."

"Don't mention it," Cillian said, shrugging it off.

The two stood in awkward silence for a moment before Cillian piped up again.

"The fireworks will be starting up in about ten minutes," Cillian told Anna. "Are you going to watch?"

"Oh... we'll probably be too busy in the truck for me to go out and see them. We have prep work and then cleaning to do," Anna replied. She saw the disappointment on Cillian's face.

"Liv and I can handle it," Erin yelled from inside the truck.

"What?" Anna said with surprise.

Erin peeked her head out the back of the truck.

"Liv and I can take care of the truck. Everyone will be watching the fireworks and then leaving after they are finished. I don't think we'll be too busy for the rest of the night. Go enjoy the fireworks with your friend," Erin grinned.

"I don't want to leave you guys short," Anna insisted.

"As your employer, I am telling you to go," Erin laughed. "If you really have to, you can come back after the fireworks and help us clean and close."

Erin disappeared, then reappeared holding Anna's purse.

"Thanks, Boss," Anna said with a sneer.

"No problem." Erin held Anna's purse for a second and leaned in to whisper in Anna's ear.

"Have some fun, and let me know how it goes," she told her friend.

Anna turned to face Cillian and let out a big breath.

"Let's go," she smiled and followed alongside Cillian as they walked out toward the ponds.

Cillian shortened his stride to keep pace with Anna's walk, allowing him to stay by her side as they made their way across the grass towards the ponds. He watched as Anna looked around at the sights of the festival. Neither said a word to each other as they moved until they neared the beer tent.

Loud music emanated from the tent before raucous cheers began. Cillian paused outside the tent and saw that the Sheahan-Gormley School of Irish Dance dancers had started their annual routine. Crowds gathered inside and outside the tent, hoping to get a peek at the action. Cillian instinctively grabbed Anna's hand and pulled her toward the tent so she wouldn't miss what many considered the festival's highlight.

"You'll want to see this," he noted to Anna, leaning close to her ear so she could hear him clearly. Cillian picked up the hint of Anna's perfume from the nape of her neck. The scent was familiar to him, the same she wore all those years ago when they knew each other better.

Cillian moved through the crowd outside and got to the entrance to the tent where Whitey stood guard. He had kept the group outside since the inside tables looked full and the dance floor was packed.

"Any room, Whitey?" Cillian yelled over the din.

"Always for you, brother," Whitey indicated as he let Cillian and Anna pass. Cillian kept a firm grip on Anna's hand, and she gave no indication of wanting to let go. The couple moved to the left of the dance floor for the best view and to stay away from the blasting music coming from the nearby speakers.

Cillian looked over and saw Anna watching intently as the girls in their hard shoes and school dresses and the boys, smartly dressed in their vests and ties, went through their routine. She beamed as they moved in unison, and the crowd clapped along, hooting and hollering along the way. When the performance ended, the throng erupted in applause.

"That was amazing," Anna said, smiling at Cillian. Cillian couldn't help but notice that she retook his hand after she stopped applauding.

"Those kids are fantastic," he told her. "The Cosantóir – we do what we can to support the school so any kid who wants lessons can get them, no matter the finances."

"That's so nice that you do that," Anna replied, seemingly surprised.

"Don't look so shocked," Cillian laughed. "We're not all heavy drinking and knife fights, you know."

"Oh, I didn't mean it like that," Anna said, flustered. "It's just…"

"I'm teasing a bit," Cillian remarked. "I know how it looks to most people, but those are the ones that don't know anything about us and assume the worst. Our club has outlived that reputation. Do you want something to drink?"

"Please," Anna said. Cillian noted that the tent was stifling with the crowd. "Just some water would be great."

"Back in a sec," Cillian nodded.

He moved through the crowd until he could reach the corner of the bar. Thanks to his height, he grabbed Rory's attention, and the bartender crept down to him.

"What can I get you, Preacher?" Rory yelled.

"A pint and a water, please," Cillian replied. Rory nodded, and Cillian turned to look at Annabella. She stood nervously as the crowd moved around her. One of the dance floor area lights seemed to place an aura around her that made her glow. Rory put a water bottle and a plastic pint cup in front of Cillian, and Cillian slid a ten onto the bar.

"Your money's no good here," Rory said, pushing it back.

"Bullshit, Rory," Cillian insisted. "Take it."

Cillian turned to leave the bar and spotted Liam standing next to Annabella, chatting with her. Cillian hustled over to try to intercept his efforts.

"This eejit bothering you?" Cillian said, half-joking. He handed Anna her water bottle.

"What? Oh, no," Anna said as she looked between the two men.

"He's just afraid I'm going to steal you off his arm, darlin'," Liam laughed. "Don't worry, Preacher. She's all yours. I was just asking about her girl."

Cillian cringed at Liam's remarks and tried to laugh them off as Anna watched.

"We're going out to watch the fireworks," Cillian told him. "You heading out there?"

"Nah, there's nothing new with them for me, and there's plenty of drinkin' still to be done, brother. Go enjoy yourselves; you earned it."

Cillian nodded and began to leave the tent. Anna had grasped onto his hand again so he could lead her. Cillian looked down at her hand in his and caught Liam smirking at the two of them as he walked away.

Just as they got outside the tent and all its noise, one of the younger Cosantóir members, Rocky, came up behind the couple, startling Anna.

"Preacher," Rocky said breathlessly. "Liam bade me bring these chairs to you and your lady, so you had places to sit."

"Thanks, Rocky," Cillian answered. "You didn't need to do that. We can sit on the grass."

"No, Liam insisted," Rocky intimated.

Cillian knew that probationary members were at the beck and call of the senior members if they wanted to earn entry into the club. He allowed Rocky to follow them as he carried the chairs until they found a flat, comfortable spot that had an excellent view over the ponds.

Rocky quickly set up the chairs, pulling one out for Anna to sit on just as if they were visiting a fancy restaurant. Cillian took the other chair and set it next to Anna.

"Need anything else?" Rocky asked, awaiting instructions.

"We're good, Rocky. Thanks," Cillian nodded. He hoped the young member would move along now to have some alone time with Anna. Rocky raced off back to the beer tent, and Cillian sat next to Anna.

The area was dark enough where the show would start shortly. Liam glimpsed the silhouette of Anna in her chair as she sat back, sipped her water, and breathed in the fresh air.

"It's nice to sit down," Anna said, trying to start a conversation.

"I'll bet," Cillian added. "Your truck has had quite the line all day. Every time I walked over there, it was busy."

"You came by more than once?" Anna asked.

Cillian was caught and nodded.

"I did a few times as I was making my rounds," Cillian admitted. "Ever since I saw you last night, I've wanted some time with you to... to catch up."

"Twenty years leaves a lot of catching up," Anna told him with a smile. "I think we are both very different people now."

"True enough," Cillian agreed. "It was just such a surprise to see you here, after all this time. The odds of us both ending up in the same place at the same time... it's almost like it was..."

"God's will?" Anna said with a smile.

"Well, not exactly what I was going for," Cillian added. "But fate, for sure."

Cillian leaned closer, wanting to ask more questions, but just then, the sky lit up with the first color burst of the night. Accompanied with loud Irish music, the display of lights and explosions all but obscured the chance of any conversation taking place. Anna's attentions were turned toward the sky now as she took in the show.

Cillian found that he spent more time watching her and her reactions than the fireworks in the sky. Everything about her stirred those same feelings he had so long ago, feelings he fought tooth and nail for several reasons. When Anna had slipped out of his life for what he thought was for good, his life veered course drastically. There was still something there... electricity, connection, or something... and he needed to know if she felt it too.

The fireworks went on for about twenty-five minutes, with plenty of oohs and aahs from children and adults alike. Cillian had made sure the company handling the display this year went the extra mile, putting a bit more into the budget for that part of the festival than past years to wow the crowd. The finale began with constant explosions, including the last two rapid-fire moments that created a large green shamrock in the sky, followed by a replica of the Irish flag. The applause that followed the ending was nearly as thunderous as the fireworks themselves.

When the show was completed, Cillian saw Anna lean back in her chair with a big smile on her face.

"That was fantastic!" she beamed. "Loud, but fantastic."

"They did a great job, as usual," Cillian admitted.

He rose from his chair and offered his hand to help Anna up from hers. He gripped her fingers as she rose, and they stood face to face. Even in the darkness, Cillian made out the features of her face, her eyes sparkling brightly. The two stood looking at each other until Rocky appeared to disrupt the moment.

"I can grab these, Preacher," Rocky indicated, pointing to the chairs.

"Oh... thanks, Rocky," Cillian answered as the mesmerizing spell was broken.

Anna smiled and placed her purse over her shoulder as Cillian walked by her side, out of the darkness and into the gleaming lights of the festival.

"Why do they call him Rocky?" Anna asked as the couple strolled, and Rocky sped past them with the chairs. "He doesn't look like Stallone or anything."

"Oh... it's not that Rocky," Cillian explained. "With the Sandhogs, his job is to help drill through the rock formations."

"Sandhogs?" Anna questioned. "I thought your gang... I mean, the club was the Cosantóir."

"It is," Cillian told her. "The Sandhogs are what we're called at work. We dig tunnels. In the Cosantóir, almost everyone gets a nickname. Rocky's real name is Peter, but no one I know calls him that."

"So you dig tunnels for a living?" Anna said with surprise.

"I do," Cillian replied. He looked up and saw they were getting close to the Erin's Edibles food truck and wanted to slow down so they had more time together.

"That's quite a change from... well, from before," Anna added. "I'm sure there is a story behind that."

Cillian shook a bit inside. There was a story behind it; he just didn't know if it was one he could share with Anna.

"There is," he said abruptly as they arrived at the back entrance to the food truck.

Anna glanced into the truck and saw Erin and Olivia hard at work cleaning the equipment.

"I should probably get in there and help them out," Anna acknowledged.

"Sure," Cillian responded, not wanting to let her go just yet. "Do you... do you have to work tomorrow? The festival is over, and... well,

I'm kind of on a 'forced' vacation for another week. Maybe we can get together when it's not so loud and crowded."

Anna smiled coyly at Cillian.

"No, we're doing cleaning tonight and then cleaning again on Monday, so I am free tomorrow. The only thing I wanted to do is go to church if I can figure out where to go."

"I'd be glad to take you... I mean, go with you... to St. Anastasia's in the morning. That's where I go," Cillian told her.

"Oh, I didn't realize you were allowed to... I mean that you still went..." Anna fumbled over her words.

"It's okay," Cillian reassured her. "Just because I'm not a priest anymore doesn't mean I stopped believing or going to church. Do you mind going to the early mass? It's less crowded, and they hold it in the old church."

"No, that would be fine," Anna told him.

"Okay," Cillian said happily. "I can pick you up if you like. Or I can meet you there, whatever you are comfortable with."

Cillian tried not to seem too eager.

"If picking me up isn't too much trouble, that would be grand," Anna said, trying to put on her Irish. She giggled when she said it, bringing out a laugh in Cillian as well.

"Nicely done," Cillian offered as he turned up his brogue. "Mass is at 8, so I'll pick you up at 7:45. You said you're on Church Street, right?"

"Yes, I am," Anna answered. "15 is the number. It's a little white house on the corner."

"I know it well," Cillian said. "Close to the Harriman Square Deli. They have good breakfast sandwiches. I'll see you then."

"It's a date. I look forward to it. Thanks for the fireworks. Have a good night, Cillian." Anna smiled as she walked up the steps and into the truck.

Cillian walked away from the truck, passing by the front and noticing the two women inside, both watching him as he moved. He turned and gave them a slight wave as they laughed and beamed at him.

Cillian sighed deeply, letting the nervous energy he had inside out. He then thought back onto what Anna just said to him about it being a date. Cillian steeled the nerves away and stepped firmly toward the beer tent.

Maybe not a traditional date, but it's a start, he thought to himself with more confidence.

Chapter 11

Anna was startled out of bed when her phone started playing music at 7 AM. She bolted upright and fumbled on her nightstand to try to locate what was making all the noise. Instead, she knocked her phone and the glass of water she had there onto the floor.

"Shit!" she exclaimed, putting her feet on the floor and right into the wet spot on the carpet. She got down on all fours to spot her phone underneath her bed, still blaring music from her playlist as her alarm. She finally spotted the glimmer of the screen in the darkness under the bed and reached for it, just sliding the phone toward her with her fingertips. When she had it in her grasp, the voice behind her startled her even more, causing her to bang her head on the nightstand as she rose.

"Shit!" she yelled again and dropped the phone down on her bed. It was still playing "Sweet Caroline at near top volume.

"Mom," Makenna said as she trudged over to the phone on the bed and turned the alarm off. "What are you doing? It's 7 AM on a Sunday."

Between her damp feet and the pain she felt in her head, Anna was unsure why she was getting up so early herself. It was then she remembered Cillian.

"I'm sorry," she said, rubbing her aching skull. "I... I'm going to church this morning and meeting... someone."

Makenna sat down on the bed next to her mother.

"Are you meeting the priest?" she asked.

"He's not a priest anymore, Mac," Anna insisted. "And yes, I am meeting him. In fact, he's picking me up. I need to pick out something to wear and get in the shower."

Anna suddenly felt rushed and tore through her closet, looking for something appropriate to wear.

"None of this is going to work," she said with frustration as she flipped hangers. "I still have stuff in boxes too. I can't find anything. This was a bad idea."

"Mom, chill!" Makenna insisted. "Go take your shower. I'll find something for you." Makenna pulled her mother away from the closet and pushed her into the small hallway toward the house's lone bathroom.

Even though there was a great temptation to linger in the hot shower as the water soothed her aching muscles, panic ruled the moment. Anna sped through her shower and morning routine before returning to her room wrapped in just a fluffy green towel. She was more than a bit surprised to see Makenna had called in Reese and Deirdre to help her out.

"The cavalry is here," Reese said as she directed Anna to sit down at her vanity.

"Girls, really, I don't need all this," Anna attempted to tell them.

"Mom, you haven't been on a date in twenty years," Makenna insisted as she came up behind her mother and looked at her in the mirror.

"It's not a date," Anna insisted.

"Whatever," Makenna replied. "I think you should leave your hair down and curly like this. It looks great."

"Are you sure she shouldn't wear it up like this?" Reese added, lifting up the back of Anna's hair. "It would show off her neck more, and it might be too hot today to wear it down."

"How about this one?" Deirdre said as she pulled a white dress from a box. The dress had a long slit on the left leg and a plunging neckline.

"She's going to church with a former priest, Dee," Reese insisted. "Not to the bar at a swanky hotel."

"What? I would wear this to church," Dee stated, holding the dress up against herself and looking in the mirror.

"That's exactly the problem," Reese answered and grabbed the dress from Dee to hang it back up. "This one is much better," Reese said. She plucked a spaghetti strap floral A-line dress from the back of the closet. "Throw a light shawl over your shoulders, and you are all set."

Makenna took the dress from Reese and brought it to her mother.

"I remember this dress," Makenna said to her. "You used to wear this when we would picnic. You haven't put this one on in a long time."

"I guess I had forgotten about it," Anna told her.

A knock on the front door froze everyone in the room.

"He's early," Reese said.

"You two go entertain him," Makenna ordered her friends. "Let's get moving, Mom."

Reese and Deirdre scampered from the room and shut the door behind them. Anna's heart raced a bit as she put on just the slightest bit of makeup. She sprang from the chair at her vanity to quickly dress before the bedroom door swung open again, this time, Reese and Dee with Erin in tow.

"Is the whole neighborhood coming over to get me ready?" Anna said, bewildered. "I'm just going to church."

"We both know it's not just a going to church thing, Anna," Erin told her. "I just came by for moral support."

"What happened to sleeping in on Sundays?"

Anna had slipped into her dress and was rummaging through the closet to find shoes to wear.

"Don't be nervous," Makenna said, attempting to calm her mother down.

"I wasn't nervous, but with the four of you here, I am now!"

Another knock on the front door caused all the women to stop talking and moving.

"That must be him," Reese said quietly.

"Why are you whispering?" Makenna replied.

"Could someone go answer the door, please, while I get my shoes on?" Anna barked.

The three younger women raced out to the door while Erin stayed behind to be with Anna.

Anna stood in front of her vanity mirror and put on her gold cross necklace. The necklace had been a gift from Cillian many years ago. Leo had insisted she stop wearing it just at the beginning of the marriage. She smoothed out her dress and smiled at herself.

"You look great," Erin complimented. "You have nothing to worry about."

"I'm not worried about anything," Anna answered firmly.

"Then why do you keep fussing with yourself in the mirror?"

"I just want to look nice," Anna told her. "It's my first time at this church. I want to make a good impression."

"Okay," Erin said with a chuckle. "And it has nothing to do with the good-looking biker escorting you there. I barely know the guy, but I'd be swooning like a teenager too."

"Erin, stop," Anna asserted. "I barely know him as well. We haven't seen each other in a long time. He's a lot different than what I remember."

"He can't be too different, or you wouldn't be going at all."

"Well, I guess that's what I need to find out," Anna answered honestly. Anna took another deep breath and turned to Erin. "Okay, I'm ready."

Erin opened the door, and Anna walked out, taking a few steps from the small hallway and into the living room. She spied Cillian sitting in the recliner with Makenna and Reese sitting on the couch opposite him while Dee sat on the floor. All faced him as if they were engaged in a police interrogation.

"So, did you ever put someone in the hospital like you guys did with James?" Deirdre asked eagerly.

"Well..." Cillian began to answer but then rose from the chair when he saw Anna enter the room.

"I didn't realize there would be an audience here this morning," Cillian said with a smile.

"Neither did I," Anna said with an eye roll. She took a cursory glance at her watch and looked back up. "We should go," she told Cillian as she headed toward the door.

"How long are you going to be out?" Makenna asked as if she was the mother.

Anna looked at Cillian and then back at her daughter.

"Oh, I don't know. Probably not long."

"I was hoping that maybe we could go around the area a bit and spend some time together. I mean, since you aren't too familiar with the town and all," Cillian interjected. "If that's okay with you, of course. If you had other plans..."

"She doesn't," Makenna said quickly. "I'm going back over to Grandma's today. Take all the time you want."

Anna blushed as she felt all eyes on her, awaiting a response.

"Sure, that would be nice," she told Cillian.

Cillian held the door open for Anna as she departed the house, and he followed right behind her, stepping fast to catch up to her. Once he was beside her in the driveway, Anna turned to him and smiled. She spied from the corner of her eye that Erin, Makenna, and the girls were all staring at them through the screen of the front door.

Cillian dutifully opened the passenger door to his car so Anna could get in, and they were on their way. Cillian drove the short distance to the church less than a mile from Anna's front door.

"If it wasn't so hot, it would have been a nice walk over here," Cillian said as he drove up the slight incline to park in the church lot.

"Maybe next time," Anna said, realizing what she had said as it came out of her mouth.

"Maybe," Cillian grinned.

Anna opened the passenger door before Cillian could get around to open it for her. Still, he took her hand to assist her out of the vehicle.

"Careful, there are some holes in the lot that need fixing," he mentioned to her.

Anna felt Cillian's grasp of her hand start to loosen, but she kept her hand there, wanting that connection. Cillian led her up the path to the church, and they tucked into the back row of the nearly full church.

Anna couldn't help but notice that Cillian, and by association she, were getting many looks. She was unsure if that was because she was an unknown person to the congregation or if people always looked at Cillian that way. She noted he was dressed smartly in a dark suit and tie, much better dressed than many patrons in attendance that morning.

"People keep staring at me... at us," Anna whispered.

"Yeah, I get that a lot," Cillian reassured her. "They just aren't used to seeing me here with..." Cillian halted himself. "Well, with anyone."

The mass began on time, and Anna enjoyed every aspect of it. She hadn't been to church in months, mainly since all the problems with Leo occurred and came out into the open where they lived. Anna had felt shunned by many of the people she thought were her friends within their congregation in Westchester. It became too uncomfortable for her to attend something she had always loved doing, and now she realized how much she had missed it.

She watched as Cillian's voice boomed out during responses and singing, which seemed to garner even more looks from those in attendance. On one occasion, his singing was loud enough where it elicited a giggle from Anna. Cillian looked over at her, and she noticed his cheeks redden.

When it came time for Communion, Anna panicked a bit. As someone divorced, she wasn't permitted to receive the sacrament and feared judgment from those in attendance. However, as the music played and those who wished to receive went toward the altar, she noticed Cillian hadn't moved either. It didn't dawn on her that he couldn't or wouldn't partake as well, but she felt some comfort in having him beside her while Mass proceeded.

As Mass ended and the priest led the processional outside, Cillian waited for many parishioners to leave before leading Anna into the aisle and out the doors. Father Mike greeted the congregation as they went, and Cillian paused to shake the priest's hand and say hello. Anna stood next to him and listened in as he talked to the pastor.

"Nice to see you today, Cillian," Father Mike indicated. "You were on time and quite exuberant today," he laughed. "And I see you brought a friend."

"Father Mike, this is Annabella Mazza," Cillian introduced.

"Actually, it's Foley now," Anna said as she corrected Cillian. She shook the priest's hand warmly. "It was a lovely Mass."

"Thank you, Annabella," Father Mike added. "I am so glad you were here to join us. You wouldn't happen to be related to Marcella Foley, would you?"

Anna was a bit surprised by the question.

"Why yes, I am. She's my mother. Do you know her?"

"I do, I do," Father Mike uttered, saying little else, a cue Anna had picked up on for years when people talked to her about her mother. "She's been part of the parish for years. In fact, she's right over there."

Father Mike pointed, and Anna spotted her mother chatting with another older woman.

"We should go," Anna whispered frantically to Cillian as she tugged on his sleeve.

Cillian nodded and said his goodbyes to Father Mike as Anna then led him down the stone steps. She stumbled briefly on the bottom, kicking a loose stone, but Cillian grasped her firmly to prevent her from falling over completely, leaving her in his arms. She glanced up and saw Cillian's gaze locked onto hers, and for the first time in a long time, she wasn't worried about who was around her, what they might say, and what her mother was thinking.

However, all that changed when the familiar voice broke the spell Anna was under from Cillian's eyes.

"Annabella? Is that you?"

Anna straightened up, standing next to Cillian, as she watched her mother come closer to her.

"Hi, Mom," Anna said with a forced smile. "I didn't know you came to this church."

"You didn't know?" her mother responded incredulously. "I've been talking about it for years. They really need to get those steps repaired. Are you alright?"

Anna watched as her mother's gaze shifted from her over to Cillian. Anna cringed at the thought that her mother might recognize Cillian from years ago.

"I didn't realize you would be here with... with a gentleman," Marcella said with more than a hint of disapproval.

"I decided to come at the last minute," Anna said. "And I should probably get going..."

"You should at least introduce me to your friend, Annabella. Don't be rude."

Anna watched as Cillian extended his hand toward Marcella.

"Hello, Mrs. Foley," Cillian grinned. "We actually know each other. I'm Cillian Meehan."

Anna shifted her gaze to her mother's face, which showed no hint of recognition yet.

"The name doesn't ring a bell," Marcella said as she shook Cillian's hand.

"Well, I look a bit different from the last time we talked," Cillian offered.

Anna was grateful that Cillian clipped the conversation there and left it, but her mother continued on.

"Meehan, huh? I don't recall any from around here or in my younger days," Marcella went on. "Though I do remember that priest from down at St. Brendan's... I think his name was Meehan. Hmph... I never liked him... I think he performed your wedding to Leo. You remember him, Anna?"

"I do remember him," Anna squeaked.

"Are you related to him?" Marcella asked as she looked Cillian over again.

"Mrs. Foley, that was me," Cillian admitted.

"No, that can't be you," Marcella scoffed. "He was a scrawny young man, clean-shaven, had an Irish brogue... and he was a little too close to you, Anna. I never liked that. That can't be you."

Anna was more than a little uncomfortable with her mother's comments, but Cillian seemed to take it all in stride.

"Unfortunately for both of us, that was me," Cillian laughed.

"You can't be a priest and look like this," Marcella stated.

"Mom!" Anna said sharply.

"It's okay, Anna," Cillian said calmly. "I'm not a priest anymore, Mrs. Foley. I left the priesthood a long time ago."

"I see," Marcella said, clicking her tongue. "Were you tossed out when they were getting rid of priests?"

"That's it," Anna said boldly. "Come on, Cillian. We're leaving. Mom, I'll talk to you later."

Anna tugged Cillian's arm and put hers through his as she left her mother with her jaw open and staring.

Anna stomped off to the car, barely able to contain her anger. Cillian opened the passenger door for her as she climbed in.

"I am so sorry," Anna said when Cillian got in and started the engine. "I had no idea I would run into her, let alone that she would act that way."

"Anna, calm down. It's okay," Cillian reassured her. "She's not the first one to question me about all that stuff. It's just part of who I am for some people, I guess."

"I know, but first the interrogation at my house, and then this... it's not fair to you. I just wanted to have a nice morning at church."

"And we did," Cillian replied as he drove.

"I understand if you just want to take me home and call it a day," she resigned.

"No way," Cillian asserted. "It's just the start of the day, and we have a lot of catching up to do. I hope you're ready."

"I guess it can only get better from here, right?" Anna added hesitantly.

Chapter 12

Cillian drove away from the church lot, a bit rattled but determined. The morning had been fraught with surprises, particularly running into Anna's mother outside the church. The two had clashed from nearly the moment they met over twenty years ago. Cillian, then a young priest, had taken an instant liking not just to Marcella's husband, Donal, but also to Anna. Donal was a sanitation worker and proud to let people know it. Cillian knew it was an embarrassment to Marcella how her husband would preach about the work he did. She also didn't take kindly to Donal's use of language and his drinking. Still, Cillian found the man to be one of the most honest and interesting people he knew. He spent a lot of time with Donal and with Anna, who was heavily involved with the church at the time.

Cillian worked his way through the traffic in Monroe, away from the church and hopefully far from any problems for Anna. He saw that she fumed over the meeting with her mother.

"That was certainly an interesting meeting," Cillian offered. "To be honest, I don't know how your mother and I haven't run into each other before. I try to go to church every weekend, and I'm around town a lot. We're not that big of an area."

"Mom mostly keeps to herself and her rich friends," Anna said as she stared out the window. "Even if she saw you, she probably wouldn't have even acknowledged you, let alone recognize you. She's still a snob."

"I don't know about that," Cillian said as they waited at a traffic light.

"Oh please, Cillian," Anna said with frustration. "You don't remember the way she used to talk to you when you were a priest and would come over to the house? Or even the way she would talk down to my Dad? She flaunted it every chance she got and still does. To Marcella Foley, money is what makes you a better person. It's no wonder she likes Leo so much."

"Your mother was brought up a different way," Cillian interjected. "Much different from the way I was, anyway, and clearly from the way your Da was raised."

Anna chuckled at Cillian's statement.

"What's so funny?"

"I'm sorry," Anna told him. "I didn't mean to laugh. I just haven't heard anyone call him 'Da' in a very long time. My mother used to hate it when I did it. I forgot how..." Anna cut herself off.

"Forgot what?"

Cillian noted the redness on Anna's cheeks already before she spoke.

"Oh, this is embarrassing," Anna began. "I was going to say I forgot how much I always liked the Irish brogue my Dad had, but also the one you had... I mean, still have, I guess. Oh, never mind."

Cillian let out a hearty laugh.

"Mine isn't nearly as strong as you probably remember it," Cillian said. "It's softened quite a bit over the years, but spending 24/7 primarily around Irishmen keeps it going. I think I used to turn it up some to try to impress your Da."

"You didn't need to," Anna told him. Cillian could see that she was looking right at him now as he drove. "He loved having you around. He always told me he thought the world of you and hoped I... well, that I would end up with a man like you. Ugh, this is so embarrassing."

Cillian's heart swelled at the statement.

"Your Da was one of my favorite people, without a doubt," Cillian nodded. "One of my saddest days was when he passed."

"Mine too," Anna said softly.

The ride quieted for both of them as Cillian drove along 17M and made his way into Chester, the next town over.

"Hungry?" Cillian asked.

"I could eat," Anna said as she gazed out the window.

"I know a nice little place," he told her as they moved down Main Street past some closed shops until they reached what looked like a barn.

Cillian parked the car in the gravel-covered lot and raced to the passenger's side of the vehicle to open the door for Anna, but she had already stepped out.

"You don't have to get the door for me every time, Cillian," Anna told him as she slammed the door shut.

"I'm just trying to be gentlemanly," he answered.

"Gentlemen," Anna said as she looked at Cillian and smiled. "I forgot what you guys are like. It's nice to be around one."

Cillian led Anna to the front door of Meadow Blues Coffee and opened the door for her, bowing gracefully as he did so.

"My Lady," he said, fashioning his brogue even more.

Anna giggled and gave a curtsey as she nodded and entered the coffee shop. The sound of John Coltrane emanated over the speakers while the intoxicating aroma of fresh ground coffee permeated the air.

Cillian inhaled deeply and smiled.

"Boy, you're serious about your coffee," Anna noted as she watched him.

"I think you can say there are a few things I am serious about – biking, working, Guinness, coffee, and faith," Cillian replied.

"Oh, we have a lot to talk about," Anna laughed.

Cillian saw Anna staring at the chalkboard, looking overwhelmed at all the choices for beverages.

"I don't know how I can choose from all this. Why don't you just pick something I might like?" Anna requested.

"Are you sure?" Cillian said cautiously. "I drink just black coffee. Is there anything special you might want?"

"I trust you," Anna said as she put her hand on Cillian's arm and smiled.

"Fair enough. Why don't you grab us a table out in the back so we can enjoy the sunshine while it's still a bit cooler out?"

Anna nodded and went off out the back door. Cillian spied every step she took as her dress swayed slightly as she walked. The only thing that broke the spell he was under was the barista getting Cillian's attention.

"Cillian?" the young man repeated. "You want your usual?"

"Oh, sorry," Cillian offered. "Yes, please. A large hot coffee, black. Can I get a sausage, egg and cheese, a ham, egg, and cheese, and... geez, I don't know what kind of drink to get her."

Cillian looked at the barista, who smiled back at him.

"She's with you? I'll pick something for you. If she doesn't like it, we'll switch it out. No problem."

Cillian nodded and moved to the side so the next customer could order while he waited. He peeked his head outside and saw Anna sitting back in one of the Adirondack chairs, eyes closed, basking in the sun. Memories of the days that he spent at Anna's parents' house in Westchester when they would sit out in the backyard and talk when Cillian would come over for dinner flooded back to him.

"Here you go," the server told Cillian, handing him his beverages and sandwiches. Cillian stepped outside to overlook the farmland behind the coffee shop. The crystal clear sky allowed a view that seemed endless. He walked across the patio to where Anna sat, facing the open fields.

"I haven't sat at a view like this in years," Anna replied. "This is so beautiful."

"One of the perks of our area," Cillian responded. "I could sit out here for hours."

"Do you have a view like this at your place?" Anna asked as she gratefully took the beverage from Cillian's hand.

"Hardly," Cillian scoffed. "My home is somewhat lacking in a view. I really just have a room at the Hog House."

"The Hog House? What is that?"

"It's the house for our motorcycle club," Cillian explained. "A few of us live there. It's mostly a... social club." Cillian tried to be as tactful as possible.

"That doesn't sound very nice," Anna said before she took a sip of her drink. "Oh wow. This is delicious. What is it?"

"They call it Momma Megan's Mocha," Cillian told her as he sipped his coffee and put his feet up on the table in front of them. "It's a mocha latte with dark chocolate and salted caramel drizzle."

"Hmmm," Anna hummed with another sip. "These could be dangerous."

"You think that is good? Wait until you have this."

Cillian handed a sandwich to Anna before unwrapping his own.

Cillian eyed Anna as she took a bite of the ham, egg, and cheese sandwich. Crumbs from the English muffin dotted the front of her dress as she worked to move the strands of melted cheese from her chin to her mouth.

"Sorry," Anna said through a full mouth. "Not very ladylike, I'm afraid. That's wonderful."

"Glad you like it," Cillian answered. "I'm sure it doesn't rival what you can cook up. I remember some of your home-cooked meals after Mass on Sundays."

"Thanks, but it's been a long time since I did any cooking like that. Leo had staff around the house, so I never got to hone my skills. I think I'm a little rusty."

"I guess that means you never went to CIA," Cillian asked as he took a bite of the fresh sausage patty on his sandwich.

Cillian saw Anna turn and stare at him.

"What? Do I have cheese on me?"

"No," Anna said with a smile. "I can't believe you remember I wanted to do that. I only told a few people about it. No, I never got the chance to do it. Leo wanted a wife that stayed at home, and with Makenna born, I can understand that. It would have been fun, though."

"It's not too late to do that now," Cillian offered.

Anna laughed out loud at the suggestion.

"Unfortunately, I don't have the $30,000 a year it costs to go there," Anna admitted. "I brought it up once to Leo after we first got married. He just laughed it off. Even with the sale of the house, all the money I got went into paying for the new home here. It's going to be rough going for a bit, but once I get on my feet, things will be easier."

"What about scholarships and financial aid? Or maybe your Mom can help you," Cillian asked.

"Fat chance on my mother helping with it. She still thinks I should have just stayed with Leo. I think it was all just a pipe dream," Anna told him. She took the last bite of her sandwich. "Everything happens for a reason, right? Isn't that what you used to tell me all the time?"

"The Lord has made everything for its purpose, even the wicked for the day of trouble," Cillian told her. "Proverbs 16:4. I know that's what

I used to quote you. However – Jeremiah 29:11 says, 'For I know the plans I have for you, declares the Lord, plans for welfare and not for evil, to give you a future and a hope.' That might be more applicable now."

"I'm impressed that you still remember all that," Anna said. She sat up in her chair and leaned closer to Cillian.

"It becomes ingrained in you," Cillian remarked. "Read it enough, and you would remember it too."

"So, what happened to Father Meehan that led to this?"

Cillian winced slightly at the question.

"I'm sorry," Anna said to him, speaking softer. "If you don't want to talk about it, that's okay. I just... well, I knew you back then, and I know how much you enjoyed working with the church and teaching. It seemed ideal for you. I can't believe something would come along that could change all that."

"It's a fair question," Cillian told her. "I just don't know if I'm ready to answer it yet. I can tell you that I loved doing God's work and the people I met." He smiled at Anna as he said this. "That being said, I also love the life I have carved out for myself now. I like the work, and I love the people around me. In a way, the Cosantóir is a lot like the life I had before. There's a bond, a brotherhood, a spiritualness if you will, that it brings to me. After I left the church, I searched for something like that and couldn't find it anywhere. It was when I came across Conor O'Farrell and the Cosantóir that I realized it was where I am now."

"What year did you leave the church?" Anna asked.

"In 2001," Cillian answered as he crumpled up the empty sandwich wrapper he had.

Anna sat back in her chair.

"So it was right after I got married and moved away," she said quietly.

"I... I guess it was."

"Cillian... did you leave because of me?" Anna said seriously.

Cillian rose from his chair and extended his hand to Anna to help her up.

"Let's go," he said, quickly changing the subject.

"Where?" she asked.

"We still have exploring to do," Cillian replied. "There's more to see in Harriman and Monroe than just the grocery store or fast food places, and it's still early in the day. Besides, it's getting to the time where our fair Irish skin is going to fry in the direct sun."

Cillian led Anna back to his car, and they drove off on his version of a local tour. They traveled around the local area, stopping at Roe Orchards to pick up some locally-grown apples and cider. Cillian drove over to Sugar Loaf, a small artisan town nearby, to walk on the shady sidewalks and visit local craft shops. The whole time, he and Anna talked and laughed, rehashing what they used to do, the good and the bad, and what they have been up to over the many years since they saw each other.

Cillian decided to skip lunch and indulge in ice cream at Wally's, the local ice cream choice. The long line was a bit predictable for a summer afternoon in August, but it was well worth it. Cillian treated Anna to a hot fudge sundae while having some black raspberry ice cream of his own. They managed to find an empty picnic table in the back where there was some shade, so their treats didn't melt quite as quickly. He gave Anna a good laugh when there was a mustache of ice cream resting on his upper lip. He watched as she took one of her napkins and gently dabbed the ice cream off his face. Anna looked into his eyes as she touched him and inched closer to him.

"So, where to now?" she asked eagerly.

"I'm not sure," Cillian told her. "I think I covered a lot of places today, and it is Sunday. Not as much is open, and the local parks will be crowded. Is there anything you want to do?"

Anna sat back on the bench and look at Cillian.

"We can go back to my place," she offered. "I have a lovely little patio out back that is shaded with lots of trees. We can relax there. I'm... I'm not ready for the day to end yet."

Cillian nodded in agreement.

"That sounds great," he told her. He stood up from the seat, took Anna's hand, and led her back to the car. The short ride to her place on Church Street was made a bit longer by the Sunday traffic, including many of the trucks and vendors breaking down from the festival as they drove past the Goose Pond area.

Cillian pulled into Anna's driveway and parked behind her car.

"I guess Makenna and her friends are gone," Anna said as they emerged from the car and walked toward the front door. "We'll have the place to ourselves."

Cillian trailed behind Anna and followed her as they moved through the house and then out the back door and onto the stone patio. Anna had taken the time to hang some plants and clean up the garden area a bit, to begin with. However, most of her patio furniture and the like were still stacked up in the adjacent garage.

"Damn, I forgot the furniture is still in there," she said, pointing to the garage.

"It's okay," Cillian told her. "I can pull it out for you."

"Are you sure?" she asked. "It might be a bit grimy in there. I don't want you to ruin your suit."

Cillian took off his suit jacket, undid his tie, and placed both on the stone wall around the patio.

"It should be fine," he told her. "I work in dirt and grime every day. Maybe not in a suit, but it's nothing I can't handle."

"You don't mind if I run in and change, do you?" Anna said as she stood at the back door.

"Not at all. I'll have all this out in a few minutes."

Anna disappeared back into the house as Cillian went to work, dragging out the glass table and chairs. He went back in for the cushions for the chairs, stacking them up so he could barely fit through the door leading back to the patio. He emerged from the garage and dropped the cushions, giving himself a view of Anna as she bent and wiped down the glass table with cleaner she had brought out with her. Cillian froze as he looked at Anna in a pair of shorts, showing off her long legs. He swallowed hard and cleared his throat.

"Oh, I just wanted to spray this down," Anna said as she turned to face Cillian. Cillian picked up two sets of cushions and placed them on the chairs positioned next to each other so they could both sit.

"You want something to drink?" Anna offered. "I don't have any Guinness, I'm afraid, but I can offer you some iced tea, homemade."

"Sounds perfect," Cillian croaked, his throat suddenly dry and parched.

"Back in a sec," Anna said happily and moved inside to get drinks.

Cillian sat down, feeling the heat more in the last minute or so than he had all day.

Anna reemerged with a tray holding two glasses, a bowl of ice, and a pitcher of tea. Cillian rose and took it from her, placing it on the newly-cleaned table, before Anna took up the glasses to pour. She passed a glass to Cillian before filling one for herself. She stood in front of Cillian and made a toast.

"Thank you for the best day I have had in a long time," she offered, clinking her glass with his.

"You are very welcome," Cillian replied. He took a quick drink, draining half the glass, as he watched Anna sip hers. She then turned around and noticed one of her hanging plants just barely staying in place.

"I knew that hook was going to be a problem," she lamented. "It was too loose. I'm going to need to replace it."

Anna dragged the stepstool over so she was positioned underneath the plant. She stood high on her tiptoes to reach the hook and was able to just barely twist it.

"Why don't you let me get that?" Cillian told her as he rose and approached her.

As he got closer to Anna, he saw her lift her right foot to stretch higher, causing her t-shirt to rise up and bare her midriff. Anna stumbled, slipping from the step and falling. Cillian closed in to catch her and then move her head away just in time as the planter came crashing down to the stone patio, shattering and spreading soil everywhere.

Cillian held Anna in his arms, one hand under her neck with the other holding her bare waist tightly.

"You saved me," she said breathlessly. "Thank you."

"Of course I did," Cillian replied. He looked down into Anna's face, saw her smile lightly as he held her, and she began to bring her face closer to his.

Instinct took over for Cillian now, and he did something he had been waiting more than twenty years to do – he kissed her.

Chapter 13

Anna was caught entirely off-guard by the kiss from Cillian, but once she felt his lips on hers, she shut her eyes and got swept up at the moment. It was everything she imagined it would be – soft lips that firmly let her know she was thoroughly kissed. Instinctively, she wrapped her arm around Cillian's neck to hold him there, connected to her for the first time in the way she had always wanted.

"I've been waiting a long time to do that," Cillian said as he pulled his lips from hers. He leaned his forehead against Anna's and closed his eyes.

"I think I've been waiting just as long for you to do it," Anna sighed.

"Really?" Cillian asked with surprise.

"Really," she smiled. With that, she reached and pulled Cillian's lips down to hers again. Anna's heart raced like it hadn't in many years. She knew that it had been a long time since she felt anything from a kiss she received, and she didn't want this one to end quickly.

Anna stood up and faced Cillian, running her hands over the dress shirt he still wore. Just the feel of the strength she felt in his pecs and abs lit a fire inside her. Part of her wanted to tear the shirt open then and there on the patio. Cillian's body trembled slightly under her touch, and she saw that this strong man had closed his eyes and was clearly trying to control himself. Anna got on her tiptoes and lightly kissed Cillian's neck, reveling in the short stubble that was there and his scent – subtle, strong, manly – and that heat she experienced rapidly spread through her body.

"You're too tall for me to keep this up out here," she giggled. "Maybe we should take this inside," she purred into Cillian's ear.

She took Cillian by the hand and led him into the house. Thoughts of forgetting about the bedroom and just having him take her on the couch, the kitchen table, or even in the doorway raced across Anna's mind. All she knew for sure is that she had to have him, and it had to be now.

When she crossed the threshold into her bedroom, she stopped at the foot of the bed and sat. Cillian still stood in front of her in his dress shirt and slacks, almost frozen in place as Anna felt his eyes go over her body. She reached down and pulled her t-shirt over her head. Cillian looked at her in a way that no man had in a long time, and a smile crept across her lips.

Anna's eye line was right at Cillian's waist, and she wasted no time reaching for his belt and unbuckling it. Her hand slid down from his waist, across his zipper without undoing it, and her hand lightly gripped Cillian. A gasp escaped his lips as Anna touched, and the telltale twitch she felt in her grip let her know he was just as aroused as she was.

Anna's right hand undid the trousers' zipper, and one tug had them falling onto the floor. Cillian mindlessly kicked off his shoes and stepped out of the pants, leaving his white dress shirt dangling over the navy blue boxer briefs that fit his body perfectly. She rose from the bed and quickly opened the buttons of his dress shirt, allowing Cillian to shrug it off and let it fall to the floor. Anna's hands began to roam again, this time over the muscles she imagined before. Her imagination proved correct, as Cillian had the fine definition of a man who takes care of himself physically. Her fingertips glided over each area slowly as she inched closer and closer to his waist again.

"Anna," Cillian gasped. Her fingers hooked into the waistband of his briefs as she looked up at him. Cillian's hands now gripped each of hers, holding them in place. "Wait," he managed to croak out.

"I've been waiting too long," she said playfully but then noticed the serious look on Cillian's face.

"What's wrong?" she asked, her body aching to keep going.

"There's something you need to know about... about me," Cillian replied.

"What is it?" Anna worked to slow her breathing down. She slid over a bit on the bed as Cillian now sat next to her.

"I was a priest for a long time, and before that was in school and seminary," Cillian explained. "I don't have a lot of experience with... with this."

"But you haven't been a priest for many years," Anna replied. "Surely there have been other women. I mean... not to disparage your club, but the stories about the parties and motorcycle clubs are kind of legendary."

"Here's the thing," Cillian said. He took Anna's hand in hers and held it. "When a priest gets a dispensation to leave the church, they do get to leave the order. What most people don't know is that once you are ordained, you're ordained for life. The dispensation releases you from church roles and responsibilities, but your vows... your vows and ordination are forever."

"So... you're supposed to stay celibate?" Anna asked, wondering where the conversation was going.

"Technically, yes," Cillian responded. "And I have. The only way to be released from that is to get a special dispensation from the Pope, and it's not something that is usually given."

"Oh," Anna answered, unsure of what else to say. "I'm sorry... I didn't even think about it... I'm so embarrassed..." Anna rose from the bed and went to grab her t-shirt to put it back on and cover up, but Cillian held tightly to her hand.

"Anna, wait," Cillian said to her. "You didn't let me finish." He pulled her back, so she sat next to him again.

"In all those years, going back to seminary right up until today, there has only been once where I considered breaking my vows. That was when you and I were becoming... close. The day you told me about your need to get married. Somehow I restrained myself then and bottled everything up. I've held that in for so long. And now..."

"What about now?" Anna asked.

"Now... in this moment... I know it's time... It's right."

Cillian had enfolded Anna into his arms before either had a moment to say anything else. He kissed her deeply again, and this time he did not let up. Anna pressed her body close to his, returning Cillian's kisses over and over. Within minutes, the two lay on the bed together, hands exploring each other's bodies for the first time.

Anna realized Cillian's tentativeness and took the lead, guiding his hands to the places she most wanted to be touched. It was a far cry from what she had grown accustomed to with her ex-husband, who typically took what he wanted, thrust a few times, groaned, came, and went to sleep. For Cillian, she unclipped her bra and slid out of her shorts, taking his hand in hers so she could show him just what was right for her.

Anna reached the point where she couldn't wait any longer. She shed her thin, damp panties before tugging Cillian's briefs down, so she saw and felt him. His warm hardness in her hands sent electricity through her body as she teased him with the base of her thumb on the tip of his cock. The move elicited a guttural groan from Cillian's lips, and Anna relished in the surge of power she felt, making her even more excited.

"I need you... inside me," Anna whispered to Cillian.

Cillian nodded and rolled, so he was on top of Anna. Her hand held his dripping shaft as she spread the precome up and over him, making him groan again.

"Anna, I don't have any protection," Cillian admitted. "I didn't think... I mean, I didn't know this..."

"It's okay," Anna gasped, trying to regain control of her breathing. Anna thought closely, trying to remember if she had any condoms. "Don't go anywhere or lose anything," she laughed.

Anna jumped out of bed and padded across the carpet, out of the room, and into the bathroom. There were two packing boxes still closed that held some items, and she prayed - which she found ironic at this point - that the box of condoms she bought because she insisted Leo wear one was still in there. She tore through the tape and flung open the box, tossing aside small sample size boxes of toothpaste, lotion, and shampoo that she hoarded from hotels over the years before she found the blue box of condoms at the bottom.

"Thank you," she said silently with a glance up and a smile.

Anna raced back to the bedroom to see Cillian lying still on the bed. She held up the box triumphantly and prowled her way back to the bed, straddling Cillian. She pulled a foil wrapper out of the box, tore the package open with her teeth, and removed the condom. All it took was one or two light strokes from her index finger to bring Cillian's cock back to its rigid state. She slowly and steadily unrolled the condom onto Cillian. Before Cillian could do anything, Anna took control and straddled his torso before slowly enveloping him inside her.

Just that move alone was nearly enough to push Anna over the edge. It had been so long since she felt like this, had something that was more than one-sided sex, that she wanted to make the most of it. Anna began to rock back and forth slowly, finding the angle and rhythm that sent chills throughout her body. She ground her pelvis against Cillian as his hands firmly gripped her waist. He let her guide the action and response. Anna peered down at Cillian and saw he did his best to keep watch on her but struggled to keep his eyes open with each movement they made together.

Anna picked up the pace, knowing that she was getting close, and sensed Cillian was as well. She leaned back a bit, and Cillian hit the ideal spot inside her. Anna panted loudly with each gyration and thrust before the rush inside her let her orgasm flow. The moment it hit, and she tightened on Cillian's cock, she heard his groan and felt him throbbing inside her as he came himself. Anna did her best to hold steady on top of him as wave after wave of pleasure coursed through her, and she collapsed her head onto Cillian's chest.

The two lay together quietly, each trying to regain composure. Anna felt Cillian's hands run through her hair and then caress her cheeks as she looked up at him. He rolled her to the side and kissed her over and over before he stopped and pulled her body close to his. Anna rested her head on Cillian's shoulder and sighed.

"How many more condoms do you have in that box?" Cillian asked as he kissed the top of Anna's head and held her.

Anna laughed loudly.

"I think we have enough for today," she smirked. "But damn the electric bill; I'm putting the air conditioning on," Anna quipped before jumping across the room to switch the AC on. She quickly climbed back into bed and assumed her position, snuggled closely to Cillian.

Chapter 14

It was hours later when Cillian woke with a start. Anna was curled up next to him, the top sheet for the bed tangled around her as she slept. Cillian trailed his index finger over the bare shoulder next to him, tracing the outline of her body down to her hip. He saw that Ann shivered lightly as his finger moved, and he straightened the top sheet on her so that she was covered while the air conditioner blew and kept the chill in the room.

A glance outside the window allowed Cillian to see that dusk was approaching. The two had been with each other for quite some time in the bedroom before settling in to rest. He tried not to disturb Anna as he sat on the edge of the bed and pulled his briefs and pants on. He scanned the room for his shirt, but when he couldn't find it easily, he decided to forgo it and just padded out of the bedroom to the bathroom.

Cillian then strode into the kitchen, getting himself a glass of water from the tap. He spied pictures of Anna and Makenna on the refrigerator and in small frames scattered on the windowsill. The array allowed Cillian to see Anna and Makenna over the years together and how happy they always looked.

He moved outside to the patio where the now tepid pitcher of iced tea sat on the table. The air was cooler than it had been when the sun shone earlier. Cillian straightened up, bringing everything inside, and then fixed the hanging plant that had started everything the best he could without making too much noise. He casually looked around the property at the garden and the lawn. He saw that Anna had her work cut out for her in maintaining everything. The grass was slightly overgrown, some of the garden spots had areas where weeds took over, and the trees and bushes needed some care to make them more pleasing to the eye.

Returning toward the patio, Cillian spotted a fire pit off to one side of the patio. He tugged on the steel object to drag it to a more appropriate spot and gathered the few logs that remained tucked away in the covered area of the patio. He then returned inside, grabbing some of the loose newspapers strewn about from unpacking, and grabbed the lighter next to the candles on the table so he could start a fire.

Cillian had the dry wood sparking up in no time, and a comforting fire started up for him to sit around. He sat back in one of the patio chairs and lightly rocked back and forth as he considered how things had played out today. Never in his wildest dreams did he think he would be in this position just a few days ago. Yet here he was, with the woman he had thought about for most of his adult life. As elated as those thoughts made him, he also realized he had crossed a threshold that there was no turning back from, both concerning Anna and his view of the church and his faith.

Cillian watched the flames dance back and forth and sipped his water, lost in thought. The sudden bang of the screen door behind him caused Cillian to spin around. There stood Anna, on the top stone step that led down to the patio, clad only in his dress shirt that came down nearly to her knees.

"I got worried that you had left," Anna said with concern before walking down toward Cillian. She draped her arms over his back and kissed the back of his neck lightly. Anna rested her chin on Cillian's shoulder and gazed at the fire.

"I didn't even realize I had a fire pit," she laughed.

"I found it off in the corner," Cillian replied. "I hope you don't mind."

"Not at all," Anna said as she came around to the front of Cillian's chair and parked herself on his lap. "It's romantic."

Anna nestled her head on Cillian's shoulder as they both sat silently for a minute. It wasn't long before Cillian noticed her looking out of the corner of her eye at the tattoos that covered his arms.

"I just never imagined you would have had all these," Anna spoke. "It seems so different from the man I knew."

"That man from all those years ago is mostly gone now, Anna," Cillian said honestly. "I hope you're okay with that."

"I don't think he's completely gone," Anna told him. "Yes, physically, you are not the same, and believe me, I have no problem with that," she laughed. "But I think your heart is the same. You're still a caring person willing to help. That 'priestly' part of you is there."

Cillian flinched when Anna said this.

"No, no, it's not," Cillian said firmly. He rose from his chair, helping Anna up, and squatted in front of the fire, moving the logs with a sturdy tree limb he had found to act like a poker.

"Are you okay?" Anna asked with concern.

"The priest part of me left a long time ago, Anna, and I'm pretty sure what we did today obliterated any of the remnants that might have existed."

Anna came closer to Cillian and took his free hand in hers.

"Just because you don't wear a collar anymore doesn't mean you can't have some of those same feelings inside you, Cillian. You can be gentle, kind, charitable, and spiritual without being a priest. You would tell that to the congregation and even your students all the time years ago."

Cillian kept at the fire and held Anna's hand without replying.

"Do you... do you regret what we did?" Anna asked warily.

Cillian pivoted and looked into Anna's face. Concern was there before him.

"No... I think I'm just experiencing some guilt over it."

"Guilt's not far from regret, Cillian," Anna said honestly as she let go of his hand.

"You have to understand, Anna," Cillian tried to explain. "Those vows I took mean something... meant something, I guess... to me. What I did completely changes not just my relationship with my faith, but me, and there's no going back from that now."

"And is that such a bad thing?" Anna said with a tinge of anger. "Whether you want to believe it or not, Cillian, things changed for you the moment you decided to leave the priesthood, just like they did from the day I decided I was getting a divorce. You know what that means for me with the church, don't you? Yes, it changes how I look in the church's eyes and maybe the eyes of some others, but I'm still allowed my faith, just like you are."

Cillian stared blankly into the fire, and Anna moved next to him again.

"Sit," she said, pointing at the chair. Cillian sat down and looked at Anna before she knelt in front of him. "What happened between us... it was wonderful. Honestly, it was something I had thought about a lot when I was younger. I had a massive crush on you when I was younger. You would have to have been blind not to see it."

"I knew," Cillian admitted. "But..."

"But things were a lot different back then," Anna interjected before Cillian could say anything else. "Nothing would have or could have happened without both of us completely upheaving our lives. I knew that, even though I was only twenty. We stayed good friends through all that, right up until the time Leo moved me out of the parish and made me disappear. At least that was what I thought. Even with facing all I have met since then, I still have my beliefs. I don't have to be within the four walls or even call myself Roman Catholic to be there. Cillian, I've always been able to share things with you. You know parts of me that no one else is aware of to this day. I never imagined I would get another chance to have you as part of my life."

"I never imagined it either," Cillian replied. "And it is what I want. But there's..."

Before Cillian finished that thought, he found Anna's lips on his. He brought his hand up behind her head and held her there until both were out of breath.

"But nothing," Anna whispered.

Cillian rested his forehead against Anna's and nodded.

"Now, let's enjoy this fire together for a bit," Anna said as she sat back on Cillian's lap, wriggling herself around. "And then maybe go inside after that and enjoy some other things," Anna said as she nibbled on Cillian's earlobe.

Cillian pulled Anna close as she put her arms around his neck. He prayed she was right and even found himself looking skyward before returning his gaze to the fire.

Morning bled through the slits between the blinds enough to rouse Cillian from his sleep. He rolled to his left and saw Anna was not there. He sat up quickly and reached for his phone on the nightstand. He quickly saw it was 9:30 in the morning already. Cillian struggled to recall the last day where he ever slept this late. He was about to get out of bed when Anna walked through the door, carrying a cup of coffee and a big slab of coffee crumb cake on a small plate.

"Good morning," she said, beaming as she handed the porcelain mug to Cillian.

"I'm sorry I slept so late," Cillian apologized as he took a sip of coffee.

"I thought about waking you, figuring you would be late for work, but you looked so peaceful there I didn't have the heart to do it. I hope it doesn't mess up your day."

"Actually, not at all," Cillian admitted. "I'm off the entire week anyway, so I have nowhere I need to be."

Cillian took a big bite of the cake, feeling crumbs bounce off his bare chest as he savored the taste of cinnamon in his mouth.

"This is delicious," Cillian said, covering his mouth so he didn't spray Anna with crumbs. "Where did you get it?"

"Get it?" Anna scoffed. "I made it this morning while you were snoring away. It's an easy recipe."

"You made this today? How did you have time?"

"I slept for a while after our last..." Anna giggled as she made a tumbling motion with her index finger. "Then I got up about seven feeling... invigorated. I had to do something with all that energy, and you were sound asleep, so I baked. It felt wonderful – the baking and the stuff we did."

Cillian smirked before he finished the crumb cake in just a few more bites. He then pulled Anna close to him as he sat on the bed. He leaned forward and kissed her stomach through the tank top she wore and tried to pull her forward onto the bed with him.

"As much as I would love to lay around with you all day, I can't today," Anna lamented. "Erin is picking me up at ten. First, we have to go and scrub down and empty the truck, and then I am going back to her place so we can go over the schedule for the next few weeks and talk about menus, plans, things like that."

Cillian looked at her with disappointment.

"Don't worry," she said to him. "We can get together tonight."

"I'd love to," Cillian replied. "I do have a few things I need to take care of today anyway, and I should check in with the club to finalize everything with the festival. I can meet you here at, say six? We can go out and grab dinner."

"Or I can cook dinner for us," Anna answered.

"I thought you were doing that later this week anyway? That's what Makenna told me," Cillian said with a wry smile.

"That's right," Anna recalled. "Well, we can have dinner in more than once, you know. Is Wednesday okay with you for dinner with Makenna?"

Cillian thought for a moment and then realized what Wednesday was.

"Ummm..." he hesitated.

"Wednesday is no good?" Anna asked.

"It's not that it is no good," Cillian answered as he got out of bed and grabbed his briefs. "It's... well, it's kind of my birthday."

A look of surprise leaped to Anna's face.

"Your birthday?" she exclaimed. "I completely forgot that you were born on September 1st. Now I have to cook for you that night... unless you already have plans."

"No, I don't have anything planned," Cillian told her as he plucked his shirt off the doorknob to Anna's closet. "That would be wonderful."

"Fantastic!" Anna said, clapping her hands. She stepped toward Cillian and reached to kiss him.

After he finished dressing, Cillian walked to the front door. Anna picked up her purse and followed him outside. He walked to Anna's car and went to open the door for her, but it was locked.

"I don't need my car," Anna told Cillian.

"Why not?"

"Because..." Ann began before another voice interrupted them from behind.

"Because Erin only lives three doors down, and that's where the truck is," said Erin with a wide grin on her face. "Good morning, Anna. Good morning, Cillian."

"Morning, Erin," Cillian replied.

"Nice suit," Erin told him as she touched the jacket slung over his shoulder. "Looks like your Sunday best."

"I should probably get going," Cillian said sheepishly as he moved to his car.

Anna hopped over next to him just as he climbed into the car. Cillian rolled down the window to speak with her.

"Thank you for an amazing day," Cillian said honestly.

"Right back at you," Anna answered. Anna leaned in and gave Cillian a deep kiss. He saw her smile as she pulled her head out and watched as she turned toward Erin, who was still grinning.

"I'll see you tonight," Cillian told her as he backed his car out of the driveway and began his ride back to the Hog House.

Cillian mindlessly drove the short distance back to Hog House, his thoughts more occupied with Anna and what occurred the previous night. He pulled into his usual parking spot in the back of the house and made his way up the back porch. At first, he was taken aback by how quiet the place was before realizing that it was Monday and most members were at work already.

Before he could get to his room to change clothes, he was stopped by someone calling his name.

"Preacher!" the female voice said. He spun and saw through the half-opened door that Maeve was sitting in her room knitting.

Cillian walked in and did his best to straighten his wrinkled suit, smiling at Maeve.

"Morning. Maeve," he said cordially.

"Good morning to you," she smiled, putting her knitting down on the basket next to her chair.

"I'm surprised to see you here. I thought you and Conor were at the house."

"We were, but after his PT appointment this morning, he was feeling particularly ornery and wanted to see what was going on at the house. A couple of the boys helped him up the ramp in his chair before they left for work. He's out in the rec room holding court to anyone who will listen, no doubt," Maeve smiled.

"Ahh," Cillian replied, feeling a loss for words.

"We missed you yesterday," Maeve added. She picked up a travel mug and sipped her coffee, spying Cillian over the edge of the cup.

"Yesterday?" Cillian asked, wracking his brain to make sure he didn't miss an important meeting or appointment.

"Yes, it was Sunday," Maeve answered. "You usually stop by after church. Conor was beside himself without his donuts. I'm sure he tried to call you... more than once, in fact."

Cillian glanced at his phone and saw several text messages and missed phone calls.

"Sorry. I think I switched my phone off."

"No problem. Conor certainly doesn't need the donuts. I was just worried about you. Is everything okay?"

"Fine, fine," Cillian replied. "I was just out most of the day and lost track of time."

"I guess so," Maeve smiled. "So, how is Annabella, anyway?"

Cillian did a double-take.

"Oh, don't look so surprised, Cillian," Maeve scoffed. "Liam told Conor and me that you two went off to watch the fireworks together Saturday night. He sent Rocky out to take care of you. I have to say I was a bit shocked when I heard that's who you were with. It must have been quite a bombshell when you saw she was around here."

"I... I can't believe you even remember Anna's name," Cillian said in awe. "I don't think I have talked about her much."

"You did, years ago, right in this very room, with me," Maeve said. She pointed at the seat opposite her so Cillian would sit. "It's nothing to be embarrassed about. A woman who has that kind of effect on you never leaves your memory. It wasn't long after Aoife passed. You were helping me get through it and deal with Conor and his troubles. We both said a lot of things that night that we probably haven't shared with many people. She left quite an imprint on you, Preacher. It's only natural you would want to see her."

"Maeve, I..." Cillian struggled to find the words he wanted to say to explain himself.

"Cillian, you don't owe an explanation to anyone about what you said or did last night. That's your business. Goodness knows you of all people have earned that respect the way everyone uses you as a sounding board."

"Thanks, Maeve," Cillian said, relieved. "I'm sure I'll want to talk about it at some point."

"Door is always open for you, A chara: two ears, no waiting."

Cillian rose from his chair and gave Maeve a kiss on the cheek.

"Now go clean yourself up," Maeve bade him. "You look a fright. The boys will be questioning you up and down if anyone sees you in your church suit."

"Yes, Ma'am," Cillian laughed.

He walked off to his room and, once inside, stripped out of his suit. He resolved to drop it off at the cleaners later to get it looking better and then climbed into the shower. When he got out, he wrapped the white towel around his waist and walked back into his bedroom. He lay on the bed and closed his eyes to relax, and his thoughts immediately returned to Anna. He replayed each moment of the last night in his head, going over every contour of her body, every touch, every sound that came from her lips, the scent of her – everything – and he knew he wanted more, despite what his brain might try to tell him.

Anna had watched Cillian pull away before she began walking toward Erin's house, leaving Erin standing on the walkway. Erin raced to catch up, and Anna barely got three more paces before Erin spoke up.

"So, are you going to say anything?" Erin inquired.

"About what?" Anna replied innocently.

"Well, let's see – a man you haven't seen in twenty years sweeps back into your life weeks after your divorce is final. You go off to watch fireworks with him, he comes to pick you up for church and to spend the day with you, and then I see him leaving your home in the same suit he was wearing the day before."

"I guess that about covers it," Anna said nonchalantly.

"Anna!" Erin yelled. "Come on! Details!"

Anna smiled and kept walking until they reached Erin's driveway. Anna spotted Olivia already hard at work emptying out the truck to store nonperishables and clean thoroughly. She spied Olivia looking at her as she got closer.

"Spill it, Anna," Erin begged.

"Spill what?" Olivia asked as she stacked bins of supplies.

"Anna had an overnight guest last night," Erin grinned.

"Ooh, the hot biker?" Olivia said as she stepped toward Anna.

Erin nodded as she and Olivia now stood in front of Anna, demanding a response.

"Okay," Anna relented. "We spent all day yesterday together. He showed me around town and the area. We caught up a bit, sat outside at the house, and..."

"It's what comes after the 'and' that we're interested in," Olivia said anxiously.

"Will you two stop?" Anna insisted. "Don't we have work to get to?"

"Stop being so coy, Anna," Erin insisted. "I saw him leaving your house this morning and that kiss he gave you when he was going. That wasn't a 'thanks for the morning coffee' kiss on the cheek."

"Yes, he spent the night last night," Anna relented. "Can we get to work now?"

"Something tells me he was too big to sleep on the couch," Olivia laughed.

Anna turned red and was frustrated.

"Alright, alright. Enough of the teasing, Liv," Erin added. "We're just giving you a hard time, Anna. We don't mean anything by it. It's your business."

"Thank you," Anna sighed.

"It was good, though, wasn't it?" Erin said with a grin.

"Amazing," Anna answered as she set about moving boxes from the driveway and into the garage.

Anna, Erin, and Olivia spent a long day cleaning the truck inside and out, followed by going over the menus for the catering gigs Erin had lined up for the next two weeks.

"We have a small party on Wednesday night," Erin said as she pulled up the next project on her computer screen. "It's just a private party at a home over in Mansion Ridge. Eight people, an excellent menu, and it should run about three or four hours that night. I've done parties for them before. They are a nice couple."

"And they tip really well, too, which is always great," added Olivia.

Anna nodded in agreement before she stopped.

"Did you say Wednesday?" Anna asked.

"Yeah. Is that okay?"

"Well, I had told Cillian I would cook for him that day. It's his birthday, but I'm sure I can reschedule it for another night."

"Cook for him, Anna," Erin insisted. "It's no big deal. Liv and I can handle this one by ourselves. We've done it for them plenty of times."

"No, I should be there. It's what you're hiring me for," Anna told her.

"Yes, it is, but I think you need him more than you need to cook for a small party. Besides, I have another party on Sunday that we'll need you for. We're doing the brunch wedding reception. That's a big one."

"Are you guys sure?" Anna said, looking at both the women.

"Anna, trust me," Erin told her. "There is going to be plenty of work once we get into the fall and winter. We have weddings, holiday parties, and more already lined up. It's times like this I wish I had a regular space I could use with a commercial kitchen and a small dining area. We could do so much more. Maybe someday."

"We'll get there," Olivia added positively.

"I think we've had a pretty productive day, ladies," Erin said as she rose from her desk chair and plucked a few bottles of iced tea from the fridge. "I'd offer something stronger, but Olivia still has some growing up to do," she laughed.

"Hey, I'll be twenty-one at the end of September!" she exclaimed.

"And until then, it's iced tea."

"That's cool," Olivia said as she popped the top of the bottle. "I have to get going anyway. I need to pick up my niece from the sitter and get home so I can start dinner before Beatriz gets back from work."

Olivia took a quick sip from the bottle, grabbed her purse, and was ready to go.

"I'll see you on Wednesday, Erin," she noted. "Enjoy time with your man, Anna," she added with a wink as she headed out the door.

"She's a great kid," Anna said as she sat at the dining room table.

"She's unbelievable," Erin added. "She works for me, helps take care of her niece, and works part-time at the Quik Chek, a lot of time during the overnights. She's a go-getter, tough as nails, but one of the nicest people you will ever meet."

Anna yawned and stretched, leaning her head back.

"Keeping you awake?" Erin asked.

"I'm a little tired after this weekend and today. My body is still getting used to everything."

"I bet it is," Erin teased.

"Not this again," Anna said, rolling her eyes.

"Come on, Anna. I'm just teasing you. Honestly, I'm happy for you. I'm glad you can connect with someone and move forward with your life. I guess you really like him."

Anna sighed happily.

"I think I always have. It just got buried along the way. I got so blinded by the life I was in with Leo that I lost sight of everything I ever wanted or needed out of life. For the first time in a long time, I think I can say I'm feeling good about everything."

"Good," Erin affirmed. "If anyone deserves it, you do."

"Thanks," Anna said proudly. She rose slowly from her chair and smiled. "Now I'm going to head home and take a shower. I think my whole body smells like frying oil. See you tomorrow to go work on some recipes?"

"Sounds like a plan. See you in the morning."

Anna walked down the street slowly toward her home. The heat of the day had worn off slightly, but between it and the sticky feeling she had from all the work done today, she couldn't wait to feel the hot water of the shower on her body. As she reached the driveway, she noticed the presence of the green motorcycle parked next to her car. Her heart jumped a bit at the thought of seeing Cillian unexpectedly at the house this early.

The banging coming from the backyard let her know he was out back, so Anna walked around the back of the house to the porch area. Cillian stood on a stepstool, adding the finishing touches to the plants she wanted to hang along the eave of the patio. His back was to her, but with his shirt off, Anna could see not just the glistening sweat on his body but the definition he had from his shoulders down to the base of his spine. She gave a quick catcall whistle at the sight to get his attention. Cillian spun around and smiled at her.

"I could get used to coming home to that sight," Anna smiled.

"I hope you don't mind," Cillian said as he moved from the step ladder to in front of Anna. "I just thought I'd fix your hanger, but then I saw the wood was rotted all around, so I picked up some new boards and replaced them for you. Everything should hold better now."

"You got all that here on your bike?" Anna asked with surprise.

"No, no," Cillian laughed. "A couple of the brothers helped me out and drove the supplies and tools over. I rode on my bike myself. Safety first, you know. By the way, your back door was open. I hope you don't mind I went inside, but you really should lock that before you leave. We're a small town, but you never know who might come by."

"Oh, I think the lock on that door is broken," Anna said, looking at the old door. "I don't even remember getting a key for that one. I'm not too worried about it."

"I can pick up a new lock for you tomorrow if you want," Cillian replied.

"Oh, no. I'm sure you have better things to do than go around my house and fix everything wrong. I'll get to it."

"Hey, I'm free this week with nothing much to do. I don't mind at all. Tomorrow I'll see if I can get that old lawnmower in the garage working and clean up the property a bit for you."

Anna pulled herself close to Cillian, wrapping her arms around his waist and pressing her head to his bare chest.

"You might not want to do that," Cillian joked as he put his arm around Anna. "I'm pretty sweaty."

"Hmmm, I know, and I don't mind at all," Anna purred. "Besides, my hair probably smells like French fry oil from all the cleaning we did today. I need a shower."

"I do too," Cillian answered. "Why don't you go first, and then I'll shower, and I can take you out for some dinner. No cooking tonight."

"Fine, but you don't have to wait for me to finish to get in the shower," Anna said slyly.

"I don't know; your shower looks pretty small," Cillian told her.

Anna looked up into Cillian's face and waited for a beat to see if he would catch on.

"That's the point," she whispered into his ear as she kissed his cheek. She sauntered to the back steps and let herself in the back door. Anna started stripping out of her clothes, leaving them in a trail like bread-crumbs for Cillian to follow into the bathroom while she turned the shower on.

Chapter 15

Cillian needed another shower after initially entering the shower with Anna. The space was tight, but once Anna's hands started roaming all over his body, he found it easier to lift her up as she wrapped her legs around him. He held her against the shower wall as the water pounded down upon them until both were gasping with pleasure. He felt Anna's heart race as she pressed her body tightly to him, gripping his shoulders and muffling her moans into his neck and chest.

Once he rinsed off, he reluctantly left Anna to shower herself while he dried off and dressed. He had smartly brought an extra shirt with him and had left it out in one of the saddlebags on his bike. He slid into his jeans and walked out across the lawn to the driveway, barefoot and shirtless. He opened the saddlebag and pulled out a dark blue short sleeve Henley and began to put it on. Once it was over his head, he heard a loud muffler of a car idling at the top of the driveway and spun around to get a look. All he could see were the tinted windows of a large white Ford F-150 as the car sat near the top of the gravel drive. When the pickup did not seem to be moving, Cillian slowly began to approach the truck. He stepped lightly on the gravel before one poked his bare feet as he got closer to the truck.

"Damn!" he exclaimed and looked down. As he broke his focus on the truck, he heard the tires squeal as it abruptly pulled away before he could get too close to it. Cillian gazed through the blue-gray exhaust fumes, trying to look at anything on the truck, but he could not see anything else as it tore down the street. He made his way back down the driveway toward the house, where Anna greeted him at the front door, clad only in her terrycloth robe.

"Everything okay?" she asked.

"Yeah, I just went to get a clean shirt," he told her, not wanting to worry her over what could be nothing. "I noticed a lot of weeds around the driveway, too. I can clean those up for you tomorrow up to the mailbox."

"Hmmm, you are so handy at a lot of things," Anna said with a wicked smile.

"I'm glad you think so," he answered as he opened the screen door. Cillian's hands went right around Anna's waist to pull her to him for a kiss. His hand snaked down and untied the loose knot at the front of her robe so that it just barely opened and he could slip a hand in to touch her bare skin.

"Hmmm, you do have quite the appetite," Anna told him as Cillian planted soft kisses on her neck.

"I guess I'm trying to make up for lost time," he growled to her.

"Well, I'm no expert, but I would say you're doing a fine job," she laughed. "But maybe we want to move away from the front door, so the neighbors passing by don't get an eyeful. I still haven't met most of them yet."

Cillian moved back into the house and went to the kitchen while Anna dressed. He poured himself a glass of iced tea from the fridge and looked out the window over the sink onto the side yard. His mind drifted back to the truck and how it sat outside the house, watching him or the house or both. It made him uncomfortable, and it was something he wanted to keep in the back of his mind.

Anna appeared in the doorway connecting the short hall and her bedroom. Cillian turned to look at her and found himself beaming at how beautiful she looked standing before her. He walked closer to her, looked from her face down, and caught sight of the gold cross she was wearing.

"You still have it," he said quietly. Cillian lightly picked up the cross that hung just above Anna's cleavage, holding it between his thumb and index finger.

"Of course I do," Anna answered. "It's always been special to me. Leo never wanted me to wear it. I think he was always a little jealous of you, even if he never said so. I kept it tucked away in my jewelry box. Every once in a while, I would come across it, and it would remind me of you. It made me wonder where you were and what you were doing."

Cillian's heart swelled at Anna's statement.

"I always wondered where you were as well," he confessed. "There were a few times I thought about trying to contact you. I would see one of the Mazza Sanitation trucks driving around and think that it wouldn't be that difficult to find you."

"Hmmm," Anna said as she put her arms around Cillian's waist. "I wish you had. But, for future reference, maybe don't tell me that seeing a garbage truck made you think of me."

"Oh, no, I didn't mean it like that," Cillian fumbled. "It's just that..."

"Easy, Cillian," Anna replied, laughing. "I was just teasing you." Anna pushed herself closer to Cillian so that her body pressed against his.

"Let's get some dinner," Cillian proposed as he led Anna out of the house to the driveway. He held her hand as they reached her car, where Anna stopped walking and let go of his hand.

"Where are you going?" she asked him.

"To my bike," Cillian replied, lifting up his helmet. "Where are you going?"

"I thought I would just drive us."

"It's only down the road," Cillian told her. "Let's just take the bike."

"I don't know," Anna answered nervously. "I've never been on one, and I'm wearing a skirt."

"Come on, it will be fun," Cillian told her as he got the second helmet out. "I promise I'll protect you. If you don't like it, I won't ask again."

Anna walked to Cillian with some trepidation. She picked up the helmet, working on getting her hair to fit underneath it comfortably, before standing next to Cillian, who was already seated on the motorcycle.

"Now what?" she asked.

"Climb on and put your feet up on the footrests," Cillian told her. "Then hold onto my waist."

Cillian waited until Anna was seated and had wrapped her hands around his waist before starting the bike. The engine of his Harley roared to life and clearly startled Anna as she gripped Cillian's midsection tighter.

"Hold on," he said into the Bluetooth headset of his helmet.

"I can hear you," Anna giggled. "Trust me, I'm not letting go."

Cillian pulled out of the driveway and sped the short distance down the street. Before they even reached the stoplight, he turned the bike into the small strip mall parking lot and parked it.

"That was it?" Anna said with shock.

"I told you it was quick," Cillian laughed, turning the engine off.

"That wasn't bad at all," she said as she hopped off.

"Good, maybe next time we can go for a longer ride," Cillian smiled. He locked his helmet in place and then took Anna's from her, watching as she shook out her hair and it cascaded down to her shoulders.

"I think I would like that," Anna replied. When Cillian turned, she was standing right in front of him. "Besides," she whispered, "I like long rides."

Cillian both blushed and surged with arousal.

"You're insatiable," he said quietly as he took Anna's hand.

"And I do believe I made you blush, Mr. Meehan," Anna told him.

Cillian led the couple into An Artistic Taste, a small, elegant restaurant located in Harriman. It was a place he went on occasion by himself when he wanted something more refined for dinner, and the dining room and friendly staff provided him with the comfort he sought. He was greeted warmly at the door as a regular and brought directly to his favorite table by the window.

"Can I get you something to drink," the waitress asked while handing menus to the couple.

"Two of the peach mint lemonades, please," Cillian stated, ordering for Anna. "I hope you don't mind. Trust me; you'll love it."

"Sounds good," Anna smiled as she perused the menu.

The drinks arrived, and Cillian watched as Anna sipped hers first.

"Oh wow. That's really good."

Cillian smiled and clinked glasses with her as they drank and ordered dinner. While they waited for their meal, Anna looked around at the décor of the place and sighed.

"I always hoped to have something just like this someday," she told Cillian. "Just a little place in a community where I could do modern food people would love."

"Now you have the chance to do that," Cillian told her.

"You mean to dream about," Anna told him. "I have a long way to go to get here."

"Dreams have to start somewhere, Bella," Cillian told her. She looked up right away at Cillian.

"Bella... no one's called me that since my Dad... and you," she reminisced.

Cillian noticed her eyes getting cloudy.

"I'm sorry," Cillian told her. "I didn't mean to make you sad about it."

"No, that's not it at all," Anna said as she dabbed her eyes with her napkin. "It's special to me, and I love that you said it."

The two dined well, with Cillian watching Anna savor each bite of the butternut squash ravioli that she had ordered. At the same time, he feasted on his large plate of paella, eating each succulent piece with fervor. Not much was discussed as the food took center stage for the moment.

When the entrees were done, Anna made sure to soak up what little was left of the sauce on her plate with a small piece of bread she had saved.

"Whew, that was amazing," she said, pushing the clean plate away from her.

"I hope you saved room for dessert," Cillian told her.

"There's no way..." Anna said as she shook her head.

"We'll split a piece of the flourless chocolate cake, please," Cillian asked the waitress.

"I know, I'm full too," Cillian admitted, "but you have to try this. Chef Andre makes an amazing cake, and it comes with this bourbon berry stuff..."

"It's called a reduction, Cillian," a voice said to him from next to the table. Cillian and Anna looked up to see Chef Andre standing there holding the nicely presented piece of cake with Venetian vanilla ice cream. "I tell you that every time you come in here."

Cillian laughed heartily and stood up, giving the chef a brief hug before he sat back down.

"All I know is that I could eat a vat of it," Cillian told him. "Andre, this is Annabella Foley. She's..." Cillian hesitated, unsure of just how he should introduce Anna to someone.

"An old friend who just moved to the area," Anna interrupted, letting Cillian off the hook.

"It's a pleasure," Andre answered, shaking Anna's hand. "It's nice to see Cillian with someone in here instead of sitting by himself. Good to know you have some nice friends," he joked.

"Anna here is a promising chef herself," Cillian told Andre as he dipped his fork into the cake.

"Oh?" Andre asked, turning to Anna.

"Not really," Anna said quickly. "More of a wannabe than anything else. Your place is fantastic, and your food is incredible."

"Well, thank you, Annabella," Andre replied humbly. "Now you have to be sure to bring her around more often," Andre said to Cillian. "I'd be happy to give you a tour of the kitchen sometime. For now, though, you better try some of the cake before Cillian finishes it."

Cillian looked up with a streak of chocolate smeared on his face and half the piece of cake already gone.

"He's not wrong," Cillian admitted.

Cillian gladly let Anna finish the cake before they finished up and left. The sun had gone down, and evening settled in, making things a bit quieter in the area.

"Are you ready to call it a night?" Cillian asked as he handed the spare helmet to Anna.

"I don't know," Anna said. "I think I'm too full right now to sleep... or do anything else."

"You're too much," Cillian laughed.

"We have many years to make up for," she said as she got on the motorcycle and gripped her hands around Cillian, placing them a bit lower than his waistline this time.

"Do that, and we'll have an accident for sure," Cillian warned.

"Spoilsport," Anna pouted.

"I know where we can go," Cillian said as he drove off down Church Street and headed out toward River Road. He pulled into one of the empty spaces up front outside of Millie Malone's. He spotted a few cars there but also spied a green bike there as well.

"I didn't know this place was even here," Anna said as she dismounted from the bike.

"Every town needs a place like this," Cillian told her as they went inside.

The bar was dotted with just a few patrons on a Monday night. Cillian saw Finn seated at his typical seat at the far end of the bar and waved before heading over.

"What brings you out here?" Finn asked as he rose and shook Cillian's hand. "You usually get your drinks at Hog House."

Cillian noticed Finn's eyes had swung over to just behind Cillian where Anna stood. He saw the smile creep across Finn's face.

"Finn, this is Annabella Foley," he said as he stepped aside to let Anna move forward.

"Nice to meet you, Annabella," Finn said, shaking her hand.

"Just Anna is fine," she said with a smile before sitting at one of the barstools.

Cillian sat next to her, leaving an empty seat between himself and Finn.

The bartender appeared in front of Cillian and smiled.

"How are ya, Preacher?" Darren asked with his brogue in full force. "A pint for you, I'm sure... and for your lady friend?" he asked with surprise.

"Oh, I'll have a pint as well," Anna said.

"A woman after my own heart," Darren said, feigning being shot by an arrow. "She's clearly a keeper."

Darren went off to pour the Guinness while a young lady appeared behind Finn and kissed him on the cheek.

"Darren, the faucet in the ladies' room is dripping," she mentioned as she went to sit. "Cillian!" she exclaimed, coming over and hugging him. "So nice to see you here."

"Hello, Siobhan," Cillian replied. Siobhan glanced over at Anna.

"I'm Siobhan," she said, reaching her hand across Cillian's body to shake with Anna.

"Anna," she said with a smile.

"I'm sorry," Cillian added. "I meant to introduce you."

"You have to excuse them, Anna," Siobhan explained. "These Irish bikers don't always live in the real world where manners and decorum reside."

Cillian sat back down, shaking his head.

"How come everyone seems so surprised to see you with someone?" Anna asked him.

"Because he's never with anyone," Darren said as he placed pints down in front of the couple. Cillian shot Darren a stern glance, and Darren backed off.

"I've got to run to the back for a sec," Darren said as he raced off.

"It's not often Cillian is out with people who aren't in the Cosantóir," Finn explained. Finn picked up what was left in his pint and toasted.

"Slàinte Mhaith!"

All four toasted and sipped their pints.

"Wow, it's been a long time since I've had a Guinness," Anna said, wiping a bit of foam from her lips. "I forgot how much I liked it."

"Are you in the area, Anna?" Siobhan asked. Cillian cringed a bit, worrying that Anna would be peppered with questions now.

"I just moved here, over on Church Street," Anna said. "My mother has lived in the area for a long time, though."

"You bought Mrs. Cromartie's place?" Siobhan said with a smile.

"I did," she answered proudly.

"And how do you know Cillian?" Finn asked curiously.

"We're old friends from years ago," Cillian said before Anna could answer. "We ran into each other at the festival."

"It's the first time we saw each other in twenty years," Anna added, looking into Cillian's face and forcing a smile out of him.

"Oh, so you knew him way back when he...," Finn began before Cillian cut him off.

"Yes, she knew me back then," he added before picking up his Guinness.

"I'll bet you have some great stories about him then," Finn said, leaning forward. "He hardly ever talks about his life of long ago."

"Maybe coming here was a bad idea," Cillian bemoaned.

"He was a wonderful man," Anna said proudly. "Just like he is now. Well, not just like it. He had a bit less gray back then, and I never saw him ride a motorcycle or wear a leather jacket."

"Fair enough," Finn laughed.

Darren reappeared with a tray in his hand and laid it on the bar.

"I made some snacks," Darren said proudly. Cillian stared down at the platter of charred bits.

"What are they supposed to be?" he asked.

"Jalapeno poppers," he said proudly.

"In an Irish pub?" Siobhan quizzed.

"Hey, people have been asking about food, so I thought I would get the kitchen going again. I'm trying some stuff out. Just taste one and let me know what you think," Darren asked.

All four looked at each other, wondering who was going to be the guinea pig. Finally, Finn sighed and motioned toward the tray.

"I'll try it," he said, picking one up. He examined the pepper closely, picked a few burnt pieces off the top, smelled it, and wrinkled his nose. He then closed his eyes and took a bite. Finn quickly reached for a napkin and spat it back out.

"Gaw, Darren, what did you make?" Finn quickly grabbed his Guinness and finished off what was left in the glass.

"What?" Darren said honestly.

"It's awful," Finn replied. "It tastes like... I don't know what it tastes like, but it's not good."

The other three of the group backed off from the tray.

"Hey, it's the first try," Darren admitted. "I didn't exactly have all the ingredients I needed, so I improvised."

"We're any of those ingredients fresh?" Finn asked as he wiped his tongue with a bar napkin. "Stick to pouring pints, please." Finn pushed his empty glass forward.

Cillian laughed and looked over at Anna, who was studying the unappetizing appetizer.

"You need to use a better cheese, maybe wrap them in bacon," Anna added. "You could even make some with pulled pork, but you overcooked them too. What did you use?"

Darren handed the fresh pint to Finn, who gulped at it.

"I used the stove," Darren said sheepishly. "What was I suppose to use?"

"I think she's asking about ingredients, you eejit," Finn replied.

"Anna's a cook," Cillian added.

"Not really," Anna immediately said. "I'm just an amateur, honestly."

"That can't be worse than what he is," Siobhan joked as she pointed to Darren.

"Hey, I'm trying to bring in some more business here," Darren said. "Having places like Chili's and Friday's around here keeps me from getting more customers who want to eat, too."

"Well, stop being a cheap bastard and hire a real chef," Finn scolded.

"I... I might know somebody interested," Anna said softly. "Do you know Erin Riley?"

"I do," Siobhan piped up. "She catered a couple of our fundraisers at A Safe Place. Her food is great."

"I work for her," Anna said. "I know she's looking for a spot to run her business from instead of her house. She might be interested."

"When can she start?" Finn yelled.

"Do you think she'd want to work out of here?" Cillian asked.

"I know she wants a permanent spot, and this might be ideal," Anna told him. "It's close by for us, would give us a place to host parties and do cooking. We could even bring the food truck around to have outside."

Darren reached behind the counter and handed Anna a business card.

"Have her give me a call," Darren told her. "I'd love to meet with her and see what we can work out."

"I will," Anna smiled.

Cillian drained the rest of his pint and placed his glass down.

"We should get going," Cillian prodded, helping Anna off her stool.

"But I didn't even get to ask any questions about your past," Finn lamented.

"Exactly," Cillian grinned.

"It was nice to meet you, Anna," Siobhan told her. "I hope we get to see you more." Siobhan gave Cillian a knowing look.

"I hope so too," she smiled.

Cillian led Anna back to his bike, and the two made the short ride back to Anna's house. Cillian helped Anna off the bike and walked her back to the front door. He glanced up and saw the motion light for the walkway did not come on.

"Something else to fix," he pointed.

"I know, I'll get to it," Anna said as she unlocked the front door.

Cillian stood on the top step outside the front door and hesitated.

"Are you coming in?" Anna asked.

"Are you sure?" Cillian said cautiously. "I can go back to my place if you want. I've been in your face for a few days now."

Anna took Cillian's hand and pulled him inside.

"If I didn't want you to come in, I wouldn't have invited you," Anna told him. "I know this is all new for you, Cillian. You have to put some faith in me. I know what I want."

Anna tugged on Cillian's belt to pull him even closer to her. Cillian took the cue and bent to kiss her deeply.

"Hmmm, that's more like it," Anna cooed as she kicked the front door closed with her foot. She took Cillian's hand and began to lead him through the living room toward her bedroom.

Cillian watched as she flipped on the light to her bedroom and then lay on her bed, giving him a come hither look and wiggle of her index finger.

Cillian moved to the bed, putting himself to Anna's left side. She turned to face him, placed her right hand on his cheek, and kissed him again.

"Thank you for tonight," Anna told him as she looked into his eyes.

"I didn't really do anything except take you to dinner."

"You did more than that," Anna replied. "You treated me well, introduced me to your friends, maybe even found a great opportunity for my future, took me on my first bike ride... I'd say we covered a lot for one night. For the first time in a long time, I felt like I was part of something."

Anna cuddled up to Cillian, placing her head on his shoulder and one hand on his chest.

"Me too," Cillian said quietly.

Chapter 16

Cillian rolled to his right with the intent of putting his arm around a sleeping Anna. When his hand just got a handful of pillow and bedsheet, he pried his eyes open and saw she was gone. He sat up, stretching and yawning, and picked up his phone to see the time. It was already nearly 10 AM as he rose, slipping back into his gray boxer briefs, as he walked into the kitchen. All he found was a small plate on the table with a homemade apple fritter and a white porcelain mug next to it. A small notepad next to the dish had a note from Anna:

I let you sleep in again. After all your hard work yesterday, you deserved it. I'm at Erin's working until about 5. PLEASE don't feel like you have to do work around my house!! Relax and enjoy your time. I'll see you later.

Bella

Cillian liked that she signed her name 'Bella,' letting him know it was okay for him to refer to her in that way again.

He had the foresight to pack another day's worth of clothes in his saddlebag and went out to retrieve the items so he could dress for the day. Even with the late August heat still kicking in, he knew he would be comfortable wearing his jeans and boots than anything else. He changed and got himself ready for the day, intent on tackling more work on the property even though Anna may not have wanted him to do so. However, when he picked up his phone, he noticed a text message unread.

Sorry I haven't gotten back to you. I'm still alive and kicking. Come see me.

Seanán

Father Clarke had finally returned his message, letting Cillian worry a little less about him. However, he still found it unusual that the elderly priest would text him instead of calling. Cillian gathered his belongings, packed up his motorcycle, and headed out to the New York State Thruway south toward Westchester.

Traffic was much lighter this time of the morning, with most of the usual rush already across the bridge and in their places of work. Cillian drove across the Tappan Zee Bridge - it would always be Tappan Zee to him, no matter what the new sign might say - until he reached exit 4 and got off to move toward Valhalla, where St. Brendan's Church and school were located.

The parking areas were relatively empty since the school was still on summer recess and morning mass at the church was complete. Cillian pulled into an empty slot closest to the parish office and made his way up the steps toward the office.

It was only natural that he got more than a few odd looks as he entered the air-conditioned office. Two women spied him the moment he walked in, and one warily approached him, looking him over in his leather jacket and jeans, his face covered with two days of stubble.

"Can I help you?" the older woman asked cautiously.

"Good morning," Cillian began, hoping to disarm the woman as quickly as possible with a friendly smile. "I was wondering if Father Clarke is around this morning?"

"I'm not sure if he is in his office," the woman responded curtly. "Do you have an appointment with him?"

"No, no, I don't," Cillian admitted. "I'm an old friend of his. He had contacted me and asked me to drop by."

"Father Clarke doesn't entertain many visitors these days," the woman said in a hushed tone. "Perhaps if you called first and set up an appointment to meet him..."

"If I could just talk to him for a moment, I'm sure he can straighten it out," Cillian pled. "I've come a long way, and I would hate to miss him."

A younger woman appeared in the corridor leading to the offices and looked at Cillian.

"Father Meehan?" she asked, tilting her head at him.

Cillian recognized the voice as the one he spoke to on the phone a few days ago.

"Evelyn Byrne, right?" Cillian recalled, hoping he got the name correct.

"That's right!" the woman exclaimed joyfully, glad he had recognized her. "It's so nice to see you."

Evelyn turned to the older woman.

"Patricia, this is Father Meehan. He worked in this parish years ago."

"Only it's not Father anymore," Cillian quickly corrected. He could see Patricia eyeing him closely as if she was not buying the story.

"Oh, right. I'm sorry," Evelyn corrected herself. "Are you here to see Father Clarke?"

"Yes, but there seems to be some question regarding his availability," Cillian said, taking a slight jab at Patricia.

"Oh, well, he isn't in his office, but I can take you over to the rectory if you want to see him. I think he's in his room right now."

"That would be great. Thanks," Cillian said with relief. He looked over at Patricia, who still had a stern face on.

"Thanks for your help," Cillian said as politely as he could.

Cillian followed Evelyn down the corridor and then out the back door. They walked down the stone path that led directly to the dormitory for the priests. Cillian could see that the area had been spruced up since the last time he was here. He was confident the rooms had to be more comfortable than when he was assigned to the parish and faced bare gray walls sparsely furnished with particle board furniture. They entered the rectory with the only sound the squeak of the door closing behind them.

The rectory had enough room to house up to eight priests, but he only saw names on two doors.

"Not many people here now, I guess," Cillian asked Evelyn.

"No, sadly, we only have three priests right now," Evelyn said quietly. "We had five last year, but two left once the school year ended."

Cillian felt like she was passing judgment on him for leaving, but he had grown used to that reaction over the years.

"Father Clarke is at the end of the hall," she added, pointing to his room as they neared it.

Before she knocked, she turned to Cillian.

"It was a big loss for this parish when you left," she said to him. "Having a younger priest here and at the school... it made things better for all of us around my age. We had someone we felt could relate better to us. Don't get me wrong; I love Father Clarke. He's a wonderful man, but he's very set in his ways. You were always different with us, and it meant something. I just wanted you to know that."

"Thank you, Evelyn," Cillian said honestly. "That means a lot to me. I enjoyed my time here."

Cillian could see she was tempted to pry more but thought better of it. She knocked loudly on the heavy wood door before opening it.

"Father Clarke?" Evelyn boomed.

"Yes?" Cillian heard the familiar voice crackle in the air.

"You have a visitor, Father. Is it okay if I let him in?"

"If it's Death, tell the bastard I'm not ready yet."

Cillian chuckled while Evelyn gasped.

"As feisty as ever," she said softly to Cillian, opening the door further to let him in the room. Cillian spotted the old man sitting in a chair near the large bay window that overlooked the grounds behind the rectory where the Stations of the Cross were placed. Father Clarke let out a slow, throaty cough and turned to face the doorway.

"Don't just stand there, boy," he barked at Cillian. "Come over and sit."

"Thanks, Evelyn," Cillian said to her.

"Lunch is in an hour, Father," Evelyn shouted. "Do you want to eat here or in the dining room?"

"What are we having?" he shot back.

"Alice was making a lovely salad..."

"Bah," Father Clarke grumbled. "How about a BLT, extra mayo?"

"You know you can't eat that, Father," Evelyn scolded. "Will you be staying for lunch, Mr. Meehan?" Evelyn asked.

"Run while you can, boy," Father Clarke warned. "That salad will give you heartburn and the runs all day."

"I don't think so, but thank you," Cillian said politely.

"Okay. Just ring me if you need anything," Evelyn replied as she closed the door.

"She's quite nice," Cillian said as he sat back in the worn maroon leather chair. He recalled that Father Clarke always had these chairs in his office back when he was pastor.

"Eh, if anything, she'll be the death of me, making me eat all this healthy stuff, exercise, having doctor visits. I'd be better off if they just let me be."

"Not likely, Seanán," Cillian laughed.

"You'll have to speak up, boy," Father Clarke said. "My hearing is worse than ever."

"Don't you have hearing aids?"

"Sure I do... somewhere," he said, pointing at his dresser. "It's too much trouble to find them and use them. Besides, I can hear well enough to what I want to listen to. So what brings you here?"

Cillian was surprised by the comment.

"You asked me to come to see you," Cillian answered. "I got a text from you this morning."

"Oh, right," Father Clarke nodded. "That contraption is the only thing that entertains me these days." The priest shakily reached for the cell phone positioned on the small table just to his right. Cillian spied it and the amber-colored ashtray under the dimly lit lamp on the table.

"You're smoking in here?" Cillian said with surprise. "I thought you quit those cigars."

"I did," Seanán smiled. He reached into his vest pocket and pulled out a black briarwood pipe. "Let's go for a walk. The warden will smell the smoke in here if I use this inside."

Cillian watched as Seanán lifted himself up from the chair, grabbing onto the security of the walker positioned next to his chair. Father Clarke then pointed to the far corner of the room by the large bookcase.

"Can you grab my walking stick for me?"

Cillian moved over and picked up the worn blackthorn walking stick that he knew well. Seanán had the shillelagh long before he needed it for support, often bringing it into classrooms with him to frighten the parochial students by cracking it quickly onto a desk or chalkboard. The story was that more than once, he broke a slate that needed to be replaced.

"You don't want your walker?" Cillian asked as he approached with the stick.

"I can't smoke and walk with the walker now, can I, boy?" the priest said with a wink.

"You want your biretta?" Cillian asked, picking up the hat off the dresser.

"No, I don't wear that anymore," he huffed. Father Clarke shuffled over to his coat rack, plucked the black Stetson fedora, and placed it on his nearly bald head.

"Gotta protect what I have left," Father Clarke said, looking up at Cillian. "You might want to invest in one yourself, you know."

The pair exited the room. Cillian began to walk back towards where he entered the rectory until a whistle from Father Clarke halted him.

"No, no!" he said sternly. "If we go that way, they'll catch us. Out the back door. I guess you've forgotten."

Cillian smiled as he walked back toward Father Clarke. They made a sharp right and went down a small set of steps that led to the basement door. Seanán nodded at the door as Cillian pulled it open. The priest bade Cillian enter first to pull the chain to turn on the bare overhead bulb in the room. The area was as dusty and dank as Cillian remembered it. Old lawn equipment sat strewn around with cardboard boxes set up like a maze. A small tool bench sat near the far door that Father Clarke pointed to.

Cillian approached the door and saw it was locked with a key. He turned to Seanán and shrugged, but the clever old priest reached into his vest pocket and removed a shiny key.

"I keep hiding it in different places, so they don't find it," he proffered.

"You're too much," Cillian said as he unlocked the door.

Cillian crept out first to look and make sure no one was around. When he saw nothing, he took Father Clarke's arm and led him to the pathway. Before they could even start walking, Seanán had lit his pipe. The familiar smell of the Peterson Irish Flake tobacco Father Clarke preferred permeated the immediate air.

"Ahh, that's how to start a day," Father Clarke grinned. "Heavenly. You don't happen to have a flask of whiskey with you, do you?"

"No, it's a little early for me," Cillian answered.

"Bah, you boys never thought it was too early when you would sneak out here for a nip and a smoke," Seanán chided.

"You knew about that?" Cillian said with surprise.

"What, do you think you were the first priests to do that? Eejits."

Cillian steadied Father Clarke as they moved slowly along the stone path that circled the back gardens of the church grounds. Seanán puffed on his pipe, stopping once in a while along the way to look at some of the flowers blooming along the way.

"The garden has never looked as good as it was when you were here tending it, Cillian," Seanán said honestly. "You had a deft hand and knew just what would look best."

"I think it's holding its own," Cillian added. "You didn't have me come down here just so you could sneak out for a smoke and complain about the garden, did you?"

Seanán removed the pipe from his mouth and looked at Cillian.

"Still with the bikers, I guess, huh?" he said, pointing the pipe at Cillian's jacket.

"I am," Cillian said. "And I still work with the Sand Hogs, too."

"Honest work, at least. I'm glad to see you're still toilin' with the earth. That biker club, though – a bit blasphemous. Probably break all the

Commandments regularly. And those tattoos – you never should have done that, Cillian."

It was rare that Seanán ever referred to Cillian by name, even when he was a priest. It was always either 'Father Meehan' or 'boy.'

"What's going on, Seanán? Why am I here?"

"My time's up, boy," Father Clarke said as he moved forward, striking the tip of his walking stick firmly on the stone.

"Seanán, you've been saying you're dying since I was in the parish."

"Not dying," Seanán looked at him thoughtfully. "They're pushing me out—forced retirement. I got my letter from the archdiocese last week. They're moving me to the Cardinal O'Connor Residence in the Bronx to live out my days."

Cillian was shocked by the statement.

"But you've been here for what, forty years?"

"Forty-eight to be exact," Father Clarke said proudly. "It's hard to believe they let me stay that long, but we had one of the largest parishes in the state at one point. As long as we thrived, I got to stay. I knew the writing was on the wall five years ago when they brought in Father Maron to be the pastor. I was just here to show up on Sundays and holidays, give last rites to the older parishioners who knew me, maybe baptize a few here and there. It had to happen eventually. All things change, boy."

Father Clarke had hit home with Cillian when he talked about change. In the blink of an eye, Cillian's perspective on life had changed drastically when Anna came back into it.

The two walked on a bit further until they came to a stone bench under a few trees between two of the Stations. Seanán sat down and patted the bench space next to him, so Cillian sat as well.

"I hated that you left this place, you know," Father Clarke said as he stared straight ahead. "Of all the priests that have come through here in my years, you were the one I thought would be the best. The parishioners loved you, the students admired you, and your understanding of the faith was unmatched. I always figured this parish would be yours when I left."

"You know why I left, Seanán," Cillian said firmly. "Like you said, all things change."

"Circumstances clouded your faith, Cillian," Father Clarke admonished. "Between what happened here and the trouble with the Foley family…"

"What trouble?" Cillian said.

"You and the Foley girl," he said. "Everyone could see it, Cillian. You were crossing a line you weren't supposed to cross. It was good for you when they left the parish. I thought that would solidify things, but then that other mess happened."

"I don't want to talk about this," Cillian said, standing up. "I never did anything inappropriate with Annabella. We were friends – nothing more. To insinuate anything else is wrong. I took my vows seriously."

Seanán looked up at Cillian.

"Took? As in past tense? Those vows are supposed to be for a lifetime, Cillian. What have you done? I can hear your confession if you want."

"This is insane," Cillian ranted. "I thought I was coming down here to see an old friend, someone I trusted, looked up to, and respected. Now you come at me with this? What I do now is my business, no one else's."

"That's not true, and you know it," Seanán said as he rose to face Cillian. "What you do now is still between you and God, yes. When you were ordained, your relationship with Him changed. Going back on that, either back then or now, alters everything for you. You know that."

The two stood silently staring at each other.

"What if it's love?" Cillian said.

"Is it?" Seanán asked him.

Cillian hesitated a moment before answering.

"I think it might be... I mean, I think it always has been."

"It's with her, isn't it?" Seanán said. "She's back in your life. She's a married woman, Cillian."

"No, they divorced. It was finalized weeks ago, and we ran into each other."

Seanán shook his head.

"That doesn't change anything, you know. Not in the eyes of the church. There's no going back from this for you."

"This conversation is over."

Cillian approached the older priest and hugged him.

"Let me know when you get to your new residence. I can come to visit you if you still want me to. Do you need help getting back to your room?"

"No, I can manage," Father Clarke said solemnly. "God bless, boy."

Cillian turned and walked up the pathway beyond the rectory and crossed the lawn in front of the parish office. He looked back only once to see Father Clarke seated on the bench they were at.

Probably finishing his pipe, Cillian thought.

He climbed on his motorcycle and raced out of the parking lot to the stop sign. His first instinct was to head back to Harriman, to Anna's house, and put his talk with Seanán out of his mind. Instead, he turned before getting onto the highway to make another stop.

Cillian drove slowly as he approached the entrance to Kensico Cemetery. He followed the tree-lined road up and around, catching a glimpse now and then of visitors stopping to see family or friends and tourists taking in the area to visit the many famous gravesites throughout the cemetery.

Cillian knew precisely where he was headed. He passed the predominant loop of Ossipee Avenue, where Lou Gehrig and his wife were buried, until he reached the other side. He brought his bike to a stop and dismounted, walking the short distance to a shaded area of graves until he reached the one for Donal Foley.

He stood before the grave for a moment, thinking hard about how to say the Irish Sign of the Cross Prayer in Gaelic before saying it aloud:

"Suaimhneas síoraí tabhair dó, a Thiarna, agus go lonraí solas suthain air. Tabhair maithiúnas dár ndeartháir agus tabhair ionad sosa faoi shíocháin dó.

Cillian sighed and crouched down in front of Donal's grave.

"Hello, Donal," he began. "I know it's been a long time since I visited you, and I'm sorry for that. I'm always sure to think of you and place you in my prayers. You're a man I genuinely miss. I... I just wanted you to know that I saw Annabella... that is, I'm seeing her. It's difficult to explain what's happened over the last twenty years, but just know that I am keeping my promise to you. Be well, my friend."

Cillian reached into his pocket and took out his wallet. Inside, he always had a coin tucked in. He removed the silver Irish pound and placed it on Donal's headstone, making sure to sweep away the bits of tree branch and bark that had fallen recently.

Cillian got back on his bike, driving past the small crowd now taking photos at the Gehrig gravesite, and made his way to Thruway to head home. The day had not proceeded as he had hoped. He was disappointed in his interactions with Father Clarke, a trusted friend and mentor, for many years. The entire ride across the Tappan Zee and back up the highway to Harriman, he was lost in his thoughts and if any of the decisions he had made, past or present, made sense for his life.

Chapter 17

C illian returned to Anna's home and worked with fervor on the
garden, removing weeds and overgrown brush. He threw himself
into the work, hoping it would block out his conversation with Father
Clarke. The priest's voice echoed in his head, reminding him how his
life was forever changed. The truth of this stung as he pulled on tangled
roots strangling nearby plants. He spent most of the day wrestling with
one yard area that left him covered in sweat and grime that needed forty
minutes in the shower to wash off.

When Anna returned home, Cillian embraced her tightly.

"Whoa, that's some hug," she said as she placed her hands on Cillian's
cheeks. "Everything okay?"

"Just a long day," Cillian sighed. "I tangled with deep roots by the
side garden for most of the day, and it was a losing battle. I'll bring some
different tools over tomorrow that hopefully can take care of it for you."

"Oh no, you won't," Anna chastised. "Tomorrow is your day. Erin
gave me the day off so we can spend it together and I can make you a nice
dinner. You're not spending all day getting all sweaty... at least not out
in the yard," she grinned.

Cillian gave her a weak smile before he sat down at the kitchen table.

"You really look beat," Anna said with concern. "Do you look like this
when you are down in the tunnels every day?"

"Sometimes," Cillian replied. "It's hard work, and the new technology and machines do most of the heavy lifting, but there are days where it gets pretty bad, and we're hundreds of feet underground. I think today in the sun all day wore me out a bit. I'm not as young as I used to be."

"Oh please," Anna said. "You're in better shape than most twenty-somethings I see today. They couldn't do half of what you can do."

Anna came over to Cillian and sat on his lap, kissing his neck and nuzzling against him. Cillian closed his eyes and relished the feeling before reaching over and caressed her cheek with his thumb. When he opened his eyes, he caught a glimpse of Anna looking right at him.

"Hey, if something's wrong, talk to me," she said softly.

Cillian hesitated before answering.

"Everything's fine," he said, kissing her lips. "I'm just tired."

"Well, go lay down for a bit, and I'll make us some dinner."

Anna opened the fridge to look around.

"There's not much in here, but I'll go shopping in the morning for things for tomorrow. I can whip up a quick stir fry if you want," she said, with her head still in the refrigerator looking around.

"Sounds perfect," Cillian smiled. He rose from the chair and walked behind Anna, embracing her.

"Go sit in the recliner and close your eyes," she told him. "Dinner won't take long."

Cillian moved to the living room, kicked off his boots, and sat. The leather crinkled beneath the weight of his body as he slumped into the chair. He lifted his feet up and shut his eyes again, hoping to get a few minutes of rest. When he closed his eyes, he saw Father Clarke chastising him for what he was doing and how he broke his vows.

Cillian was startled awake when Anna lightly shook his shoulder to rouse him. He sat upright in the chair, surprising Anna.

"I've been calling you," Anna said concernedly. "Dinner's been ready. Are you sure you're okay?"

"Yep," Cillian said with a stretch. "Let's eat."

Cillian ate heartily at the chicken and broccoli stir-fry Anna had crafted. Everything was cooked to perfection.

"It's delicious," Cillian told her as he went in for a second helping.

"Thanks," she answered. "I told Erin about meeting Darren last night and what we talked about. She was pretty excited and was going to try to arrange to meet with him tomorrow. That would be great if we could start to use that space. We were already talking about some menu ideas, with a mix of traditional Irish fare and modern American offerings. I think it has real potential."

"That's great," Cillian said. Anna reached over and took Cillian's left hand in hers.

"I can't believe all of this is coming together," Anna beamed. "After being stuck for so long, I finally feel like things are looking up. I guess God was listening after all."

Cillian recoiled a bit when Anna made her proclamation. He did his best to hide his feelings and sat back in the chair, pulling his hand away slowly from Anna's.

"Thank you for dinner," Cillian said politely.

"Not a problem," Anna said. "I think I have a good plan for dinner tomorrow. If I remember correctly, you're a big fan of lamb, right? I'll see what I can get. I wish I had a grill to cook on outside, but we'll make do. Maybe we can pick one up this weekend. What do you think?"

Cillian stared at Anna with surprise before the look came over her face as she realized what she had said.

"That didn't come out exactly right, Cillian," Anna said. "I meant, I should get one to use. I wasn't trying to push you into..."

"It's okay," Cillian replied. "It just caught me a little off guard, is all."
Anna paced in front of Cillian and looked at him.

"I know it's only been a few days together, and I'm coming out of
my marriage and all. I'm guessing relationships are a relatively new thing
for you as well, from what you have said. But I feel like we have been
connected for so long. It just felt natural for me to think of us that way."

"Anna, really, it's fine," Cillian told her. "You're right. It is all new to
me, and I'm still working my way around, but one thing I know for sure
– I'm happier when I'm with you."

"Good," she nodded. "Let's just leave it at that for now," she said,
feigning a zipper across her lips. "Do you want some dessert? I'm sure
I could whip something up."

"No, no, I'm full, and you worked all day. You should relax a bit too."

"I know, but I feel energized today. I think you bring that out in me.
After twenty years of not doing things I want to do, now I have the
freedom. I want to make the most of it."

"How about we just go sit outside for a bit?" Cillian said. "It's a bit
cooler out now that the sun has moved off."

"Sounds good to me," Anna answered as she let the dishes soak for a
bit.

Cillian and Anna sat on the back patio until the sun started to set.
Anna carried the burden of the conversation, letting Cillian know about
her day, what she did, and what plans she and Erin were making for the
future. Cillian said little and gave no hint of what had occurred for him
during the daylight hours.

Once it was completely dark out, Anna got out of her chair, took
Cillian by the hand, and led him inside to her bedroom. What started
out as slow undressing quickly turned into a frenzy of clothing being
tossed aside. Cillian grasped Anna's body hungrily, putting aside all the

turmoil he felt inside and redirecting the energy into his actions. He laid Anna beneath him and kissed her from head to toe, lingering on her neck, between her breasts, behind her knees, and finally between her thighs. Anna moaned and writhed beneath Cillian as he went after her ravenously with his mouth and tongue. Even after she came, Cillian moved further, rising up atop her, ready to enter her aching, quivering body. Sweat dripped off Cillian's forehead, and he saw a sheen on Anna's body to go with her damp, tousled hair. Cillian blocked everything out of his mind, concentrating solely on this moment before Anna put her hand on Cillian's chest to get his attention back on her face.

"Cillian," she panted. "Look at me."

Cillian focused his gaze on Anna, and some of the fury he felt in his body subsided. He struggled to control the pace of his breathing.

"We don't need one if you don't want to," she said, her body shaking. "You can."

Anna began to wrap her legs around Cillian to draw him into her, but Cillian stopped.

"No," he said breathlessly, using all the inner strength he had to roll off her and lay by her side.

"I can grab one," Anna said as she reached for the drawer of her nightstand where she had placed the box of condoms.

"It's okay," Cillian said, stopping her with his right hand. "Can we just lay here for a bit?"

"Yeah, sure," Anna added with a hint of disappointment in her voice. She placed her head on his shoulder and a hand on his chest, feeling his rapid heartbeat slowing down.

"What happened today?" Anna asked quietly.

"What do you mean?" Cillian answered, staring at the ceiling.

"Something is up with you today," she told him. "You've been... I don't know, distant like your head is somewhere else. And then all this. Don't get me wrong; I loved what you did, believe me," she chuckled as she propped herself up to look at Cillian. "But there was something about you just now. It was frantic, out of control."

Cillian turned toward Anna and smiled at her.

"Nothing, really," Cillian said. "Do you remember Father Clarke from St. Brendan's?"

"Sure, he was the pastor when we were there until we moved away. Why?"

"I've kept in touch with him over the years. He was always a mentor to me, and we remained friends. I heard from him today, and they're forcing him to retire. He was down about it, and I don't think I was much help in consoling him."

Cillian left his remarks at that.

"That's too bad that he has to retire like that," Anna told him. "He was such a fixture at the church. I'm sure you did your best to listen to him. You always have. Sometimes you can't fix everything; I've found that out over the years."

"Yeah, I think I see that as well now," Cillian sighed.

Cillian held Anna until he heard a light snore escape her lips. He looked down to see her fast asleep in his arms. He did his best to stealthily slip out of bed and get dressed. It was only when Anna felt the weight of Cillian sitting on the bed to put his boots on that she stirred from slumber.

"Hey," she said groggily. "What are you doing?"

"Go back to sleep," Cillian said, patting her bare leg sticking out from beneath the top sheet. "I'm going back to my place."

"Are you sure? It's late. Why not just stay here?"

"I need to check in with the club and make sure everything is okay, and I'm out of clean clothes here," Cillian said as he walked to the other side of the bed and squatted down, so he was eye level with Anna.

"I'm okay if you don't have any clothes to wear," she smiled.

"You're too much," he said softly and lightly kissed her lips. "I'll be back tomorrow for dinner anyway."

"That's right!"

Anna glanced at the clock and saw it was just after midnight.

"It's already your birthday," she said to Cillian. "Happy Birthday."

Anna reached over and gave Cillian a deep kiss.

"Sure you don't want an early present?"

"It's very tempting, but I think I'll rest up for later on."

"You don't know what you're missing," she said as she lifted the bed sheet to expose her naked body.

"Oh, I know, believe me," Cillian laughed. "I'll see you later, Bella."

Anna smiled and rolled over, grasping the pillow and pulling the bed sheet back on.

Cillian opened the bedroom door, creaking it a bit.

Anna moved a bit and spoke, "Love you," she said sleepily, not turning around.

Cillian froze at the door, unsure of how to react. He slipped out without saying a word.

The quick ride back to Hog House was filled with thoughts for Cillian. Not only was he still dealing with the turmoil and emotion of the day with Father Clarke, but what Anna had said to him before and when he was leaving stuck with him.

Cillian drove up the dirt hill to the house and parked his bike. There were more than a few motorcycles still outside, unusual for a Tuesday evening. This nullified any chance Cillian thought he might have of slipping back to his room without notice.

He entered the house and walked through the entertainment room, his boots tapping on the wood floor. The only group visible was huddled at the bar, watching the Mets game.

"Preacher!" Rory noted from behind the bar. "Get you a pint?"

"No, thanks, Rory," Cillian declined, hoping to get to his room. "Extra innings?"

"West coast game against the Dodgers," Rory said. "Seventh inning, 6-1 Mets. DeGrom's pitching a gem."

"Nice," Cillian said, faking interest. He went to step toward the hall leading to his room when he heard his name called.

"Preacher!" a voice yelled. He spun around and saw Rocky, a bit tipsy, holding up a whiskey glass. "Have a drink with me to celebrate!"

"Celebrate what?"

"He heard he's coming off probation at the meeting this weekend," Whitey added as he drank his pint.

"Congrats!" Cillian said and waved, moving back toward his room.

"Come on, one drink!" Rocky implored.

Cillian spun around and moved to the bar.

"Just a shot, Rory, please," Cillian said as Rory poured him a Jameson.

"Comhghairdeas," Cillian said as he lifted his shot glass and quickly drained it.

"Huh?" Rocky said, confused.

"It's Congratulations in Gaelic, you tool," Whitey laughed. "You might want to bone up more on it."

Rocky laughed and drank his whiskey.

"Speaking of boning up, how are things going with that gal you were with, Preacher?" Rocky asked. "She looks ripe for the picking, even for a cougar."

Cillian shot across the bar, grabbed Rocky by the neck, and pinned him against the far wall, just underneath the dartboard. Cillian reached up and plucked a dart from the board and held it under Rocky's neck.

"Watch what you say, Rocky, or you won't live to see the meeting this weekend," Cillian roared.

Cillian poked the dart tip into Rocky's dimpled chin, drawing blood, just as Whitey pulled Cillian off the young member.

"Jesus, Preacher! What the fuck?" Rocky said, wiping the dripping blood on his chin. "I was just jokin', is all."

"Choose something else to joke about, you feckin' moron," Cillian spat.

Whitey led Cillian back toward the hall and to his room.

"Easy, Preacher," Whitey said as he worked to calm Cillian down. "The kid's had too much to drink. He doesn't know what he's sayin.'"

"He's as useful as tits on a bull is what he is," Cillian said as she shrugged out of Whitey's grip.

"I'll talk to him and set him straight, don't worry," Whitey pledged.

"Make sure you do," Cillian barked. He went into his room and slammed the door closed.

Cillian locked his door and sat on his bed. He pulled his boots off and laid back on his pillow. When he sat up to take his shirt off, he saw the crucifix hanging on the wall in front of him.

"What's going on?" he said in its direction.

Chapter 18

Cillian woke with a start when the pounding on the door began and didn't let up.

"What?" he yelled as he sat up.

"Unlock the feckin' door!" the raspy voice of Conor screamed back.

Cillian got out of bed and went and turned the lock. Conor pushed the door open with his right hand to guide his wheelchair into Cillian's room.

"How did you get yourself into the house?" Cillian asked. "We haven't finished installing the ramps yet."

"Perks of being in charge, brother," he smiled. "I don't think the boys were too thrilled to have to carry me in."

"What brings you down here so early?"

"I can't come to see my best friend on his birthday?" Conor started. "Cripes, man. I haven't seen you in days. You didn't even come for coffee on Sunday. Then I hear you're threatening to make shish kebabs out of one of the prospects. I think that warrants a visit, don't you?"

"He was out of line, Conor."

"Maybe. But that's not like you. I told Rocky I was extending his probationary period for another thirty days, and we'll review it then. Sound fair to you?"

Cillian nodded in agreement.

"Now, how about you tell me what's going on with you? I'm used to dealing with the bullshit fights over women with the other brothers, but not you."

"Conor, I don't think it's anything to worry about. I was just a little out of sorts yesterday."

"Does it have something to do with the woman you were with for the fireworks?"

"Jaysus, Conor, does everyone have to ask that?" Cillian added before spinning around and walking to his desk to sit.

"Everyone said it's what set you off," Conor remarked. "After last night, Maeve mentioned that..."

"Enough, Conor!" Cillian barked.

"I'll say when it's enough!" Conor shot back. "You know I love ya', brother. But when what you do impacts the club, it's up to me to straighten it out. I'm on your side; we all are. I thought the time off from work would be good for you. I know you better than anyone else around here, Preacher. We both know all the skeletons in each other closets, remember? I know what you've been through and what you lived with, and what Anna meant... or means... to you. There's no shame in that."

"You're wrong about that," Cillian said solemnly. "There is shame in it. I broke my vows, Conor. Even though it was for someone I care deeply about and have for a long time, that doesn't make it right."

Conor wheeled over to bring his chair next to where Cillian sat. Conor placed his hand on Cillian's arm.

"I know you and I don't see eye to eye when it comes to the church," Conor began. "When Aoife got sick and passed, I basically swore them off for taking her away for no good reason, so I don't see the benevolent God you do. But with that benevolence should be forgiveness, no? You're not a priest anymore, Cillian. You can't be expected to act like one always."

"There's the conundrum, my friend," Cillian replied. "I am expected to act like one. I have a relationship with God that goes beyond that of the laity, even if I don't wear the collar anymore. When I was ordained, I agreed to live my life a certain way. It doesn't matter that I left the priesthood a long time ago. That bond with God was supposed to still exist. A few nights ago, I broke that bond."

"That doesn't make you an evil person, Preacher," Conor said. "It makes you human. I never thought there would be anyone else in my life after Aoife died. I figured that part of my life was over, and all the drugs and booze I used did everything to help me bury it. I felt guilty for letting her slip away the way she did and for the way I treated her and the boys for far too long. You know all this. It was because of you being a good man, an honest man – not a priest, but a man – that helped me get through the dark times, get clean and see that Maeve could fill that hole in my life. The person you are doesn't go away because you broke a vow, Cillian. Especially if you did it because you care so much about the person you were with. What are you going to do? Beat yourself up forever, live with constant guilt and let a chance at a real relationship slip away?"

Cillian sat silently, considering what his friend had said.

"Just think some more about it before you make a decision you'll regret," Conor told him. "In the meantime, try not to kill any of our prospects. And here."

Conor reached into the side pocket of his wheelchair and pulled out an envelope, handing it to Cillian.

"Happy Birthday. I thought about getting you a bottle of something, but since I don't drink anymore, I didn't see the point."

Cillian opened the envelope and saw two tickets to a Mets game scheduled for mid-September.

"Wow, Delta seats," Cillian said, noting the tickets right behind home plate.

"I pulled some strings and dropped some cash," Conor replied. "Take that gal with you. You said she liked baseball."

"That was a long time ago," Cillian said as he put the tickets away. "I don't know if she still follows them."

"Only one way to find out," Conor told him. "Want to go out tonight to celebrate? Maeve and I can take you over to Christopher's Bistro. You can get a nice steak, and we'll have a good time."

"Can I take a rain check?" Cillian asked. "Anna is making dinner for me tonight."

"Even better!" Conor exclaimed. "We'll do it this weekend instead. Go enjoy yourself."

Conor pivoted his wheelchair so he could get through the doorway with ease.

"Do you need a ride?" Cillian questioned.

"Nah, the prospects can get me home," Conor laughed. "Maeve was going over to the yarn shop in Cornwall for a bit to do her knitting thing. Let the lads earn their keep around here. Someone get me to a car and drive me home!" Conor bellowed as his chair moved down the hall.

Cillian spent most of the day alone in his room. He finalized paperwork left over from the festival and made arrangements to make the donations with the proceeds. The Cosantóir routinely donated money to local charities and organizations like A Safe Place. They also used the money to set up a scholarship in Aoife O'Farrell's name, gave funds to the local Irish dance troupe, food pantries, and other places in need. It was Cillian's job to make sure it was portioned out appropriately.

After doing paperwork, he cleaned himself up, getting rid of the stubble on his face for the first time in days. He searched through his closet, looking for something to wear that wasn't jeans and a t-shirt like he wore to work most days or one of his suits. He finally found a pair of khakis he had tucked away in the closet and settled on a short-sleeve dress shirt to wear. However, he stayed with his boots since he planned to ride his bike over to Anna's.

Cillian still had some time before he was expected at Anna's. He walked through the entertainment room at Hog House and garnered a few glances from members located in the room. He spotted Rocky in the far corner, sitting at one of the couches facing the TV used for video games. Rocky averted Cillian's gaze as he saw him approach.

"Rocky," Cillian offered, standing next to the young man, "I just wanted to apologize for last night. I was out of line."

"It's all good, Preacher," Rocky said. "I know I spoke out of turn. I would do the same thing if someone talked that way about my lady. No harm done."

"I know it set you back as a prospect. I wish I could change that."

"Don't sweat it," Rocky said, rising and offering his hand to Cillian. "We're brothers, always."

Cillian shook Rocky's hand firmly.

"Thanks."

"Where you going, Preacher?" Rory asked as he wheeled in a fresh keg for the bar. "It's your birthday! We have to celebrate."

"I'm celebrating somewhere else tonight. I'll catch you guys later."

Cillian waved and left the house, getting on his bike and heading out toward Monroe. He drove through town and over to the small building that housed Greenery Plus, one of the local florists. He popped in and looked over the vast array of flowers, arrangements, and plants that decorated the shop. His senses were overwhelmed by the fresh aroma permeating the room.

"Can I help you?" a friendly voice asked from behind the counter.

"I think you can," Cillian answered with some embarrassment. "I'm going over to dinner, and I want to bring her some flowers. Any suggestions?"

"Is it a relative, a friend, or someone special?" the woman asked as she came from behind the counter to stand next to Cillian.

"Someone special," he smiled.

"Okay. Do you know what kind of flowers she likes?"

"I know years ago she used to like the daisies and carnations that were planted..." Cillian cut himself off before he added 'at the church' to the sentence.

"Perfect!" the woman exclaimed. "I can put together an arrangement for you if you have a few minutes."

"That would be grand," Cillian replied.

In nearly no time at all, the saleswoman had expertly put together daisies, carnations, and a couple of roses to create a sweet, colorful arrangement that was nicely wrapped together in paper. Cillian paid for the flowers and picked them up to head out.

"Thanks," he said with a nod.

"You're welcome," the lady grinned. "I hope your someone special loves them."

Cillian placed the flowers strategically in one of his saddlebags so the arrangement wouldn't get crushed on his way to Anna's. As he moved back toward Harriman, he decided to take one last stop and pulled into Federal Plaza to visit La Lima's Bakery.

The scents of fresh bread and cookies permeated the air from the time he swung the door open. He was greeted by the smiling face of the young girl behind the counter.

"Well, hello, Cillian," the girl said as she put on a fresh pair of gloves. "I haven't seen you in here in a while."

"I know," Cillian replied. "I've been off work this week, so I haven't come in for cookies, bread, or sandwiches."

"What can I get you?"

"Do you have any of the olive bread left?" Cillian asked with anticipation.

"I think I have a couple," the girl answered as she walked over to the bin of bread to pick one out. "Anything else?"

"Oh, give me a pound of cookies too," Cillian acquiesced.

"You bet. Heavy on the rainbows and chocolate pretzels, right?" the girl laughed.

"You know me too well."

Cillian gathered his trove of goodies, paid, and was back on his bike, heading to Anna's house. He pulled into the driveway and saw a BMW parked next to Anna's car, squeezed in at the end of the driveway.

He strode down the pathway to the front door and gave a solid knock on the screen door. He tried to peer inside since the front door was open, but he saw nothing and heard a young voice yell, "coming!"

Makenna appeared at the door with a smile on her face.

"Hello, Mr. Meehan," she said politely. "Happy Birthday!"

"Thank you," Cillian answered humbly. "Please, call me Cillian."

"Okay, Cillian. Come on in," she said as she opened the door.

"Mom's in the kitchen," Makenna pointed as Cillian followed her the short distance from the living room to the kitchen.

"Hey there," Anna said happily as she turned her head from the vegetables she was chopping. Anna put her knife down and walked over to Cillian.

"Happy Birthday," she said softly, giving him a kiss.

"Thanks," he told her before handing her the flowers. "For you."

"They're beautiful," Anna beamed. "It's been so long since anyone gave me flowers. Mac, can you put these in a vase?"

"Do you even have a vase?" Makenna questioned.

"Just use the glass pitcher in the cabinet there," Anna pointed.

Cillian then presented the bread and cookies.

"I picked up a loaf of olive bread from the bakery," he added. "I hope that's okay. They make the best bread around here."

"It will be perfect to go with the lamb chops," Anna added. "And you brought sweets, too? I made you a birthday cake!"

"It's just some Italian cookies," Cillian downplayed. "I couldn't resist."

"Well, I can't resist them either," Makenna said as she snatched the box and broke the string with a pair of scissors so she could dive in. "Hmmm, rainbow cookies."

"Mac, we're eating soon," her mother chastised.

"It's okay," Makenna added, covering her mouth, so no rainbow-colored crumbs spat out.

"Do you want a drink?" Anna asked. "I picked up some Guinness if you'd like one. They're in the fridge."

Cillian nodded and plucked a cold nitro can from the top shelf. Anna had even left a pint glass out for use.

"Do you need any help?" Cillian offered as he poured his beer.

"No, thanks," Anna insisted. "It feels great to be in the kitchen and cooking for someone again. Besides, it's your day. Go sit on the patio and relax. Dinner will be ready shortly."

Cillian followed orders, going out the back door to the patio. He took a closer look at the broken lock on the back door, vowing that he would fix it tomorrow. He sat down, looking over the yard before Makenna came out and sat next to him.

Cillian felt her eyes on him as he shifted his feet.

"Ready to head back to school?" Cillian said, searching for a topic.

"Yeah, classes start next week," Makenna replied. "It's my last year, so I'm anxious to get it going."

"I remember my last year of school, too," he laughed. "Everyone feels the same way."

"Oh, I didn't realize priests went to school," Makenna said awkwardly.

Cillian chuckled and held out his right hand, showing his ring.

"St. Joseph's Seminary and College in Yonkers," Cillian said proudly. "I got my Master's degree there."

"Wow, cool," Makenna said as she sipped the glass of iced tea she had with her.

The two sat quietly for another minute or so before Makenna turned to Cillian.

"I have to tell you I haven't seen Mom this happy in a long time," she said in a hushed tone. "I knew things weren't great between her and Dad for a while, but I never realized how unhappy she was until I have seen her these past few days and talked to her. She's practically giddy."

"She used to be happy all the time," Cillian remembered as he sipped his Guinness.

"Back when you were around," Makenna added. "I know it was before I was born, but from what she tells me, that's when she was happiest."

"Me too," Cillian said quietly.

Anna appeared at the back door.

"What are you two whispering about?" she asked.

"Cillian is telling me about how you were a party animal at my age," Makenna teased.

"Ha!" Anna laughed. "Hardly. You've met your grandmother, haven't you? She kept pretty tight reins on me. It wasn't often I got to slip out and do something without her knowing about it. You... you've been getting away with murder since you were sixteen. Anyway, no more telling tales. Dinner is ready."

Makenna snuck into the house before Cillian made his way up the stone steps to the doorway. Anna took hold of his hand and held him there.

"Were you telling tales?" Anna said slyly.

"Not at all," Cillian grinned.

The three sat at the kitchen table and began with a Caesar salad Anna had created before the entrée came to the table. The small table was quickly filled with seared lamb chops, glazed roasted carrots, and garlicky roasted potatoes. Anna passed a bottle of Pinot noir for Cillian to open for the table as well. Cillian filled Anna's glass and his before Makenna chimed in.

"What about me?" she pouted, staring at an empty wine glass.

"In November, when you're twenty-one, you can have some," Anna stated.

"Come on, Mom," Makenna whined. "One glass of wine! It's not like I haven't had something to drink before anyway, and I can spend the night here."

"Really? You're planning on staying here tonight? Are you sure?" Anna asked as she looked at Cillian.

"Eww, maybe not," Makenna added, taking the half glass of wine Cillian offered her.

The three laughed and enjoyed the meal. Makenna peppered Cillian with questions about the days before she was born when "her mother was fun," as Makenna said.

"Your mother was one of the few people I knew that could hang with the girls or the guys," Cillian stated. "She was just as comfortable going dancing with her girlfriends as she was going to the baseball game or playing touch football with the boys."

"Yeah?" Makenna said with surprise. "You were always very girly-girl when I was growing up."

"If your grandfather had been around when you were growing up, it wouldn't have been that way," Anna added. "My Dad always made sure I could just as easily change the tire on the car, use the ax to cut wood, or play football as I could cook in the kitchen or wear a pretty dress. He would have made sure you did too."

"I'm sorry I never got to meet him," Makenna lamented.

"Me too, honey," Anna said, taking her daughter's hand.

"Donal was a great man," Cillian added as he finished the last of the carrots on his plate. "He was real down to earth and didn't pull any punches, and he was always willing to talk about anything and everything. I loved being with him."

"I know he held you in high regard," Anna told Cillian. Anna raised her wine glass.

"To Donal Foley," she said as they clinked glasses and drank.

A knock could be heard at the front door, and all three stopped and looked in the direction of the door.

"You expecting anyone?" Anna asked Makenna.

"Nope," Makenna said, shaking her head.

"I'll get it. It's probably Erin just stopping by. Mac, can you clear the table, please?"

Makenna rose and began to clean off the table, and Cillian did the same. Cillian turned the faucet on and started to wash dishes when he heard a bit of a commotion out in the living room. He turned the water off and entered the room and saw Anna standing there with her mother.

"Makenna said she was coming for dinner, and I didn't think you would mind if I dropped by for dessert," Marcella said. Cillian caught Marcella's eyes and saw her look become stony.

"I didn't realize you had company over," Marcella affirmed.

"It's Cillian's birthday today," Anna said as she tried to defuse a potentially volatile situation.

"How are you, Mrs. Foley?" Cillian asked, wiping his hands on a dishtowel.

Marcella let out a huff and said nothing. Makenna then walked into the room behind Cillian.

"Grandma, what are you doing here?" Makenna asked.

"She said you told her you were coming for dinner," Anna bemoaned.

"I may have mentioned it," Makenna answered sheepishly.

"We've actually just finished dinner anyway, Mom," Anna told her mother.

"Surely you're having dessert," Marcella said firmly. "It's a birthday dinner, so there must be cake. I'll be happy to have some with coffee."

Marcella marched into the kitchen with Anna rushing behind her and Makenna mouthing 'Sorry' to her mother. Cillian grabbed Anna's wrist before she got into the kitchen.

"I'm so sorry," she began before he stopped her.

"Bella, breathe," Cillian said softly. "It will be fine. It's just cake."

Cillian watched as she closed her eyes and took a deep breath. She opened her eyes and smiled at Cillian.

"Maybe she's allergic to cherries," Anna said snidely.

Cillian and Anna went into the kitchen to see Makenna scrambling to get dishes done and items put away.

"Don't you have a dishwasher?" Marcella said as she sat at the head of the table.

"No, Mom, just my hands," she said with an eye roll. Cillian put his hand on Anna's shoulder.

"I'll do the dishes," Cillian told her. "You can sit with your mother. Why not take her outside on the patio?"

"And sit out there with all those gnats, flies, and mosquitoes? No, thank you," Marcella gruffed. "I'll just take my coffee here with milk and sugar."

"I'll get it started, Mom," Makenna told her, grabbing the percolator.

"It's not instant, is it?" Marcella asked. "I won't drink instant."

"It's not, Mom," Anna said, breathing deeply again.

Cillian and Makenna worked feverishly on the dishes, one washing while the other dried, as Marcella took her shots at Anna.

"The décor in here certainly is... quaint," Marcella said as she looked at the walls.

"I have plans for the kitchen," Anna said. "I'm hoping to paint and update some of the appliances eventually."

"Seems like you need a lot done around here."

"Cillian has helped me a lot this week, doing repairs and cleaning up the garden," Anna said as she got up from the table to retrieve the cake from the refrigerator.

"Oh, how nice," Marcella said. "I seem to remember you taking care of the gardens at St. Brendan's as well."

"Yes, I did," Cillian said politely as he rinsed off the last plate.

"Good to see you still do something you learned from the church."

"Mom!" Anna scolded.

"Bella, it's okay," Cillian remarked. He saw Marcella shoot him a glare.

"Her name is Annabella," Marcella corrected. "I never liked it when your father or anyone else called you that. You're not some cartoon character. It's a fine Italian name that your great-great-grandmother had."

"I didn't mean any offense by it, Mrs. Foley," Cillian said, hoping to defuse the situation.

"Never mind," Marcella said as Makenna placed a mug of coffee in front of her grandmother. "Milk, dear," Marcella corrected, pointing at her cup.

Cillian moved to the refrigerator to grab the milk when another knock on the door was heard. He looked at Anna, who moved toward the door.

"With any luck, it's the Grim Reaper coming to take me... or her," Anna whispered as she moved to the door.

Cillian placed the milk in front of Marcella, who did not even look up at him. Once again, he heard loud voices coming from the living room area, only this time louder.

Cillian slammed the fridge door shut and moved quickly to the living room. There stood Anna arguing vehemently with someone. When Cillian stepped close to her to be next to her, he saw that Leo had entered the house.

Chapter 19

Anna didn't think the evening she had planned cold go so horribly wrong, yet it did. Her mother kept at her and Cillian nonstop in her usual way. It was only another unsuspected knock at the door that saved her from having to listen to any more of the aggravating insults that spewed from her mother's mouth.

She arrived at the front door, hoping it was Erin and she would be saved, but once she opened the door and found her ex-husband standing there, the world came to a grinding halt. He stood there smiling, wearing the remnants of his day's now crumpled suit.

"What are you doing here?" Anna scowled.

"I was in the area, and I thought I would drop by and see the new place we bought," Leo cracked.

"Number one, this is nowhere near any area for you. Number two, WE didn't buy anything. I used my money to buy this house. Number three, you are far from welcome in MY home."

Anna hurried to close the door, but Leo had slipped his foot in to keep the door open and then pushed his way inside.

"You seem to forget where all that money came from, Anna," Leo bragged. "Without my cash, you'd probably be begging your mother for a room at her house. I don't know how you could even afford a dump like this after paying lawyer fees. I've bulldozed better-looking places clearing space for parking lots for the trucks."

"Get out!" Anna shouted. "You have no right or reason to be here. Just go!"

"Hey, I was invited," Leo professed.

"That's a laugh," Anna said. "There's no way Makenna would have invited you. She knows how I feel."

"I didn't say it was her, did I?" Leo smiled. "But is my darling daughter here? I would love to see her."

Leo took a few steps toward the kitchen before Anna stepped in front of him.

"Leave. Now."

It was then that Anna felt the presence behind her and saw Cillian out of the corner of her eye come up next to her.

"Everything okay?" he asked, looking at the red face Anna had and then at the familiar one of Leo.

"It will be when he goes," Anna demanded again.

"Wow, you really didn't waste any time, did you?" Leo joked. "The ink on the papers is barely dry, and you have a man in your bed already. I should have contested the divorce harder and really left you with nothing. He looks a little old for you, Annabella, but you always did have Daddy issues."

"You son of a bitch!" Anna yelled. "You're one to talk. You fucked every skirt you could get your hand under since the day we got married. And don't you dare bring up my father. If he knew how you treated me, he would have thrown you in the back of one of your garbage trucks and crushed you."

"Trash was the one thing your father was always good at," Leo said firmly. "He was one of my best workers. How I treated you? You had the best of everything. A big house in Westchester, a staff to wait on you, fancy clothes, a driver, exotic vacations – what more could a woman want?"

"Maybe a husband who didn't cheat on her every chance he got, didn't verbally abuse and humiliate her at every turn, and didn't isolate her from everything and everyone she knew. How's that for a start?"

Anna watched as Leo's eyes narrowed. She knew how to take him down a peg, and now she wasn't afraid to do it. Leo always relied on the notion that Anna wouldn't speak up and let people know how badly she was treated. She made sure it came out in the divorce proceedings, even if it didn't help her much with Leo's high-priced attorneys working her over. She then saw Leo look over Cillian.

"You're a pretty big fella," Leo said, shifting his attention. "Tattoos too, I see. I never figured Anna would go for a musclehead. I could use a guy like you for one of the trucks if you're ever looking for work."

Anna was grateful Leo didn't seem to recognize Cillian at all.

"I think Anna made herself clear in asking you to leave," Cillian announced, stepping forward. Anna glanced down and saw Cillian starting to make a fist with his right hand.

"Cillian, don't," Anna said, grabbing his arm.

"Cillian, huh?" Leo laughed. "It figures you'd run to an Irishman like your father. I'm surprised you can stay awake enough to satisfy her with all the drinking you probably do. I hope she does it for you, pal. She's always been kind of a lump and a prude in bed. I couldn't even get a blowjob out of her."

Anna never had time to react or stop Cillian from putting his hand around Leo's throat and then pinning him to the wall. The maneuver rattled the wall, knocking one of the picture frames down from its space above the couch. It didn't take long for Leo to start to turn red and then purple.

"I'm not quite as polite as Anna is," Cillian said through gritted teeth. "Now you can walk out of here on your own peacefully, or I can 'assist' you. I can't promise that no accidents will occur while I'm helping you, though. I might slip up."

Anna stepped next to Cillian and looked at his face. He held a dark concentration that she had never seen in him before.

"Cillian, let him go," Anna pled. "You'll kill him."

Makenna and Marcella were now in the room as well, watching events unfold.

"Dad?" Makenna said softly.

"I'm calling the police," Marcella said, going back to the kitchen for her phone.

"Cillian," Anna whispered. "Please."

She placed her hand on Cillian's right arm, the one that held Leo's throat. Anna felt the tension, the hate, in Cillian's body. She was finally able to break through his focus, and he looked over at her. Within seconds, he eased his grip, and Leo fell to the floor, gasping for air. Anna pushed Cillian back a few steps, and Makenna dashed in to check on her father.

Anna hugged Cillian and moved with him to the other side of the room.

"It's okay," she said over and over.

"It's not okay for him to talk about you that way or treat you the way he has," Cillian growled.

Anna noticed Marcella come back to the living room.

"The police are on their way," she said, hanging up her cell phone. "Not the actions of someone who was a priest," Marcella added as she went over to Leo.

"A priest?" Leo coughed.

"He's the priest from St. Brendan's," Marcella said.

"You're fucking kidding me," Leo said as he struggled to his feet. "And here I thought I was the one going to Hell," he chuckled. "The two of you will burn before me. You really must be scraping bottom now, padre."

Cillian retook two steps toward Leo. Anna stayed in front of him while Leo crouched down and cowered on the floor, getting behind Marcella.

"You should go," Anna said to Cillian, guiding him toward the front door. "The police will arrest you if you're here. Leo will make sure of it."

"Damn right, I will!" Leo shouted.

"Leaving you here with him isn't safe, Bella," Cillian told her.

"And she's safe here with you?" Marcella said as she confronted Cillian. "You just showed how quickly you can get set off. How do we know you won't do that with her?"

"I would never do anything to hurt Bella in any way at all," Cillian added sternly. "I don't think Mr. Mazza here can say the same."

"Ha! Bella. There it is," Leo said as he finally rose. "You've been trying to steal her going back twenty years. The best thing we ever did for her is getting her away from you. I can't wait for the cops to get here."

"We?" Anna said quietly.

Leo just looked at her and turned his attention back to Cillian.

"You have anything else you want to say or do, priest?" Leo barked from behind Marcella.

Anna went back to Cillian and led him out onto the front steps.

"Please, go before they get here. I don't want to see anything happen to you."

"I can deal with the police, Bella. It wouldn't be the first time," Cillian told her as they walked toward his motorcycle.

"I'll call you when things settle down here, okay? I promise nothing is going to happen. He won't do anything while the police, Makenna, and my mother are here. Go."

Cillian sat down on his bike, and Anna leaned in and kissed him.

"Bella, I'm sorry for all of this. What you said last night to me... You know I..."

Anna placed an index finger up to Cillian's lips to hush him.

"I know you do. I always knew," she smiled, her eyes getting wet.

Cillian started up his bike and got out of the driveway, kicking up dirt and gravel onto Leo's polished black Ferrari.

Anna marched back into the house and found Leo sitting in the recliner as Marcella approached him with a glass of red wine.

"Don't treat him like a welcomed guest," Anna snapped.

"Annabella, what he has just been through is traumatic," Marcella answered. "That biker could have killed him."

"Who invited him here, Mom?" Anna said sharply to her mother.

Marcella handed the glass to Leo and turned to her daughter.

"I did," she said proudly. "I called Leo because I thought he might want to see where you are at and be able to change your mind about living this way. It's disgraceful, Annabella. A broken family, a divorce, you living in this hovel... think about how it looks and how it impacts those around you, too."

"You can't be serious," Anna said, bewildered. "How it looks to those around me? You mean how it impacts you, Mom. Makenna stands by my decision. You're the one who can't deal with it because your precious rich friends and the gossipers at church will talk about me. It has nothing to do with me."

"I hate to see you throwing your life away over a minor discretion, is all," Marcella replied.

"A minor discretion? He was fucking his assistants, co-workers, strippers, prostitutes, even my friends! That's a bit more than a minor discretion."

"Annabella, don't use that blasphemous language with me," her mother intoned. "He's your husband. It was your duty..."

"He was my husband, Mom," Anna corrected. "That's over, and it's not changing."

A loud knock on the door broke up the yelling as Makenna went to allow the police to enter. Two officers entered the room and began their investigation, taking statements from all at the house. Leo insisted he wanted to press charges against Cillian. When the officers asked Anna where they might find him, she was prepared to answer.

"I have no idea where he went," she said honestly.

"Seriously, Anna?" Leo said in disbelief.

"I don't know where he lives; I've never been there. We only met out at places or here. Besides, who knows if he was going home anyway."

"He's one of those bikers," Marcella chimed in. Anna shot her mother a dirty look.

"You mean the Cosantóir?" the young blonde officer asked.

"That's them," Marcella said. "Nothing but trouble, those criminals."

The older officer, Officer Agee, nodded at Marcella.

"You mean the group that just did that festival and donates time and money all over the place?" Officer Agee added as he took notes.

"I'm sure that's some kind of cover for what they really do over there," Marcella said. "Go see for yourself and get him. There are probably several laws being broken there as we speak."

"We'll go check it out," Officer Agee assured. "Mr. Mazza, do you need medical treatment? I can call an ambulance."

"No, I can handle it," Leo said, puffing out his chest. "He's lucky he jumped me, and I couldn't retaliate."

Anna couldn't stifle a "Ha!"

The police readied to leave, and Anna walked out with them to the car.

"What are you going to do?" Anna asked as they moved to the squad car.

"I'll go over and talk to Mr. Meehan," Officer Agee said as his partner climbed in the car.

"He was only protecting me," Anna told the officer.

"From Mr. Mazza?" Officer Agee asked. "Is there something else you want to tell me, Ms. Foley?"

Anna looked back at the house and then to the officer.

"No... it's just that Leo is my ex-husband, and I want to make sure that..."

Officer Agee lowered his voice.

"If you are in any kind of danger, Ms. Foley, let me know, and we'll remove him from the property. If you have something, you want to press charges about... if he abused you or threatened you in any way, I can take care of it."

"No, it's nothing like that tonight," Anna admitted.

"Look, I've known Cillian for years and have worked with the Cosan-tóir on many things. I know what they're about, and I know Cillian wouldn't react that way without a damn good reason."

Officer Agee reached into his breast pocket and pulled out two cards.

"One is my card with my phone number on it. You can call me if you need me. The other card is for A Safe Place. They are a safe haven here in Harriman that helps women and families in your position. You can always get someone on the phone there, and they can get to us at the station if need be."

"Thank you," Anna said as she tucked the cards in her pocket.

Anna watched the police car leave her driveway. She spotted some of her new neighbors outside, looking at the commotion. Erin was already on her way over.

"Everything okay?" Erin said worriedly. "I just got home and saw the flashing lights."

"Leo showed up while Cillian was here. Cillian took exception to some of the things Leo had to say."

"And Leo didn't have to leave in an ambulance?"

"I convinced Cillian to let him go, and my mother called the police. Cillian left before they got here."

Anna pulled out her cell phone and typed out a text message to Cillian: *The police are coming to you. Be careful.*

Leo walked outside just as Anna finished sending her message.

"I just got off the phone with my lawyer," Leo bragged. "That asshole will be rotting in jail, no doubt. Oh, look – it's like old home week around here," he said as he saw Erin. "You've filled out nicely, Erin."

"Go to hell, you slob," Erin shot back.

"What is it with the Irish around here?" Leo chuckled. "Nothing but backtalk, sass, and cursing."

"I guess you just bring out the best in us," Erin told him.

Leo approached Anna, and Anna stepped toward Erin, who put her arm around her friend.

"Relax, Annabella, I'm not doing anything. I'm going now. I'm sure I'll see you both again soon."

Leo looked at the scuff marks on the finish of his car and tried to wipe them off.

"Fuck, I just got this detailed," Leo complained.

"What a shame," Erin added sarcastically.

"See you around," Leo smiled before he backed out of the driveway and sped off.

"What do you think that means?" Erin said as she steered Anna back toward the front door.

"I don't know, but it can't be anything good," Anna told her.

Cillian had received Anna's text while sitting in his room at Hog House. However, he was already expecting the police to show up at some point and made preemptive plans of his own. He walked out to the bar and sat down on one of the stools. He had barely taken a sip of his Guinness when Liam came walking in with Demon, Whitey, and Finn in tow.

"What's going on, brother?" Liam asked as they gathered around Cillian. "I don't think I've ever gotten an SOS from you."

"The cops are on their way here," Cillian said calmly.

"Local or state?" Liam asked.

"Locals," Cillian responded.

"How come?" Finn added.

"I got into it with the ex-husband of the woman I'm seeing," Cillian said, trying to be upfront about it. "He mouthed off to her, and I grabbed him and pinned him to the wall. I may need your help, Finn. I'm pretty sure they are going to arrest me."

"You got it," Finn told him.

"You know who the guy is?" Whitey asked.

"Yeah... Leo Mazza."

"Mazza Sanitation?" Liam said. Cillian nodded.

Finn looked to Liam for some guidance.

"He does sanitation for almost all of Westchester County," Liam explained. "Their trucks are at our job sites pretty routinely down there. The guy must have some serious bucks."

"And probably some pull and expensive lawyers to boot," Whitey added.

"No doubt," Cillian said, taking another draw of his stout.

"I don't mean to change the subject here," Demon threw in, "but are we going to completely overlook that Preacher is seeing someone?"

Cillian glanced at Demon.

"Can we focus on this, for now, Darryl?" Cillian asked.

No sooner was this said when the two Harriman officers came walking across the room toward the bar. The men parted a bit so the police could get closer to Cillian, but they never left his side.

"Gentlemen," Officer Agee said with a nod. "How are you, Cillian?"

"Not bad, Ron, how are you? Can I get you a drink?"

"On duty," he said. "Maybe another night. You know why we're here?"

"Because I didn't kill that slimy bastard when I had him?"

"Easy, Preacher," Finn intervened. "Officer, I'm Finn O'Farrell, Mr. Meehan's attorney."

"Wow, you are prepared, Cillian," Officer Agee smiled. "Relax, counselor. I just want to talk and get your client's side of things."

"Okay, but I'm not leaving his side," Finn stated.

"Fair enough. Can we have some space from the rest of you, though?"

Cillian looked at Liam and nodded.

"We'll be at the end of the bar," Liam let everyone know. He walked close to the young officer, towering over him enough where the rookie backed up a few paces.

"What happened, Cillian?" Officer Agee asked.

"The guy had it coming, Ron," Cillian said, looking at Ron. "He barged into her house, insisting that he stay. Then he had a few choice degrading things to say to his ex before I had enough and grabbed him. I never hit him; I just held him in place until he calmed down."

"You mean almost passed out," Ron noted.

"Semantics," Cillian chuckled.

"Jesus, Cillian, I expect a problem now and then with the club, but never with you. This is one I can't just sweep away. Mazza is insisting on pressing charges. He's probably already lining up his lawyers to sue you, too. The guy seems like a scumbag, and from what the ex says, she has reason to be afraid of him."

"What did she say?" Cillian said with concern.

"Not much, really, but I could tell she's hiding something. I gave her my card and the number to A Safe Place if she wants to use it."

Cillian looked at Finn.

"I'm on it. I'll call Siobhan," Finn said as he pulled out his phone.

"I need to go see her," Cillian said as he rose from his stool and took a few steps. The young officer put his hands up to physically stop Cillian.

"Move, junior," Cillian growled.

"I can't do that," the officer said shakily, placing his right hand on his gun. Liam, Demon, and Whitey were up and standing around Cillian in seconds.

"Don't make that mistake, kid," Liam said firmly.

"Alright, everyone back down!" Officer Agee yelled. "Banks," he said, turning to the young officer, "take your hand off your gun. I got this. Liam, back up. Let's not make this worse than it has to be. Cillian, you know I have to take you in. Don't make me cuff you."

Finn leaned next to Cillian and whispered in his ear.

"I talked to Siobhan. She's on it. 15 Church Street, right?"

Cillian nodded.

"Just go with them," Finn said out loud. "I'll follow you down there."

"You need me to do anything, brother?" Demon asked as he walked alongside Cillian as the officers led him out to the police car.

"15 Church Street," Cillian said, and Darryl simply nodded.

"Darryl, don't make me have to come out there after you," Ron warned.

"All he did was give me the address of a friend," Darryl added innocently, putting his hands in the air.

Cillian marched out to the squad car and waited for Officer Banks to open the back door.

"Do you have any weapons on you?" The cop asked him, turning Cillian so Cillian could place his hands on the hood of the car.

"I have a pack of gum inside my jacket pocket. It's pretty minty. Maybe you want to try some," Cillian joked.

"Just get him in the car, Banks," Officer Agee ordered.

The police car drove down towards the station, passing Anna's home on the way. Cillian peeked out to see that Leo's car and Marcella's were now both gone from the driveway, providing him with a bit of relief.

Cillian was ushered out of the car and into the small station, where he was placed in a holding cell. Finn had already arrived to defend his client and be there for anything that may be needed. Cillian kicked back in the cell, laying on the undersized and uncomfortable cot, his only thoughts about Anna and how he could help her.

Chapter 20

A nna did her best to keep her mind occupied and on anything besides what had occurred at the house the previous night. She had not heard anything from Cillian and worried about what was going on. She assumed he had been arrested since Leo made it clear he wasn't going to let that go. After witnessing what went on, Makenna spent the night with Anna instead of going back to her grandmother's house, much to the dismay of Marcella.

Ten AM had rolled around, and Anna prepared to walk down to Erin's for today's work. They had a catering gig to prepare for the weekend. Anna knew Erin had met with Darren to discuss possibilities at Millie Malone's. She was anxious to learn the outcome and do anything that might take her mind off the turmoil in her life.

Anna crossed the lawn in front of Erin's house and knocked on the door. When there was no answer, Anna tried the door and saw it was open. She let herself in and called out for Erin with no response. It was then she heard a bit of a commotion coming from Erin's kitchen. Anna rushed there and saw Erin yelling into the phone.

"I have no idea what you are talking about!" she screamed. "This was all worked out months ago. You guys extended my credit line because you knew I was busy and expanding. It's a done deal. How can things change just like that? No, I want him to call me back ASAP. No flunkies; give me Mr. Collins!"

Erin slammed the phone down and looked up at Anna. Anna could see the concern on Erin's face immediately.

"What's going on?" Anna asked.

Erin walked to the refrigerator, grabbed two bottles of water, and slammed the door shut, rattling the contents inside and the items on top of the fridge. She handed a bottle of water to Anna before slumping onto one of the kitchen stools.

"My business is grinding to a halt today, is what's happening," Erin said with disgust.

"Why?"

"I went to the restaurant supply store today to pick up some new equipment and things for the job this weekend. When I get to the counter to bill it to my account, they tell me my account is on hold and suspended. They said it was some credit issue. I called the bank, figuring it was just some mix-up somewhere, but then the bank tells me they recalled my credit line this morning. They were performing an audit on my account because of some fraud allegations. All I do is get the runaround from people down there. I can't pay for anything right now. They've even frozen my personal accounts. How could this happen?"

Anna consoled Erin, who was practically in tears.

"I've spent years building this, Anna. It was my dream. Darren was excited to have us come in and take over his kitchen, but without any funds to do anything, I'm finished."

Anna stepped back and looked at Erin.

"Where's your restaurant supply store?" Anna asked.

"I use the one in White Plains," Erin said, wiping her eyes. "I've dealt with them since I started."

"And your bank?"

"Chase Bank. I use the branch in Monroe, but they're everywhere."

"And they are also the institution that Leo deals with," Anna remarked. "All of his stuff goes through them – payroll, financing, investments, you name it. I'll bet the restaurant store is serviced by his trucks, too."

"But why would he do something to me?"

"Because he knows it will hurt me," Anna told her. "He'll try to take down anyone or anything that keeps him from getting what he wants."

"How could he get things done that fast?" Erin asked.

"He was probably making calls as soon as he left here last night—money talks for him. Erin, I'm so sorry. This is all my fault."

"It's not your fault your ex is a greedy prick. So what do we do?"

"I don't know," Anna replied. "For now, I have some money I stashed away. There's a little left from the divorce settlement in one account, but I have more that I squirreled away for years as my escape money. Maybe I can get some of the things we need for the weekend until we figure all this out."

"I can't ask you to do that," Erin told her friend. "I can call the family. I tell them we had an emergency and have to back out."

"That will crush your reputation two days before an event, Erin. Please, you gave me a chance. Let me try to help."

Erin nodded and came over and hugged Anna. Anna held her tightly for a moment before breaking.

"Okay, shoot me a list of what you need. I'll go over to the bank and see what I can get."

Anna headed down to the Sterling Bank branch in Monroe that held her accounts. She pulled out her checkbook and walked to one of the tellers, writing a check for $2,500. The teller processed everything with a smile, but then Anna saw the teller squinting at her computer screen.

The teller excused herself and walked over to someone else in a suit. The older women came to the teller window.

"Ms. Foley? Could you come with me to my office for a second?" The woman led Anna over to a glass office and shut the door behind them.

"I'm sorry, but there's a bit of a problem with your account," she said to Anna. Anna watched dumbfounded as she typed rapidly into her computer and pulled it up on the screen. "Apparently, there is a hold on your account—some type of legal issue going on where there is a lien."

"Who did that?" Anna asked. "I'm the only one with access to that account."

"I understand, but an attorney's office – a Mr. Ker..."

"Kershaw," Anna interrupted, knowing the name all too well.

"Yes, that's it. According to the filing, I guess there are some questions regarding the legality of how you came about the money and where it's from. It will probably take a bit to sort out. I'm surprised you weren't made aware of it when they did this."

"When did they do it?"

The woman looked through her glasses at the screen.

"The hold was activated this morning. That's odd. Usually, it takes a few days, and they have to notify you by registered mail."

"It's not as odd as you think," Anna fumed. "Thank you."

Anna stormed out of the office and got in her car. Without thinking, she drove with a furor onto the Thruway south towards Westchester. Anna didn't even remember going through tolls, dealing with traffic, or exiting the Thruway at the proper exit. The car seemed to guide itself to the Mazza sanitation office in a shiny building in White Plains.

Anna parked the car and made her way inside and up to the third floor where Leo's office resided. Anna spotted Debbie Baxter, the latest in the long line of admin assistants that Leo had hired and taken under his wing. As soon as Debbie spotted Anna, she leaped from her chair.

"Mrs. Mazza, so nice to see you," she said.

"It's Ms. Foley, and it's not great to see you, Debbie," Anna barked. "Is he in there?" Anna kept walking toward the door to Leo's office.

"He is, but he can't be disturbed," Debbie said, trying to put herself in front of Anna.

"Why, is he banging one of the officers, or is he in a meeting?" Anna asked. "You know what? I don't care either way."

Anna stomped into Leo's office, slamming the door behind her.

Leo looked up from his computer, where he was conducting a meeting with owners of a new company he was trying to gain the business of.

"What the fuck do you think you're doing to me?" Anna screamed.

Leo stared in shock before clearing his throat.

"I'm sorry for the interruption, gentlemen," Leo said politely. Anna moved in front of Leo's desk and shut his computer before shoving it off his desk.

"What the hell Annabella? That was an important meeting!"

"You think I give a shit about your meeting? What is going on?"

Leo sat back and smiled.

"Oh, I guess you and your friend tried banking this morning," Leo said. "It's a shame you aren't more careful with your money, Annabella."

"That money is mine!" she yelled. "And you have no right to do that to Erin."

"As far as your friend goes, it looked like some shady stuff going on there. I just brought it to the attention of the bank, is all. That other money, well, we both know it's hardly yours. You stole it from me. You must have been doing that for years to get that little nest egg built up."

"That was money from our account... yours and mine, you asshole."

"But the divorce settlement that you signed and agreed to said you were only entitled to the proceeds of the sale of the house – nothing else. You broke the agreement by not disclosing that account. Now the lawyers need to see what to do with it."

Anna sat on one of the leather chairs, stunned.

"Why are you doing this to me?"

"Oh, come on, Anna. Do you really think you're better off not being married to me? Look at all you have to struggle with. Come back to me, and all this other nonsense goes away. Your friend gets her business back, your boy toy gets the charges dropped, and I won't sue him… I probably wouldn't have to do anything involving that bike club, too. Do you know all the nasty things they've been accused of over the years? How these guys avoided legal problems for so long is a miracle."

"You're crazy if you think I would go back to living with you," Anna spat. "You made my life a living hell."

"I don't know how you could say that," Leo scoffed. "I'd say you were living pretty well, and I got you out of having to live the more impoverished life with your father. Your mother was going to leave him eventually if he hadn't died. She had all the money, and she was miserable. You were going to be stuck working as a cashier somewhere if I hadn't made plans with your mother."

Leo realized he had said too much.

"What are you talking about?"

"I guess you deserve to know now," Leo sighed. "When I inherited the company from my father, it made sense for me to find a wife to be with. The company wanted a family man running things. You and I knew each other. I had seen you at company parties and such with your father. You were the perfect match. I talked to your mother about it, and she was all for it, especially when she found out I would make sure your father always had a job. Besides, she wanted you with a nice Italian boy. Now, I didn't count on you getting pregnant as soon as you did. I guess that one's on me. Once that happened, though, I knew your parents would push for us to get married."

"So it was all just an arrangement?" Anna said, shocked.

"It sounds so clinical that way," Leo answered. "I made sure you had everything you needed, and I had someone on my arm when I needed it. Granted, I thought once we were married, you might put out more than you did. That was disappointing. But there's never a shortage of women who want to be wined and dined."

"So I just became a trophy wife... someone you would trot out, show off, and then put back in the cabinet on display."

"If that's how you want to see it," Leo told her. "The thing is, I never thought you would ask for a divorce. When all that started, people looked at me differently, like I was some kind of monster. All that unsavory stuff you said about me in court, Anna – that was rough, and it affected my business and my personal life. Now, if you were to come back, people would think you just made it all up, and we could get on with life."

"You are truly deranged," Anna said. "You can't seriously think I would ever go back to you."

"Have it your way," Leo responded. "But I can tell you for sure that you will lose your house, Erin will lose her business, and your favorite priest will spend time in jail. It's your choice."

"Fuck you," Anna said, knocking the chair over as she moved to the door.

Leo dashed in front of her, turning the latch on the door with his left hand before she got there.

"I kind of like seeing you this feisty," Leo said as he ran his hand through Anna's hair. "I'm up for a tumble if you are, for old time's sake. Maybe you picked up some new moves with your friend."

Anna smiled at Leo, feeling his hand in her hair, and spat in his face.

Leo gripped Anna's hair tightly, causing her to cry in pain. As her neck leaned back, he saw the cross she was wearing.

"How sweet," Leo said. "He got you a new cross already."

"It's not a new one," Anna whispered. "I never got rid of the old one. I held onto it because it reminded me of what men should be like."

Leo pulled on her hair again, reaching up to snatch the necklace off her. As he grabbed it and moved to go further, Anna quickly lifted her knee, planting it right in Leo's groin, so he doubled over. When he fell to the ground, writhing in pain, Anna unlocked the door and fled as fast as possible. She raced down the steps, avoiding the elevator, and pushed out one of the back exits to make her way to her car.

She got inside, started the engine, and sped away, breathing heavily the whole time. Shortly after, she made her way onto the highway and began to cry. Leo's confession to her rocked her to her core, and she felt around her neck for where the cross used to sit but was now in his possession.

"I don't know how much more of this I can take," she screamed aloud.

Cillian spent a few hours in holding before they could get him before a judge. Finn was able to get him released without bail, and the charge would be misdemeanor assault. As hard as the prosecuting attorney pushed, Cillian had no previous record to speak of. His reputation in the community was stellar.

Finn walked out with Cillian to Finn's car to go back to the Hog House.

"That was the easy part, you know," Finn told him. "Odds are, even if they found you guilty, you would just get probation. The real problem is going to come when he files a civil suit against you. From what you have told me, that seems inevitable."

"I know," Cillian acknowledged. "There's not much I can do about that. I'm more concerned about Anna right now than anything else. Can we stop by there so I can check on her?"

Finn brought Cillian to Anna's home. He found Darryl stationed at the top of her driveway with his motorcycle, drinking a cup of coffee.

"Were you here all night?" Cillian said as he got out of the car.

"Most of it," Darryl said. "Whitey subbed a bit for me this morning. He said she went down to Westchester. He tailed her down there, and she's on the way back now. She went to Mazza's office, Preacher."

Cillian had a deep concern about what occurred, but it was just moments later that Anna's car pulled to the top of the driveway. She stopped when she saw the bikers gathered there, but they parted so she could pull in.

Cillian went to her car as she stopped and opened the door for her. Anna flung her arms around him as soon as she could.

"I'm glad you're okay," she sniffled.

"Right back at you," he said softly.

When they broke the hug, Anna looked around and saw Whitey as he pulled in on his Harley.

"What is all this? Why was he following me?" Anna asked.

"Just a precaution," Cillian told her. "I wanted to make sure you were okay. Why would you go down to his office alone?"

"Because he's fucking with everything in my life, that's why," Anna emphasized. "He's frozen my bank accounts, frozen Erin's business, and God knows what he is going to try to do to you and the Cosantóir. I needed to understand why and to let him know I wasn't going to just take it."

"It's too dangerous, Bella," Cillian told her. "You shouldn't be alone with him."

"It doesn't matter if I'm in the room with him or not. He's got enough reach where he can cause problems while he's sitting on his couch."

"Maybe it's time we changed that then," Cillian affirmed, looking back at his brothers. "If he wants to play dirty, we can do that too. He doesn't know who he's messing with."

"Cillian, no," Anna insisted. "He's already had you put in jail once. Do you think he wouldn't do it again? Leo is used to getting what he wants, and he'll do whatever he has to, so it happens."

"What the hell does he want?"

"Me," Anna said with a shake of her head.

"What?" Cillian said, astonished.

"He wants me to go back to him. He says he'll stop everything if I do."

"He's feckin' nuts," Cillian said. Cillian was silent for a moment while he looked at Anna.

"What did you tell him?" he asked.

"I told him to go to hell, of course," Anna replied. "But... driving home... maybe it makes sense, so he stops hurting everyone important to me."

"This ends today," Cillian said, storming up the driveway toward his brothers.

"Cillian, no!" Anna shouted. "If you go down there, he'll have you arrested again. This time you'll be in his territory, and he'll make sure you don't get out."

"She's right," Finn warned as he overheard the conversation. "You attack him again, and I won't be much help to you, especially if he knows the cops and DA down there."

"I'm just going to talk to him and shake him up," Cillian insisted.

"I don't think that's a smart idea," Finn warned. "Let's take some time to think about this."

"We don't have time!" Cillian shouted. "The guy is already fecking with her and her family. If we do nothing, he'll think he just gets away with whatever he wants. If a few of us go down there, I think he'll change his mind."

Cillian looked around at Finn, Darryl, and Whitey. All seemed to have the same look on their faces, but no one wanted to contradict what he said.

"Cillian, please," Anna begged. "I don't want to lose you again. He already made that happen once."

"What are you talking about?"

"Leo..." Anna started, "and my mother. They had it all worked out from the start. It was all a ploy to get me to marry him, and it worked. Once that happened, they worked to get me out of your parish and away from you. He never loved me; he just wanted a wife to show off to his friends and business partners, and he didn't want you getting in the way of it."

"Whitey, I'm taking your bike," Cillian ordered as he grabbed the keys from Whitey's hand before the brother could react.

"Cillian, no!" Anna screamed, but by then, he was already gone down the road.

Cillian sped through town, narrowly missing some red lights and going through a few others, as he got on the Thruway and raced toward White Plains. He wove erratically in and out of traffic. His mind focused on finding Leo and doing everything he could to tear the monster down. Rage flowed through him like it never had before. Hearing Anna tell him about how a conspiracy whisked her away all those years ago caused the vehemence to spit forth even more.

Cillian looked down at the speedometer and saw he was over 100 MPH at one point as he zipped through traffic and congestion. He could see the Tappan Zee Bridge in his sights when he realized he didn't know exactly where to go to find the Mazza offices. He knew White Plains, but not much else, and it was then that the rational side of his brain began to creep back into his thoughts.

Instead of following through and crossing the bridge, Cillian found an area and crossed the median, turning back north. He drove back to exit 10 and got off on 9W toward Nyack. He worked his way through to Piermont, bringing his bike to a stop just outside a blue four-story home overlooking the Hudson. He got off his bike and strolled onto the property and up to the front porch before he rang the doorbell. He turned and looked over the manicured lawn and beginnings of a lush garden that led to the back of the house. Cillian heard the door creak open and turned to look.

"Hello, Mark," Cillian said.

"Cillian," the older man said before breaking into a smile. "Well, this is a surprise. We haven't seen you in what, two or three years?"

"I know, it's been a while," Cillian replied.

"Come on in," Mark told him, holding the door open for him to enter.

The two entered the historic home and creaked across the hardwood floors and into the living room.

"How have you been?" Mark asked. "Are you working down this way?"

"I've been okay," Cillian lied. "No, I'm on a few jobs closer to me right now. I just... well, I just wanted to stop by. How's he doing?"

"He's been good," Mark told him. "We just got back from a trip to San Francisco. We had a great time and saw some old friends. He's out on the back porch right now."

Cillian followed a few paces behind Mark down the hall, looking at pictures that dotted the walls. Several river shots out on their boat or on one of the trips they took, all with smiling faces, created a warmer atmosphere. Mark swung the back door open leading out to the porch with a serene view of the river.

"Ben? Look who came to see us?" Mark said happily. Ben swung around in the wicker chair he sat in and broke into a wide smile.

"How are you, Ben?" Cillian said as he walked over to embrace his old friend. The two men hugged before Ben pointed at the chair next to him, offering a seat to Cillian.

"I was going to make some coffee," Mark added. "Sound good to you two?"

"That would be grand," Cillian replied.

"Did you just turn up your Irish for that?" Ben laughed.

Cillian looked at Ben and saw that the short black hair he had always sported was now dotted with more gray than it had been in the past, getting closer to the smoky color of Ben's eyes than ever before.

"It's been a while," Ben said as he turned back toward the river.

"I know," Cillian said ruefully. "Probably since the wedding. I remember everything being set up beautifully here," Cillian added as he looked out over the lawn. "It was a fantastic day."

"I know," Ben said. "It's hard to believe it's been three years already, but Mark and I have been together for so long..." Ben said as his voice trailed off. He looked over at Cillian, who was lost in the view.

"I see you've kept up with the garden," Cillian said. "It looks fabulous."

"Thanks," Ben said. "We have landscapers come in and do most of it now. I can't do as much as I used to with it thanks to these," Ben said, gazing down at his hands. "How about you?"

"Me? No, I have hardly done anything. Hog House doesn't really have a garden to do anything with. It's nothing but clay and dry and earth up there. Besides, I haven't done much since I left the parish. I just... lost the passion for it, I guess."

"That's too bad," Ben said as he sat back in the chair. "We always kept the best garden there. Father Clarke used to brag about it all the time, though the only thing he ever did was toss his cigar butts in there."

Cillian chuckled a bit and sat back and sighed.

"You look like shit, friend," Ben told him. "Why are you really here? Don't get me wrong – it's great to see you, and you're welcome any time. I can tell you have something going on."

"I don't know how you handled it, Ben," Cillian said as he got up from his chair and walked to the porch railing. He looked down the four stories to the lawn and garden that led out to the river.

"Handled what?"

"All of it," Cillian turned. "Your beliefs, your faith... love," he said, pointing as Mark came through the door with coffee mugs.

"Sounds like I walked in on something heavy," Mark laughed as he handed Cillian a mug.

"Sounds like Cillian finally has his crisis," Ben said as he took his coffee from Mark. Mark bent down and kissed Ben lightly.

"I can leave you two if you want," Mark offered.

"No, stay, Mark," Cillian added. "I could use your input too."

Mark sat on the arm of Ben's chair and put his arm around him.

"I think you already know the answer to your question, Cillian," Ben said. "You know I didn't deal with it well. It was the most challenging thing I ever dealt with. I had grown up with my parents, only wanting me to be a priest. I thought it was what I was meant to do, and I loved it. But when I met Mark, it made me question everything about myself and my faith. Feeling that way about someone, wanting to be with them, and knowing that all about it was wrong... it was utter hell for me, to the point I couldn't take it anymore."

Ben held out his arms, showing Cillian the scars on his wrists and arms that he knew of all too well.

"If you hadn't found me in the rectory that day... well, things would have been much different."

"Divine intervention in an ironic way," Mark smiled.

"That day changed both of us," Cillian told him. "It wasn't much long after that I left. It wasn't because of what you did, Ben. It was because I couldn't be a part of it any longer. Here I was, preaching about how much we should care about and love each other, but everything about what we were standing for was speaking against it."

"I always felt guilty about you leaving," Ben admitted. "You were the epitome of what a priest was for me, Cillian. I looked up to you and still do because of the person you are. I thought it was my getting kicked out and my attempt that took you away from what you loved."

"No, that's not true," Cillian stated. "Did it open my eyes more? Yes. But it wasn't the only reason I was ready to leave."

"So, that brings us to now," Ben said. "What's making you question everything now? You've been out for twenty years, living your life."

Cillian lowered his head for a moment before looking up and at Ben and Mark.

"Do you remember Annabella Foley?"

Ben looked at Cillian and smiled.

"Of course I do," Ben said. "You two were practically inseparable. She was a lovely girl. Remember her, Mark?"

"I remember her mother more," Mark said with disgust. "She invested with my firm until she found out I was gay. She did everything she could to smear my name. It didn't cost me anything, really, since I was never shy about it, but it made life uncomfortable for a bit. I do remember her, though. She was always at the church functions."

"You performed her wedding, didn't you?" Ben asked.

"I did," Cillian admitted. "Anyway, we ran into each other a week ago. I haven't seen her since she and her husband – well, ex-husband – moved away. We... we started seeing each other."

"Great!" Ben said. "You two always had some chemistry with each other."

"Yes, it is great. It made me happy," Cillian replied.

"Try not to look overjoyed about it," Mark laughed.

"I think I know where this is going," Ben said. "You slept with her."

Cillian nodded.

"And now you're feeling guilty about your vows?" Ben asked.

"I am," Cillian told him. "It was tearing me up, Ben. I should be the happiest I have been in many years, but I keep feeling torn about how I went back on my word. Adding to that is her asshole ex-husband and the trouble he is causing for her and me. He had me arrested last night."

"For what?" Ben exclaimed.

"I may have tried to strangle the life out of him."

"Okay, let's put the husband aside for a second," Ben began. "Focus on Annabella and how happy she makes you. When Mark and I first got together, I was wracked with guilt. It went against everything I was supposed to be about, but it was the first time in my life that I felt I was who I was meant to be. That's why I came to you and confessed, remember? It wasn't until all the shit came down with my family and the diocese and they told me they were removing me that I was lost. It took me a long time to heal from that, Cillian. It was work on my part with Mark, with a therapist, and having friends like you to show me I could be true to myself. Yes, I broke my vows, and it removed me from the church forever; I can't change that now. But that doesn't mean I have to beat myself up every day of my life for it or have no relationship with God at all. I have faith in God, myself, the decisions I made and keep making, which has made me happier. Have I made mistakes? Of course, I have – we all do. Trying to kill myself was the biggest one. Draw on the strength you have around you, Cillian. You have a brotherhood with you every day with the Cosantóir and with your friends. Don't give up on something that has the potential to make your life fantastic because of guilt or fear about your faith. You're stronger than any person I have ever known, and you only changed your outlook because you were with someone you love, didn't you?"

Cillian sat quietly for a moment to absorb all that Ben had said.

"Yes," Cillian said firmly.

"Let that guide you," Ben told him. "I was fortunate enough to get a second chance, Cillian. Not everyone can say that. Don't let her go."

Cillian sat back in his chair and smiled.

"I'm glad I came down here," Cillian told his friends.

"We're glad you did too!" Mark exclaimed. He glanced down at his watch. "It's almost lunchtime. Stay and talk with us. We hardly ever get to see you."

"I'd be glad to," Cillian replied.

Mark rose to go inside and fix lunch while Cillian stepped toward Ben. Ben got out of his seat and gave Cillian a hug.

"Thank you," Cillian told him.

"You bet," Ben said, patting Cillian's back. "It's the least I can do after all you have done for me. You stood by me when few would, including my family. Shit, you are my family!"

Cillian felt his phone buzz with a text message. He saw it was from Anna:

Where are you? I'm worried. Let me know you are okay.

Cillian quickly typed out a reply.

I didn't go to Leo. I'm good... we're good.

Chapter 21

Cillian stayed and talked with Ben and Mark for hours, catching up, laughing, and talking seriously into the night. When it finally came time to go, a burden had been lifted from Cillian. He gave Mark a hug before Ben walked him to the door.

"Promise me that you'll come to see us without a crisis going on in your life next time," Ben told his old friend. "We're not that far away. Come down, and we'll take the boat out for the day, go to dinner, or just sit around and bullshit for a while. I miss you."

"I've missed you too," Cillian replied. "You have no idea how much I needed this today."

"I do," Ben told him. "I've been on that side of it, and you helped me. Just let me know if you need anything. And bring Anna around. I'd love to see her after all these years."

"I will," Cillian said, giving Ben another embrace.

"I think you have someone waiting for you," Ben said, pointing toward the driveway. Cillian turned and saw Darryl sitting on his bike, next to where Cillian had parked.

"Hey, Darryl," Ben said with a wave.

Darryl gave a casual wave to Ben.

"We'll talk soon," Cillian told Ben as he headed down the porch steps.

Cillian approached Darryl and smirked at him.

"Have you been sitting out here the whole time?" Cillian asked.

Darryl nodded.

"You were tough to keep up with on the Thruway," Darryl admitted. "I lost you for a minute when I saw you swing around and come back toward Nyack, but when you did that, I figured you were coming here. I did get a few cars slow down and look at me sitting in the driveway here. I just smiled and waved at them. I'm shocked no one called the cops."

"Why are you here?"

"Because I didn't want you walking into a shitstorm without anyone to back you up," Darryl said. "We're brothers. You all good now?"

"Yes, thanks," Cillian told him. "Is Anna okay?"

"Last I checked, Whitey was there standing guard. Since you took his bike, he didn't have much of a choice," Darryl laughed. "Everything was all good."

"Okay, let's head back and see what we can do to fix this mess," Cillian said, climbing on Whitey's bike.

"Hey, take this," Darryl said, tossing his spare helmet to Cillian. "You're gonna kill yourself driving like that with no helmet. And you're buying me dinner. I was starving out here, man. All I had was a pack of Chips Ahoy I found in my saddlebag."

"Fair enough," Cillian laughed as he started up his bike and left to head back to Harriman and Anna.

The sun had long since set, and Anna walked out the front door to the sound of the crickets and frogs. Whitey sat in one of the porch chairs that he had pulled from the back, checking his phone. He turned and looked to the door when he heard it open.

"Everything okay?" he asked, standing up.

"Yes, thanks," Anna replied. "You know, you really don't have to stay here like this. I'm sure I'll be fine. Makenna is here with me. You've been here all day."

"It's okay," Whitey dismissed. "Preacher asked me to stay. I'm staying. One of the other brothers is going to be here to relieve me in a bit anyway. Better to be safe about it in case someone comes."

Two headlights lit up Whitey and Anna as they came down the driveway. Whitey stepped in front of Anna while reaching into his back pocket to make sure his knife was still there. Anna tensed for a moment until she saw one light go off and then the other, realizing they were motorcycle lights.

Whitey shone the flashlight from his phone to see Rocky walking toward him with Pick not far off.

"Hey," Pick waved, blocking his eyes from the flashlight. "All good?"

"Yeah," Whitey said, repositioning the light.

"Any word from Preacher and Darryl?" Whitey asked.

"They're on their way back," Pick answered. "They just stopped off for some food. They should be here in about an hour or so. We brought Preacher's bike down. I'll bring you back with me. Rocky's staying."

"You let the prospect ride his bike? You better not have changed anything, brother."

"Sweet ride," Rocky bragged.

"Ha!" Pick laughed. "He did twenty the whole here. He was too afraid to do anything."

"You sure you can handle this, prospect?" Whitey asked.

"It'll be fine," Rocky said confidently.

"You okay with this?" Whitey asked Anna.

"Really, none of you have to stay," Anna insisted.

"Not a chance," Pick added. "Liam's orders on top of Preacher asking. We're here until he says differently. Take the downtime and make sure there's no dirt or anything on Preacher's bike, prospect."

Rocky nodded obediently as Pick and Whitey walked up the driveway to leave.

"Can I get you anything?" Anna asked the young biker, resigned to the idea that they would be perched outside until Cillian arrived.

"No, Ma'am," Rocky added. "If you have a front light you can turn on, that would help."

"I'm sorry, the motion light is out," Anna told him. "I haven't had time to replace it yet."

"It's okay, I'll make do," Rocky answered as he sat in the chair.

Anna sighed and went back into the house. She found Makenna walking out of her room wearing a pair of sleep shorts and a blue tank top.

"What's up?" Makenna asked nervously.

"Nothing," Anna breathed. "Just a changing of the guard."

"Is he at least cute?" Makenna asked, trying to peer out the front window.

"Really?" Anna said, stunned. "I don't know. It's so dark out there who can tell. There's a little light from the street lamp, but that's it. He's young. That's all I can say to you. You can make your own judgment."

Makenna started walking toward the front door before Anna stopped her.

"Mac, you can't go out like that," Anna ordered.

"Like what?"

"You're wearing your pajamas, no bra... it's not a good idea."

"It's dark, remember?" Makenna said. "It's not like he'll be able to tell."

"Just stay in, please."

Anna walked over to Makenna and took her hand.

"I'd... I'd just feel safer if you were in here."

"Mom, he's not going to do anything to me."

"No, not him. I don't know about your father... or anyone he might have with him," Anna said honestly.

"You think Dad would really let someone hurt me?"

"I like to believe he wouldn't, honey. Right now, I'm not so sure. Why don't you come into my room with me? I could use the company to help me fall asleep for a bit before Cillian gets here."

Makenna nodded and closed the front door before following Anna into the bedroom. Anna lay on the bed and rolled to her side while Makenna put her arm around her.

"We're going to be okay, Mom," Makenna reassured her.

"I know," Anna said shakily.

Anna heard the familiar bang of the back door echo through the empty kitchen and sat up. The sound of feet scuffling on the linoleum floor inched toward her bedroom. Her first instinct was that it was Cillian, but she wondered why he would use the back door to enter the house. A sense of dread came over her as she heard muffled voices outside her bedroom door. The sound of Makenna's bedroom door opening sent chills through her.

"Mac," Anna whispered urgently. "Get up. Someone's in the house."

Makenna pried her eyes open and looked at her mother.

"What?" she grumbled.

"Someone just went into your room. We need to get out now. Out the window."

Anna quickly went over to the window and pushed it open, knocking the screen out forcefully. She grabbed her purse off the dresser while Makenna climbed through the window first, tumbling out onto the grass. Anna followed her and just got through as she heard the bedroom door open behind her.

"Shit!" she heard a voice yell. "They went out the fucking window!"

"Run!" Anna implored her daughter as they raced up the driveway. Anna glanced to the side and saw the overturned patio chair with Rocky's body lying still next to it. They both tried to stay on the grass, but Anna slipped on the damp lawn and fell to her knees. Before she could move again, she felt two sets of hands grabbing her.

"Mom!" she heard Makenna scream. Anna looked up and could see Makenna struggling in someone's arms near the top of the driveway.

"Makenna!" Anna yelled as she watched her daughter get tossed into the side door of a pickup truck. The truck then squealed its tires and sped off.

"No!" Anna yelled again. Hands gripped Anna from behind and pulled her to her feet. As soon as she was upright, she swung her head back as far as she could, crushing her skull against the face of whoever was behind her.

"Fuck!" the voice yelled as the hands released her. "She broke my fucking nose!"

A shadow writhed on the ground while Anna turned her attention forward to the stunned person in front of her. As he stood in a moment of indecision, Anna kicked forward, catching him in the midsection to knock the wind out of him.

Anna ran to her car, digging the key out of her purse and starting it as fast as she could. She flipped the headlights on, blinding the two young men who now lay on the lawn. Throwing the car into reverse, Anna barreled through the vehicle blocking her path, and skidded out onto the street. She took off down Church Street, never pausing at the stoplight, and made a right to drive into Monroe. She heard her car scraping and dragging metal as she went along, and then the telltale thumping of a flat tire going around the further she went.

No lights were on anywhere until she noticed the Quick Chek parking lot. She pulled her car to one of the side parking spaces and shut it off right away, killing the lights. Anna jumped out of the vehicle and raced inside, but she didn't see anyone in the store at all.

"Hello?" she yelled out.

"Anna?" a voice from her behind her questioned. She spun around and saw Olivia standing there, wearing a green polo shirt and khaki pants. "Are you alright?" she asked.

"No... they're chasing me... and they grabbed Makenna... I need help."

Anna and Olivia both turned to the front window and saw a white pickup truck and a black car with a crushed front end pull into the lot.

"Olivia, please," Anna begged.

"Get in the back," Olivia said calmly, pointing to the maintenance room down the hall. Olivia pushed Anna inside.

"Leave the light off, and don't move," Olivia ordered. She shut the door and locked Anna inside before returning to her post behind the counter.

Four young men came running into the store, scanning the place as they searched for Anna.

"Can I help you guys with something?" Olivia said calmly.

"Did a lady just come running in here?" a blonde man said breathless-ly.

"Been just me for about an hour now," Olivia replied. She glanced at the man next to him, who was bleeding profusely from his face and had a towel soaked in blood in front of him.

"Your friend looks like he needs some help," Olivia pointed out.

"He'll be fine," another man barked. He walked right over to the counter and got in Olivia's face.

"We know she came in here, bitch," the man scowled. "Her car is right there," as he pointed to the parking lot.

"That thing's been sitting there all night," Olivia said. "Someone left it here because the tire is flat."

"Check the bathrooms!" the man yelled while the two not bleeding went to look.

"If you're lying to me..." the man threatened Olivia.

"You'll what, asshole?" Olivia shot back. "There are cameras all over this fucking place, inside and out, that are recording you and your bud-dies, including whoever is still out in that truck of yours."

"Bathroom is empty," a dark-haired man said. He reached behind and jiggled the doorknob to the maintenance room.

"What's in there?" the man barked to Olivia.

"It's a closet... you know, brooms, vacuum, toilet paper. There's a mop in there if you want to wipe all the blood your dude over here is getting all over my floor," Olivia told them.

Olivia turned her attention back to the man leaning over the counter.

"Are you jokers done here now?" she said. "Because I already tripped the silent alarm button, and the state cops will be here in about two minutes. I'm sure they'll be glad to get an ambulance for your dying friend."

"Fuck you!" the bleeder spat out. "I'm not dying, am I, Frankie?"

"Tell him, Frankie," Olivia grinned.

"We gotta go before the cops get here!" another man shouted.

They ran out of the store, with one stopping at the pickup as the window rolled down. Frankie talked and pointed at Olivia while speaking with the driver. Still, Olivia could not see through the tinted windows of the truck. Within seconds, both vehicles peeled off and away.

Olivia raced over to the closet and unlocked the door to find Anna with her knees pulled up to her chin, shivering.

"They're gone," Olivia told Anna as she helped Anna up.

"Did you really trip the alarm for the police?" Anna asked as they moved toward the counter.

"Nah, that silent alarm thing is bullshit," she told Anna. "But the cameras recorded everything, I'm sure. I can call the police now."

"No, wait," Anna replied, stopping Olivia. "I know what to do. I don't have my phone, but I have this."

Anna went into her purse and dug out the business card with A Safe Place's information on the front and Siobhan's phone number on the back.

"Call her, tell her who I am and that we need the Cosantóir... now."

Chapter 22

Cillian and Darryl were just finishing up their meal at the Shannon Rose Pub in Ramsey when Cillian got a call from Liam.

"What's up?" Cillian asked.

"Get to the Quick Chek, now. There's been a problem," Liam said solemnly.

"Is Anna okay?" Cillian said as he stood up.

"She's alright; just shook up pretty bad. Whoever it was nabbed her daughter and messed up Rocky, too."

"On my way."

"I gotta go," Cillian said rapidly to Darryl, who was busy finishing his hamburger.

"What's wrong?" Darryl asked.

"There's trouble with Anna and Rocky's hurt. I'm heading to Quick Chek. That's where Liam says they are at. You got this?" Cillian said without waiting for an answer. He was already most of the way across the dining room before Darryl just said, "Go!"

Cillian rapidly left the parking lot, merging into the northbound traffic on 17 to get to the Thruway. Cillian paid little attention to what was going on, weaving in and out to get to the exit as fast as possible. He reached the 14A exit and jumped off the highway, going to the back roads with less traffic so he could go more quickly. By the time he pulled into the Quick Chek parking lot, the place was checkered with Cosantóir motorcycles, with members guarding both entrances.

Cillian pushed his way through the throng until he reached the counter. He saw Anna sitting behind the counter with Siobhan kneeling next to her. As soon as his eyes locked on hers, she stood up and ran to him. Cillian embraced her tightly as she sobbed.

"They broke in and took her, Cillian," she cried. "I can't believe he would take her from me."

"It's going to be okay," Cillian told her. "We'll take care of it, I swear to that. I'll get her back."

"Just do whatever you have to," Anna said to him.

Siobhan walked over to where Cillian held Anna.

"Anna," Siobhan said softly. "Come with me. I'm going to take you to A Safe Place. We'll watch you there, and they'll keep us informed of everything going on."

"I want to stay with you," Anna pled to Cillian.

"Bella, go with Siobhan. She'll keep you safe. We don't all the details yet. I promise I will keep you informed of everything."

Cillian leaned in and gave Anna a kiss, whispering, "I love you. I will find Makenna and make him pay."

Anna nodded as Siobhan put her arm around her and led her off. Cillian sought out Liam to get information. He found Liam standing next to the girl that works with Anna.

"What do we know?" Cillian asked Liam.

"The girl here saved Anna, for one," Liam said. "Tough as nails, this one. She stood up to those thugs and convinced them she wasn't here. I looked at the video. We got good looks at everyone who came in the store and the car and truck plates. We've got people running the information now and should have some info. Odds are they are headed to Westchester."

"Thank you," Cillian said sincerely to Olivia.

"She's my friend; of course, I would help her," Olivia answered.

"If you ever need anything, you contact me. I'm here for you," Cillian told her.

"Do you think you can corral some of these guys and get them out of here?" Olivia asked. "The cops will be here any second, which means they'll be contacting my manager and the store. I'm going to have a lot of questions to answer."

Cillian looked over to Liam.

"We can get some of these guys out of here," Liam agreed. Liam pointed his finger and whistled, and most of the brothers vacated the store just as the police were walking through. The officers seemed a bit overwhelmed by all the bikers coming and going. Not long after the troopers entered, Officer Agee came walking in the door.

"I heard it over the radio," Agee said to Liam as he came in.

"You had your chance to do something," Cillian barked, "but you took his side."

"First of all, you don't know Mazza was involved in this," Agee answered. "Secondly, you choked the guy. What was I supposed to do, Cillian?"

"So it's just a coincidence something happens one night and the next day someone tries to take his ex-wife and daughter? Come on, Ron, that's bullshit, and you know it. Besides, it's out of your hands now anyway," Cillian said.

"What's that supposed to mean?" Agee asked.

"It means that they are out of your jurisdiction now," Liam answered. "Time for the big boys to do something about it."

"Don't do anything stupid, Liam," Officer Agee warned. "You already have enough strikes against you. People are just itching for an excuse to bring you in."

"Let 'em try," Liam said. "We're out of here."

"We want to interview you guys!" the trooper yelled out.

"Why?" Liam shot back. "We weren't here when it went down. We just stopped in for some candy." Liam picked up two packs of Starburst and held them up to Olivia.

"We good?" he asked her.

Olivia just nodded to him.

"Look at the video. You'll see all you need to see," Liam barked. He walked outside, and Cillian followed closely behind.

"So, what's the plan?" Liam asked Cillian.

"Hold on," Cillian said, rushing over to Siobhan's car as it backed out of a parking space. He put his hands up to halt her and went to the passenger side window. Anna rolled the window down.

"Do you know where Leo lives now? Would he take her there?" Cillian asked.

"He might. He lives in Bronxville. I can send you the address. But I think he'd more likely take her to the hauling center in Yonkers. It's where they do a lot of the work. He wouldn't want people at his house. He's too much of an arrogant prick for that."

"I'll let you know when I have her," Cillian said as he jogged back to Liam. Darryl had arrived and was getting up to speed on what Liam had to say.

"So?" Liam asked.

"Bella says he lives in Bronxville, but she doesn't think he would go there. He's more likely to go to their facility in Yonkers."

"Okay," Liam began. "Whitey, you and Pick head down to the house. Preacher will send you the address. Check it out and see if anyone is around. Preacher, Demon, and I will go to Yonkers. If she's there, we'll get her. From the looks of the video, they are punk kids, not older than twenty-one or twenty-two. He got some locals to pick her up. If that's all it is, we'll be alright. Let's go."

Cillian pulled up Leo's home address on his phone and sent it off. He watched as Whitey and Pick tore off on their bikes. Siobhan left the parking lot with Anna and went toward A Safe Place's facility in Harriman. Cillian spied Anna give him a weak wave as she left.

"You sure you're up for this?" Liam asked Cillian.

"What do you mean?" Cillian replied. "Of course I am."

"This one is personal for you, Preacher," Liam told him. "Emotions cloud judgment with shit like this. If you don't think you can focus, I can grab someone else."

"I've been with your father in the club before you even put your first club jacket on," Cillian shot back. "I'll be fine. I know what we need to do."

"Just checking," Liam responded. He slapped Cillian on the back.

Darryl looked over at Liam and Cillian.

"I've got the place in Yonkers," Darryl said, holding up his phone. He sent the address over to Liam and Cillian. Liam pointed to the parking spot where Cillian's bike sat.

"I had one of the brothers bring it over for you," Liam said. "Rocky had ridden it over to your lady's house earlier."

It dawned on Cillian that he never asked to see how Rocky fared in the fight.

"How is he?"

"He took a beating," Liam answered. "They must have had bats or something like that. They worked him over pretty good. We got an ambulance over there to take him to Good Sam, and I sent Aidan down there with him, so I know what's going on. I don't think he ever saw them coming."

"Fuck," Cillian added. "This is all my fault."

"Hey, it's not your fault the ex is batshit crazy. We're all in this, Preacher. Teaghlach."

Cillian mounted his bike, put his helmet on, and started his engine. He set the GPS on his phone, so he knew just where to go even though he was following Darryl's lead. The whole ride to Yonkers, Cillian worked to keep his emotions checked and found a losing battle. He wanted nothing more than to have a second chance at Leo.

The three bikes pulled up to the outside gate of the Yonkers Waste Station. The plant operated 24/7, so people were milling about, leaving Cillian at a bit of a loss as to where to start the search. Cillian pulled his bike alongside Liam's and Darryl's, tucked away behind a row of empty dumpsters along the fence line.

"How are we going to find them? This place is huge," Cillian asked.

Liam looked at Darryl and smiled. "We'll just walk in and ask," Liam said. The two men began the trek to the front entrance, with Cillian close behind. The trio reached the security gate outside the parking lot nearest to the building. Without hesitation, Liam walked right up to the booth, grabbing the attention of the two guards inside.

"Evening, gents," Liam asked. "Could one of you be kind of enough to point me to Mr. Mazza's office?"

"Offices are closed, pal," one guard said. "No one's here. Come back on Monday."

"Normally, I would do that, but it's something of a sanitation emergency for my friend there," he added, pointing to Cillian. "We know he's here. Just tell me where to find him, and you can get back to your Internet porn."

"Look, 'friend,'" the guard added, getting up from his seat. "I told you he ain't here. Hop on out of here before I have to use this." The guard pointed down to the Taser he had on his hip.

"Geez, you're not even man enough to get a real gun? I'm trying to make this easy for you. Last chance."

Liam took a step back so the first guard could come out of the booth. The guard stepped out and realized not only just how large Liam was but that Darryl was also out there to the side of the booth. Before he could even reach his Taser, Darryl had the man gripped around the neck in a wrestling hold. He quickly collapsed to the ground as Liam bent down and took the Taser.

Cillian saw the second guard reaching for his phone and burst into the booth, grabbing the man's hands in his. Cillian glanced down and saw the man wearing a wedding ring.

"Don't risk it," he warned the man. "You want to be able to hold your wife's hand again someday, don't you?"

The guard simply nodded in fear.

"Is Mazza here?"

"He... he came in about an hour ago. Then a white pickup came in a bit later to go to him. They are all in building one, right here." The guard pointed at the building closest to them.

"Why don't you take the rest of the night off?" Liam told the guard. "I think you've done enough for one day."

The guard nodded rapidly once more and took off in the direction of a group of parked cars.

"We need to move," Liam said. "It won't be long until that guy calls someone and lets them know we are here."

The three men jogged toward the empty building. Cillian spotted the white pickup parked out front. He recognized it as the same one he had seen slowing down in front of Anna's house earlier in the week. They entered the lobby and went right to the directory. They saw that Leo's office was positioned on the third floor.

"How do you want to do this?" Darryl asked.

"Demon, you and I will take separate elevators up. Someone will probably be waiting right around there," Liam planned. "Preacher, take the stairs. You can come up behind or slip into the office, whatever you can do."

Cillian agreed and made his way to the stairwell while Darryl and Liam boarded elevators. Cillian dashed up the steps, taking two at a time when he was able so that he reached the third floor quickly. He pulled the stairwell door open slightly and heard the ding of the elevators arrive as he did. He saw two men move to the elevators before the doors opened, giving him enough time and space to slip onto the floor behind them. He spotted the wooden doors to Leo's office, but before he entered, he saw in the glass-walled office just next to Leo's that Makenna was in there, on one of the chairs, with a man positioned right in front of her.

Cillian crept over slowly to the office, hoping to go undetected. As he moved, he noticed that Makenna had caught sight of him. Makenna quickly turned to her captor to keep his attention. Cillian reached the office door and saw it was ajar, enough for him to hear what was going on.

"I never understood why you were such a cocktease with me, Makenna," the young man said. "Ever since we were young, you were like that.

Things would have been so much easier if you had just gone along with me."

"Maybe it was just the way you know how to charm a girl, James," Makenna said to him.

"I think it's time to do something to keep your mouth busy, smartass," James snarled. Cillian heard a struggle and entered the room quickly, grabbing James and tossing him across the conference table, so he tumbled to the floor.

"How many times am I going to have to tell you to leave this girl alone?" Cillian railed. He glanced and saw Makenna's hands were zip-tied to the arms of the chair. James was up, and Cillian saw that he had a large cast on his arm from where Darryl had done his damage.

"Jesus, old man, I was hoping for a second shot at you," James said.

James scrabbled across the room, tossing a chair at Cillian that Cillian dodged easily.

"You don't want me to break your other wrist, asshole," Cillian told him. "You'll have nothing left to jerk off with in prison. They'll just have to use that pretty face of yours instead."

James let out an audible growl and leaped toward Cillian, catching enough of Cillian's body so that both tumbled to the floor. James rolled over quickly and used his cast to rain down blows to Cillian's chest and head. Cillian saw black after the second blow to the head and weakly raised his arm to deflect other attempts.

James was set to hit him again when Makenna zoomed over on her rolling chair and kicked James in the mouth, causing blood to spurt out.

"Fuck!" James yelled as he fell to the floor. He got up quickly, smearing the blood from his lips with the back of his cast. "Enough of this shit," he grunted as he pushed Makenna's chair hard enough, so it slammed against the far wall and tipped over, leaving her struggling on the floor.

James moved over to Cillian, still working on getting his bearings. He sat on Cillian's stomach and punched Cillian in the jaw.

"After I work you over some more, I'm going to leave you panting and begging for mercy. Then I'll let you watch me fuck your friend over there before I go back home and do the same to her Mom."

James raised his cast like a club, preparing to strike until Darryl walked in and grasped the arm. He took it and cracked it over his knee, splintering the cast and James' arm so that bone came through where the cast was. Cillian watched as James' eyes looked as if they would pop from his head as he screamed in agony.

"Shut the fuck up, man," Darryl said, kicking James in the mouth and knocking him unconscious. "I'm tired of listening to you cry and scream."

Darryl walked over and righted Makenna in her chair.

"You okay?" he asked her as Makenna nodded.

"What about you, Preacher?" Darryl asked.

"I've been better," he said, wiping the blood from his mouth. Cillian reached into his back pocket and tossed his knife to Darryl, who made short work of the ties on her wrists with the blade.

Makenna stood up and went to Cillian, hugging him.

"Is Mom okay?" she asked.

Cillian nodded. "Yes, we got her somewhere safe," Cillian gasped. He looked up and saw a figure move to the stairwell door and duck in.

"I'm going after Mazza," Cillian said to Darryl. "Watch her."

Cillian darted from the office and caught sight of Liam pushing the limp bodies of two men into one of the elevators.

"They're napping," Liam chortled. "Go. I'll meet you downstairs."

Cillian entered the stairwell and could hear shoes pounding down the steps. He went down one flight quickly and then looked over the edge of the stairs, catching sight of Leo's form moving as fast as he could to get out of the building. Cillian heard the sound of a door slamming shut when Leo reached the bottom. Cillian jumped down the last few stairs and threw open the door. He saw Leo stumble and skid across the shiny waxed floor of the lobby right to the front door. Leo scrambled to his feet, looking back with fear on his face as Cillian paced across the floor and toward his prey.

Leo ran to the right along the sidewalk, and Cillian moved right behind him. Cillian noticed Leo fumbling with his pocket, clearly looking for his car keys so he could make an escape. Pain coursed through Cillian's side as he began to cramp from the blows he took from James and all the running he had done, but he moved feverishly to catch up to Leo. He saw as Leo ducked into the parking lot, and seconds later, Cillian heard the engine and saw the headlights of Leo's sleek Ferrari light up.

Cillian stepped up his pace, getting to the rear of the car as Leo backed up. Cillian tried to grab on, but the car moved forward as Leo spun the tires, and Cillian's hands just slipped off the vehicle as he pulled away. Leo held his left hand out the window, giving Cillian the finger as he sped through the parking lot.

Cillian cringed as it looked like Leo was getting away. He rested his hands on his knees, trying to catch his breath, as he spied the car speeding forward. It was then that Cillian's vision switched to slow motion as a sanitation truck was backing up into the path of Leo's auto. The brake lights briefly flashed before the loud crash occurred, and smoke filled the area.

Cillian rushed toward the accident, reaching the area where the truck and car met. The truck driver was screaming in a panic, and Cillian saw the twisted metal of the Ferrari as it was jammed underneath the massive garbage truck. The roof of the car had peeled back completely. Cillian went to the other side of the truck, but there was no sign that the car made it through. He faintly heard a noise coming from beneath the truck. Cillian got on his back and shimmied underneath to where the driver's side of the car was. What Cillian saw turned his stomach. Leo was breathing as his chest worked furiously, but part of his scalp had been sheared off in the wreck. The airbag had deployed, but it helped little. Leo shifted his eyes to the left and spotted Cillian there. His breathing quickened more as he struggled for air.

"Please..." Leo croaked.

"They called 911. Just try to hold on," Cillian told him, not knowing what else to say.

"I... I won't last," Leo huffed. "I need to... to confess..."

Cillian was frozen. He knew from examining the situation that Leo would never survive until the police and fire department arrived. Even if he somehow managed to, he likely would not last in a hospital—the thought of just letting him go and leaving him there crossed Cillian's mind.

"I... I can hear your confession, Leo," Cillian resolved. "I'm allowed to do that."

"I can't move my arms... to make the sign of the cross," Leo gasped as he struggled.

"It's okay; you don't need to. Go ahead," Cillian said as he bowed his head.

"Bless me, Father, for I have sinned. My last confession was four months ago."

Leo began to wheeze.

"I cheated... I cheated and lied to my wife for many years. I committed adultery. I... broke Commandments... I stole money from businesses... cheated on my taxes. I... abused Anna... not physically, but verbally and mentally to keep her with me. And I conspired against you, Father... to keep her from you. I'm sorry. I'm so sorry. Tell Makenna I'm sorry... this is all I can remember."

Leo coughed several times, blood moving through his mouth and onto the airbag in front of him.

Cillian lay on his back, watching Leo, not saying a word.

"What's my penance?" Leo gasped.

"Say the Lord's Prayer," Cillian informed him. Cillian closed his eyes and mouthed the words as Leo tried to recite them as best he could. When Leo was completed, Cillian looked over and saw Leo's eyes closing.

"Leo, say the Act of Contrition."

Leo fluttered his eyes open again and began to mumble.

"I am sorry for my sins with all my heart.

In choosing to do wrong

and failing to do good,

I have sinned against you.

I firmly intend, with your help,

to do penance,

to sin no more."

Leo's breathing became shallower.

Cillian reached out and placed his hand on Leo's before he began reciting.

"May our Lord and God, Jesus Christ, through the grace and mercies of his love for humankind, forgive you all your transgressions. And I, an unworthy priest, by his power given me, forgive and absolve you from all your sins, in the name of the Father and of the Son and of the Holy Spirit. Amen."

A peaceful look came over Leo's face, and he opened his eyes again.

"I never meant to hurt...," he struggled to say. "In my shirt pocket," Leo huffed as he looked down.

Cillian crawled close enough where he could reach his hand inside. He wriggled it between the deployed airbag and Leo's body to locate the breast pocket. Cillian poked two fingers inside, felt something, and pulled. Out came Anna's gold cross. Cillian gripped it tightly in his fingers.

Sirens wailed as cars and trucks arrived on the scene. Cillian saw the eyes of two firefighters looking in at him and Leo.

"Are you okay?" a firefighter asked Cillian.

"Yes... I'm a... I was just taking his confession..." Cillian replied.

"You need to get out of there, Father," the man warned. "There's gas leaking everywhere. This could spark at any minute."

Cillian crawled out from underneath the truck and was pulled away by firemen on the scene.

"Is he still alive in there?" one asked Cillian as they led him to an ambulance.

"I'm not sure," Cillian coughed. "He was."

Liam arrived over where Cillian sat in the back of the ambulance.

"You alright, brother?" Liam asked.

"Yeah, I'm alright. Mazza is trapped under there. It's bad," Cillian said as he breathed in some oxygen.

"Cops are inside the building cleaning up," Liam reported. "Those boys sang as soon as they saw the police. They left Mazza and the other kid out to dry. What a feckin' mess. Did he say anything to you?"

Cillian looked up at Liam.

"Not really," Cillian answered.

Epilogue

Cillian, Liam, and Darryl spent hours on the scene talking to firemen, EMTs, and police before all three were brought to Westchester Medical Center to get checked out. Darryl and Liam had escaped unscathed. Cillian had some cuts and bruises but nothing they needed to keep him for. Makenna was brought there for observation. The police took her statement about what had happened and what James, his friends, and her father had done. She let them know that her father had planned to hold at her office and then his home, unharmed until Anna gave in and came back. James started to take things too far and caused all the problems at Anna's house, the store, and the office.

Makenna was informed during the interview that her father did not survive the accident. Firefighters could not get him out in time as they used every means possible to free him from the scene but failed. Makenna sat stoically when told, unsure how she should feel about it. She was eventually allowed to contact Anna to let her know she was safe. Siobhan brought Anna down to the hospital to reunite the family.

When Cillian was done with the countless police interviews, he was mentally and physically drained. He had sent a text to Anna earlier with just the words:

It's over.

It was only when he saw her at the ER with Makenna that he could embrace her and hold her. Makenna was admitted for overnight observation, and Anna refused to leave her side. She sat with Makenna until her daughter slept peacefully. Cillian crept into the room to check on them.

"I can't believe all this," Anna said. "It's been a nightmare. Thank God you were here for her... for us."

Cillian took Anna's hand and held it.

"Anna, I have to tell you something," Cillian began. "Before he died, I took Leo's confession."

Anna stared at Cillian.

"Are... are you allowed to do that?"

"Yes, in extreme circumstances like these were, I am. I can't tell you what Leo said... I can't tell anyone. He knew he was dying. What I can say is that I know he was sorry about the way he treated you. I don't think he was just saying it because death was near. I thought you should know."

Anna bowed her head.

"I also have this for you," Cillian added. He reached into his jacket pocket and pulled out the cross.

"Is that..." Anna said, tears in her eyes.

"Yes, it is."

Anna hugged Cillian tightly and kissed him on the neck.

"Thank you," she said quietly. "Thank you for saving Mac and for saving me. Not just today, but for a very long time."

It was nearing the end of September when everyone started to get things sorted out. The police took weeks to untangle the messes Leo had created for Anna, Cillian, and Erin. Once all that was cleared away, Erin could move forward with her business plan with Darren. The end of

September brought about the opening of Erin's Inn at Millie Malone's, and locals and the Cosantóir gathered at the location to celebrate. Erin, Anna, and Olivia worked hard in the kitchen to craft a special opening night meal of traditional Irish fare for all to enjoy.

Anna made her way out of the kitchen and sat at the long table where Cillian, Darryl, Liam, Conor, Maeve, Finn, and others sat to see how everyone enjoyed things.

"Best lamb stew I have had outside of Dublin!" Conor raved.

"That's mighty high praise coming from him, Anna," Maeve laughed. "Take the compliment while you can. You're not likely to hear too many more."

"I'm glad everyone likes the food," Anna said humbly. "It's a great start for us."

"Can I steal you for a minute before you rush back to the kitchen?" Cillian said to Anna.

"Sure," she said, putting her arm around his waist. The two walked outside and away from the front of the building to a clearing Darren had set aside that might eventually hold the food truck for special events.

"I was just wondering how everything is coming with all the paperwork," Cillian asked.

"Ugh, the lawyers are still sorting through everything," Anna answered. "Leo hadn't changed his will, so I was still listed as the primary beneficiary. Directors in the company are challenging things. It could take years before they get it all fixed. To be honest, I don't want any of it anyway. I never wanted to be part of the business. I never saw the house he moved into or anything else. They can all keep it as far as I'm concerned."

"Some of that money would sure help out," Cillian told her.

"Makenna's tuition is taken care of. That's all that matters to me. I can make the rest on my own."

"Well, I just want you to know that you don't have to do it all on your own," Cillian added. He pulled an envelope out of his jeans pocket, unfolded it, and handed it to Anna.

"What is this?" she asked.

"Open it."

Anna opened the envelope and then looked back at Cillian, speechless.

"It's an account I set up in your name. It has tuition money in it for when you want to go to the Culinary Institute. It's always been your dream, Bella. There's no reason you shouldn't get the chance to make that come true."

"Cillian, I can't... this is too much."

"I've spent the last twenty years working with the Sand Hogs, making a good living, and not doing anything with my money. I always said I was saving it for when I wanted to do something special. This... you... are my something special."

Anna's lips flew to Cillian's as he lifted her slightly off the ground to hold her.

"My father always told me to find a man like you," Anna said, smiling. "I just never imagined it would really be you."

"Faith, Bella. It's all about faith."

Acknowledgements

As is the case with each book, a lot of work goes into each one beyond me typing pages. I have a fantastic support system behind me of family, friends, community members, and co-workers that make it all possible.

Thank you to Scarlet Lantern Publishing for allowing me to write from the heart, do what I love, and create new worlds. I also need to thank all of the fabulous writers I work with at Scarlet Lantern. They are a constant source of inspiration and provide encouragement and teamwork above and beyond the call of duty.

My amazing family of my Mom, siblings, cousins, aunts, uncles, and more who rally around me and have given me support at every turn. Millie Malone's wouldn't exist on paper without all of you and the wonderful Millie herself, God rest her soul. I know she's smiling down now that she's been immortalized on paper.

The community here in Harriman, Monroe, Chester, and throughout the Hudson Valley that I have been fortunate enough to call home for the last forty years has embraced me and provided me with the chance to meet many new people, support our local small businesses, and give to the place I call home.

My group of friends near and far who are there to cheer me on and have been by my side from the start when I was just a kid writing short stories in my spiral notebook and have seen me through life's challenges has helped me become who I am today.

Most of all, I thank Michelle and Sean. They are my rocks no matter what has come my way and my biggest fans. The love I have for you has no bounds. Like Preacher says, it's all about faith, and yours in me has done wonders.

Also By M. Geraghty

The Cosantóir MC

Small Town, Biker Romances

Finn
Preacher
Liam
Demon

The **Home Stand** Series

Small Town, Sports Romances

Change Up
Spring Fever
The Sweet Spot

The <u>Celtic Sisters</u> Series

Small Town, Dark Romances
<u>A Calm in the Storm</u>

Standalone Romances

<u>For What It's Worth</u>

A Christmas, Rockstar Romance